ONE NIGHT TO WIN YOU

JULIA JARRETT

Meagen,
Happy reading!
xo Julia Jarrett

CONTENTS

For Chelle and her hot dog hill.
Don't die on it, I need you.
(and they're sandwich adjacent.)

CHAPTER ONE

Sawyer

"I've got twenty on Sawyer not going home alone tonight."

I fight back a smirk over my glass, not denying or confirming my intentions for the night. Gotta save the smirks for when they're really needed, and these two jackasses would be a waste of a good one if I unleashed it on them. Not to brag or anything, but I could weaponize that thing if I wanted. Nothing but straight-up facts. There's a reason my nickname among the wildfire crews is Lover Boy. Because while the smirk is the bait, the panty-dropping smile is the hook. I'm unstoppable in getting whoever — and whatever — I want.

Derek and Boone, two of the guys I've been to hell and back with, have seen the smirk in action more times than I can count.

"Shit, I'm not taking that bet. It's more a question of *how many* broken hearts he leaves behind."

"I didn't notice you complaining the last time we went out, cowboy." Arching my brow at Boone, I wink. "I seem to recall you had an absolutely lovely time with that brunette that didn't make the cut."

Boone slaps me on the back. "Too right, man. Too right."

My eyes survey the ballroom, decked out in shades of red and silver. This is my second year attending the British Columbia Firefighter Fundraiser gala as Mr. July in the annual calendar, and the cocky arrogance I felt walking into the room last year is back in full force this time. Find me a red-blooded male who doesn't enjoy being told he's one of the hottest firefighters in the province for two years in a row and I'll sell you some ocean front property in Arizona.

Nights like tonight are prime pickings for a guy like me who's only interested in one thing: a couple hours of mutual, consensual fun.

Derek, Boone, and I have that in common. Which is a good thing, seeing as my three brothers back home in Dogwood Cove, who used to be the ones to join me on a night out on the town, had to all go and settle down, leaving me a lone wolf. And rather than howl at the moon, this wolf is fucking lonely. Something I'll never admit to anyone. Don't get me wrong, I love my future sisters-in-law, but that's not for me. No fucking way.

I've always loved women. Short, tall, curvy or slim. Redheaded or blonde, sweet or spicy. I don't care. Women are to be worshipped and cherished.

But only for a night.

"Sawyer? Did you hear me?"

I shift my attention back to Boone. "What? Sorry, I missed that."

He just gives me a knowing wink. "Too busy scoping out your next conquest?"

"You could say that," I say, hiding the fact that I wasn't paying attention. Lifting my glass to my lips, I take another sip of rye and Coke. "What did I miss?"

"We were just reviewing the terms of our deal."

I let out a low chuckle. The fucking *deal*. I don't even remember which one of us assholes came up with it, but after last year's event, we decided this year to make things interesting, we'd add in some higher stakes.

The three of us have been friends for years, even though Boone and Derek both work on the mainland and I'm stationed in Dogwood Cove. We've fought enough wildfires together to form a bond that isn't easily broken. Briefly, my mind pictures the fourth person that should be here with us. But just as quickly, I dismiss it. Dwelling on Lance and why he's not here isn't exactly what I need to get my game face on.

"I thought it was clear," I say confidently. "We agree on a woman, then ask her to choose which of us had the hottest photo this year. Losers pay the tab tomorrow night."

Yes, it's exactly as arrogant and chauvinistic as it sounds. We might be grown-ass adults, but we still have moments of juvenile idiocy.

"You're going down this year, Lover Boy." Derek shoves me lightly in the shoulder. "That kitten they had me hold is gold, baby, pure gold. No woman can resist a guy in turnout gear holding a kitten."

"You don't have it in the bag yet, D-man. All I had covering my junk was a hose. That's fucking hot. Let's pick our mark. How about her?"

Unbidden, my eyes follow the subtle point of Boone's finger and land on a sleek black dress shot through with silver thread. The generous curve of her hips draws my attention upward, the fabric skimming the dip of her waist, the flare of her breasts. Sleeves that have a long slit from shoulder to wrist show off a hint of skin that's way sexier than I anticipated from, well, arms.

It's a good thing Boone and Derek aren't looking in my direction because the second I lock onto her face, I choke on my drink.

Holy forking shirtballs. Yep, her beauty calls for a quote from *The Good Place.*

I've seen a lot of stunning women. Hell, I find beauty in just about every woman I see. Whether it's their appearance or something deeper, every single woman is beautiful in their own way. But this one? This one is so goddamn gorgeous she outshines everyone else around her.

Blonde hair cascades over one shoulder in gentle waves, the light hitting the golden strands, making her glow as if she's heaven-sent. Long earrings compliment her long and slender neck. Deep red lips with a fucking adorable little cleft just below them. She's smiling, but it's small, hesitant almost, and I'm seized with a bizarre need to see her let her guard down and truly shine. Her eyes sparkle in the dim light of the room, and while I can't make out what colour they are, the long dark lashes framing them give her an innocent appearance that is at direct odds with the sensual vixen vibe the rest of her gives off.

"No ring, and she's here with a friend. We're two for two, green light for go, and that blue dress will look good on the floor of my hotel room."

The red that was filling my gaze at Boone's statement clears in an instant when I register the fact that he wasn't talking about my angel, but rather her friend. Who, yes, is attractive in her own way, with dark hair twisted into some complicated updo and a blue strapless dress that hugs a more slender body than blondie's.

Blondie's rockin' a petite body with the perfect amount of curves. I keep sneaking glances at her, greedily drinking in every detail I can capture from a distance without looking like a total perv.

"I dunno, bro, she's got a classy look to her. She needs a refined touch. You might find yourself sitting this one out." While I'm trying not to drool over the angel I'm staring at, Boone and Derek are still bantering like the assholes we are.

For a brief second, I feel kinda guilty about it all. This really is a dick move, the three of us competing to charm a woman just for bragging rights. Granted, we're not forcing anything. Just asking them to decide which one out of the three of us fuckers has the hottest photo. But there's an unspoken assumption that the winner will most likely get lucky with the woman as well.

As long as she's interested, of course. We do have a moral code, it just gets loosened sometimes.

But as I stare at the two women, something has me hesitating. Normally, nothing would stop me from simply walking up to blondie, unleashing the smirk, whispering something swoony to sweep her off her feet, and showing her the time of her life.

But for some reason, I'm not feeling that strategy. Maybe it's because she doesn't look like the usual fire hoes that flock to these events just for a shot at banging a guy of the month. She looks like someone who wants a man who can offer her the picket fence, two kids, minivan, forever kinda shit.

And that man is definitely not me.

The guys are moving and my feet automatically drag after them, even though I'm already willing to concede defeat. I'll accept the drink tab for our night out tomorrow if it means I don't have to go through with trying to charm the wrong woman. As we get closer, I realize the ethereal beauty I noticed from afar is even more potent up close. *Goddamn, I'm in trouble.*

"Ladies, how are we doing tonight?" Derek's smooth voice has both women smiling, although I take pleasure in noticing the brunette is staring at him with interest in her eyes while the blonde is not paying him any attention.

"Oh, we're just fine, handsome. Even better now that we have Mr. February, Mr. October, and Mr. July with us." She eyes us each in turn, and I have to give her credit, she's done her homework knowing who we are on sight. Of course, the giant posters with our calendar photos adorn the entry to the ballroom, so I guess it was kind of easy. "I'm Willow, and this is my friend Tori."

Tori. My angel's name is Tori.

I give Willow a quick smile, then turn to the woman I'm really here for, my hand reaching out. "I'm Sawyer." Her eyes lift, and this close to her, I can see they're a deep brown that match my own.

"Hi."

One word. That's all it takes for my dick to stir in my pants.

I tune out Derek, Boone, and Willow, only vaguely aware the guys are bestowing all their charm on Tori's friend. My focus is solely on her and the way her eyes keep darting over to me, then away, as if she can't quite let herself openly look at me. Christ, even in heels, she barely comes up to my shoulder, and it makes me want to see how she'd fit against the rest of my body.

She reminds me of a skittish animal, afraid to relax and trust that they're safe. *I* want to make her feel safe. Which is why, instead of my usual smirk, smile, and flirt combo, I go for banter.

"I'd ask if you come here often but seeing as it's a once-a-year event, that seems pointless."

She cracks the tiniest of smiles, so I push on.

"Can I let you in on a secret?" A small nod encourages me to continue. "My twin brother wanted to pretend to be me so he could come tonight."

Her brow crinkles. "Why?"

"Because the crab puffs are the best thing you'll ever put in your mouth. Or so he claims." I give her a wink that's hopefully the light side of flirty and not the dirty side. "I promised to sneak a few into my pocket to bring back for him as long as he pays the dry-cleaning bill for my tux."

That gets me a laugh and a subtle relaxing of her shoulders. I grin back at her and gesture to her empty wine glass. "Can I buy you a refill?"

"I thought the drinks were free?" she teases, a twinkle lighting up her eyes. Her body has shifted ever so slightly toward me, putting the tiniest amount of separation between us and the others who are still talking animatedly.

I shrug affably. "Sure, but 'can I get you another free drink' doesn't sound as charming, now does it?"

One eyebrow lifts. "You're trying to be charming?"

"Naturally. Isn't it working?" I wink at her to show I'm just teasing.

Her delicate laugh fills the air like fucking music, and I want to make her laugh again and again. Preferably when we're alone. And naked.

I wonder if she's ticklish.

Chapter Two

Tori

The sweep of Sawyer's dark brown hair is so perfectly styled, he literally looks like he stepped off a magazine cover. It should be intimidating, he's that good-looking, but something about the way he's staring at me makes it seem almost as if he's the one intimidated. By *me*.

Which is ridiculous. He's a hot firefighter who could have his pick of women. And I'm a single mom who writes romance novels for a living.

Don't get me wrong, it's not a confidence issue. In general, I have zero issues with how I look. But tonight, I'm a little more vulnerable than normal. Which is exactly why Willow forced me to get all dressed up and come to this dang event.

I'm busy trying not to swallow my tongue at just how freaking handsome Sawyer is when Willow makes our excuses to the trio of hunky firefighters and drags me with her to the bathroom, supposedly to "freshen up."

I call bullshit. She wants to make sure I'm okay if she abandons me and goes home with one of the two guys she's chatting up, or maybe both, knowing her. She's bold and brave in her sex life — heck, in all of her life. There's a reason she inspires my characters a lot more than I do.

"Remind me why I'm here again?" I whisper once we're in the glamourous ladies' room just outside the ballroom. "I could be at home eating the discount Valentine's Day candy from last week, wearing comfy clothes, and watching *The Golden Girls*. But instead, I'm squeezed into a dress that really is a size too small, sipping on lukewarm wine, making small talk." My complaints fall on deaf ears.

Willow fixes me with a glare. "Oh sure, you're having such a terrible time talking to a hot firefighter. I saw you smiling, Tori, don't deny it." She turns to face the mirror, pursing her lips as she touches up her already perfect lipstick. "And you're here because, as your best friend, there wasn't a chance in hell I would let you spend this weekend alone. Coop's at a sleepover, and you don't need to wallow in the dark thinking about *him*."

The fiercely defensive tone of her words underlines her protective nature. There's no better best friend in the world than Willow Lawson. When she showed up at my apartment tonight, dress in hand, and told me she had two tickets to the annual BC Firefighter gala, she made it perfectly clear what she expected of me.

Find a hot firefighter and let him fuck away any residual hurt my son's father left on my soul when he told me he was getting married and moving to another province. Starting a family and abandoning the one he already has. Again.

"I wouldn't think about him," I start to feebly protest. "I'd..."

Willow turns to face me, arching one brow in a perfect lift. "Uh-huh. You'd...?"

Damn it.

"Listen, honey, I love you. And I know you. That's how I know that even though Sir Douche Canoe doesn't deserve a second of your brain power, and I know you don't really want *him* but the *idea* of him, heck not even the idea of him, the idea of a life partner. I also know that finding out he's getting married hurts more than you want to admit. And that's why my job as your best friend is to distract you from that pain. If it ends up that you finally dust off the vajayjay and finally get some action, so be it. Call it revenge sex."

I snort at that. "Revenge against what? Tim made it perfectly clear from the start he didn't want a future with me and Coop. He never once lied to me or did anything bad."

"Except for abandoning his kid?"

"He didn't abandon him."

"No, just signed over full custody and walked away for the first two years of his life."

"I'm going to ignore the fact that you called it a vajayjay, or that you implied it would be dusty, because, *eww*. I am capable of basic hygiene, you know," I say archly, folding my arms across my chest. But Willow's not done.

"If you didn't want me interfering in your sex life, then you shouldn't have admitted to me that you haven't been thoroughly fucked since you got pregnant. That's over eight years, T."

I knew I'd regret my margarita-fueled confession last week. I managed to get this far without her finding out just how long my dry spell was, then drunk me blurted out my secret. I hate drunk me. "Fine. But if I end up a statistic in the morning, I'm going to haunt your ass so hard."

Willow just smirks, knowing she's won. "I thought you wrote romance novels, not thrillers. Embrace the one-night stand trope, Tori."

Yeah. Sure.

There's a reason I write romance, and it's not because my life is so romantic. It's because between the pages of a book is the only place I can find a man who treats a woman the way we should be treated.

Guys like that just don't exist. And even if they did, my hands are full being a mom and a writer. I don't have time for a relationship.

Except, maybe for just one night.

We rejoin the men, who really are, as a whole, far too pretty for their own good. *Pretty* isn't the right word, but it is the safest. Especially when my eyes land on Sawyer. Standing tall and proud, he exudes a vibe that is pure masculine confidence.

I always thought that alpha attitude would be a turnoff, and maybe in my right mind, it would be.

But I'm not in my right mind tonight.

Tonight, I want a man to make me forget myself, and Sawyer seems the perfect one to do just that.

He turns his dazzling smile my way, and my stomach flip-flops.

"Hey angel, you ready for that free drink I'm gonna buy you?"

I give him an answering grin and take the arm he's offering. "You're a big spender, aren't you?"

His rich laugh warms me and the air between us. "What can I say, I know how to spoil a girl."

"What if I don't want to be spoiled," I say, the sensuous decor and my pep talk from Willow making me bold. "What if I want to be ruined?"

Sawyer falters ever so slightly but recovers quickly, the only indication he's affected by what I said being the subtle tightening of his hold on my arm. "Then I'd say we need to make the rounds I'm here to make, and then..." His voice trails off, but the meaning is clear in the silence left behind.

"Then..." I echo softly, that one word hopefully acting as my clear consent to whatever he has in mind.

The next hour spins around me like a dizzying spell of anticipation. Sawyer is the perfect gentleman, dazzling me on the dance floor, escorting me around the room, introducing me to so many people I can barely keep names and faces straight.

When his hand grazes across my lower back, I feel the trail of heat through the thin fabric, making it hard to focus on anything else.

By the fifth round of introductions, I stop trying and simply smile as he humbly accepts praise and recognition from everyone, from the mayor of Vancouver to the provincial minister of public safety, who he whispered is some sort of head honcho for all firefighters, I guess.

"Are you some sort of firefighting celebrity?" I murmur to him as we turn from the latest group of admirers. "Am I actually hanging out with the Chris Hemsworth of firemen?"

His low chuckle is full of amusement, but also something else. Not quite embarrassment, but perhaps humility, as if he isn't as comfortable with the showering of praise as he seems.

"If you're saying I look like the God of Thunder, I'll take it."

My lips quirk up, but I don't respond to the bait.

"I, ah, well..." His hand reaches up as if to run through his hair, but then he pauses, probably remembering how perfectly styled it is. The hand gets stuffed in his pocket instead as he shifts to face me. "I've been a firefighter for a while. Fought some crazy blazes at home, and a lot of wildfires. There was one..." His voice trails off as a flash of pain and regret mar his perfect features. "Anyway. I also got roped into doing some international competitions and um, yeah."

"You won, didn't you?" I say, filling in the gaps. "You really are a firefighting celebrity."

His eyes are alight with humour as he tries to look humble but fails. "I guess so."

I thread my arm through his again and tuck myself against his side, my forward behaviour shocking me even as I find myself melting into the solid warmth of his body. "Well, I feel honoured to be by your side."

He's silent for a moment, those eyes searing into mine. "The honour is mine, angel."

It's the second time he's called me that. It's cheesy as heck, but I like it, even if there is a distinct possibility he's called every woman before me that. This is never going beyond tonight, what does it matter if I'm nothing more than a notch in a bedpost. The first man to truly interest me in years *wants me, too.* And that alone has me rising up slightly, wrapping my hand around his neck, and pulling his head down for my lips to brush against his.

I can't honestly say what my intentions are in kissing him, but Sawyer's are abundantly clear the second he takes over the kiss. He skillfully turns us so that his back is to the crowd and mine is against the wall behind us. Keeping his touch on my hip light, he slides his other hand up to my shoulder, drifting it around to my front to rest lightly at the base of my throat. I should feel cornered. Pinned down. Trapped.

I don't.

His tongue strokes my lips, and they open easily to welcome him. He kisses with confidence, the same way he's moved through the entire evening. As if he has every right to be here, and this was his plan all along. Maybe it was? I don't really care, because the fingers on my hip are tightening, gripping me with a protective and ever so slightly possessive touch that sends thrills down my spine and heat building inside me.

"Tori," he growls against my lips as his forehead comes to rest on mine. "Tell me this is what you want."

It's a command, not a question, yet I don't sense anything in him that makes me worry he'd push if I said *no*.

"I want this. I want you."

His hand falls away from my throat and my sharp intake of air cuts between us. Those deep brown eyes penetrate me, desire glittering back at me. "Why do I feel like you're going to be the one to ruin me?" he murmurs so softly, I almost think I misheard. But then he's taking my hand, threading our fingers together, and leading me through the crowd I had all but forgotten about when he was kissing me.

Oh God. Anyone could have seen us. Probably *did* see us. I'm a mom. A respected writer. I don't make a habit of making out with some random guy in a room full of strangers.

But the feel of Sawyer's hand in mine, intimate in its innocence, brings me back to the here and now. In this moment, I'm not a mom or a writer, I'm just a woman who really, *really* wants this particular man to ease the throbbing ache between my legs.

We reach the elevators and step into the first empty one. The doors slide shut silently, and I turn to Sawyer as nerves war with need inside of me. "What's your last name?"

"Donnelly." He doesn't ask why I need to know, just as he doesn't say a word as I pull out my phone and type a message to Willow.

TORI: I'm going to Sawyer's room. His last name is Donnelly and he's some kind of big deal celebrity when it comes to firefighting competitions. If you don't hear from me by tomorrow, he's where to start the investigation.

Her answer comes through quickly, which is a surprise.

WILLOW: Fuck yes girlfriend. Text me if you need a ride tomorrow.

That makes me frown; I would have put good money on her spending the night with one of the other two.

TORI: You okay? Going home alone?

WILLOW: Yeah. Got a call from management, we've got some surprising news about one of the veterans that I need to deal with.

TORI: Oh no. Is it Maverick?

Willow's work in the media department for her uncle's major league baseball team is constantly being made more difficult by Maverick King. The man is a loose cannon, so much so that Willow's told me he's close to being cut from the team if he doesn't clean up his act.

WILLOW: Shockingly enough, no it's not him this time. Don't worry about me, everything will be fine. The call just kind of killed my mood. Don't let it ruin yours. Love you, go get all the orgasms!!!

The ding of the elevator indicating we've come to a stop draws my head up from my phone screen. Sawyer steps out, holding the door open as he extends one hand toward me. "Everything good?"

I take his proffered hand and step into the hall. "Yes."

Sawyer comes to a stop, sensing my hesitation even if he doesn't know where it's coming from. "We don't have to do this, Tori. I'll take you downstairs and call you a cab if that's what you want. You're in charge."

The quiet, calm way he says that, as if it would be no imposition whatsoever for me to back out on our plans for the night, settles over me.

"Willow knows who you are in case you turn out to be a psycho murderer instead of a firefighting hero." His nod of acknowledgment and respect isn't exactly what I expected as a response, and the writer in me is brimming with curiosity. I've heard stories from Willow about guys that get insulted when she does something similar. Granted, that's always a full stop red flag that ends the evening, so maybe Sawyer's smarter than most guys. "That doesn't upset you? That I feel like I need a safety plan?"

He shakes his head slowly. "Hell, no. I have a younger sister and three future sisters-in-law. Women shouldn't *need* to be so concerned with their safety around men, but the god-awful truth is that you *do* have to be. I'm not upset you needed to text your friend information about me. If that's what it takes for you to feel safe around me, then I'm all for it. I'm just sorry it's necessary in the first place."

I close the small distance between us and throw myself into another kiss. This man, this stranger. This perfectly handsome, humble, considerate, funny stranger is already making my head spin.

And we haven't even taken our clothes off yet.

CHAPTER THREE

Sawyer

She tastes like heaven, further cementing my belief that she's a fucking angel. Her body fits against mine so well it should be a sin, so maybe she's a fallen angel? I don't care. She's mine, if only for tonight.

I knew exactly what she was doing the second she asked for my last name and a part of me was relieved to know she had the sense to do that. I've spent enough time worrying about my baby sister Kat back when she was dating to know how hard it can be for women these days.

Somehow, Tori and I make it to my hotel room. It takes a stupid amount of effort to let go of her so I can open the hotel room door. And even more to fight back the urge to spin Tori around and pin her against it the second it swings shut. But I can tell she's going to want a softer touch, at least at first.

You could say it's my superpower — knowing exactly what a woman needs and wants without them saying a word.

Which is why I lean my back against the closed door and let her wander around the room, her delicate fingers trailing over the messy bedclothes. Shit, when did fingers start turning me on? She glances back at me over her shoulder, and all I want to do is sink my teeth into the creamy skin of her neck.

"Why are you so far away?" There's a heady mix of lust and excitement in her words, but I can still detect an undercurrent of nerves. Moving slowly, I push off from the wall, shrugging out of my jacket to drape it over a chair before I start untying my tie.

"Because I need a little space from your addictive self so I can make a few things clear." I pull my tie off, my eyes never leaving hers as I give her my typical pre-hookup speech. "First of all, you're in control. We do whatever you want, nothing more. I can promise you pleasure like you've never experienced, but only if you want that. This can stop at any time. Second, protection. I get regular physicals and know I'm clean, but I wrap up — always. No matter what. Third, this is just for tonight." For once in my life, those words stick in my throat, as if my body doesn't really want me to say them. But I do anyway. "I'm not a relationship guy, so if that's what you want, then we shouldn't go any further. I'm the guy who will fuck you so well you'll be seeing stars and remembering my body for days to come, but I'm not the guy you take home to Mom and Dad."

She's turned to face me by now, and there's an unreadable play of emotions across her face. The predominant one I do recognize is relief. "That's good. Because I don't need to take a guy home. I need a guy to make me forget."

I don't get the chance to ask her what she wants to forget before she's unzipping her dress, and the black fabric is pooling on the floor, leaving her in a matching set of black lace.

My hand rubs over my face as the panty-dropping grin comes into play. "Oh, you're definitely a fallen angel, aren't you?"

Her answering smile shows no more hesitation or nerves. *Good*. I peel off my shirt, letting it fall to the floor as well, leaving me in nothing but my dress pants and shoes. I close the distance between us, but instead of yanking her up into my arms, I take it slow. Letting one hand drift down her cheek, I glide it over her shoulder, along her collarbone, down the center of her chest to her belly button, then over to her hips.

"You have an outie," I whisper, her brow furrowing before morphing into a slight wince. Pink dances across her cheeks until I take her hand and place it over my own stomach. "Same as me."

She chokes out a laugh, dropping her head to my shoulder. "Sawyer," she murmurs, and I grin as I place a kiss to the top of her head. Her hands land tentatively on my chest, short nails scratching lightly. "It's been a while for me...since I...well. Um. Did this."

It doesn't take a rocket scientist to know that was hard for her to admit in the heat of the moment. Instead of a teasing response, I gather her into a hug. "Thank you for trusting me to take care of you."

Her head tilts up, a small smile playing at the corners of her mouth. "If talking about belly buttons and hugging me is your idea of foreplay, I might have to rethink that trust. What happened to fucking me until I see stars?"

One heartbeat. That's all it takes for her words to register. My hands reach around to cup her luscious ass, digging into the soft flesh as I lift her into my arms and stride over to the bed. Setting her down, I stand up, undo my belt, then slide the zipper down on my pants to give my dick room to breathe.

"You are heaven and sin wrapped up in one perfect package, aren't you, angel?"

A blush covers her cheeks as her arm wraps around her midsection. "Hardly perfect."

I drop to my knees in between her legs, pushing them apart as I lean in to kiss her. She's so much shorter than me that even down in this position I can reach her lips. "Definitely perfect." She melts against me as I take the kiss deeper, my hands threading through her soft hair.

Drawing one hand down her body, stroking every inch I can touch, I break the kiss and look Tori in the eyes. "Perfect for me to worship. Every fucking inch of you, angel." I gently push her to lie back as I drop down, bringing her lace-covered pussy right in front of my face. Not even bothering to hide my groan, I run a finger lightly over her sex. The dampness is obvious. "Jesus, Tori." She squirms a little, which prompts me to reach one hand up to rest heavily between her breasts. "Tell me you want this, angel."

"Oh my God, just eat me already!"

Her hand claps over her mouth as soon as she says it, her head falling back as her other arm comes up to cover her face.

I'm shaking with laughter. Not at her; that was hands down the hottest thing she could have said. More at how surprised she seems to be that she said it in the first place.

"Gladly."

Yanking her panties down roughly, I glance up to see her lifting her head back up to look at me, any embarrassment melting away under the scorching stare I'm giving her as I lower my head and swipe my tongue up her slit.

"Ohh..." comes her breathless moan as her head drops yet again.

I make another pass. And another. Lapping up every drop of her sweetness that I can. When her hands tentatively come to my head, I reach up and close her fingers over the strands. "Use me, Tori. Ride my fucking face. Pull my hair, hold me here, whatever the fuck *you* want is what *I* want."

The vibration of my words against her already sensitized skin has her legs threatening to squeeze the life out of me. So, naturally, I decide they can hold my head in place instead. Lifting them up one at a time to drape over my shoulders, I tug her even closer. One hand goes up to pull down the lace covering her generous tits, and I've never been so thankful for long arms in my life.

Her hips start to rock against me as she takes my instructions to heart. The tugs on my hair border on painful, but I fucking love it. I love feeling this woman abandon herself to the pleasure I'm giving her. I really do feel like a Norse god at the sounds coming out of her mouth as I latch onto her clit and suck hard. My free hand drops down to palm my dick through my boxers, willing it to stand down. No matter how hot Tori is right now, I will not come in my pants like a goddamn teenager.

Then again, the risk of that is growing higher and higher as my angel grinds her sweet pussy into my face, her voice chanting my name. My need to watch her explode is parallel to my need to plunge my cock into her wet heat.

Sliding two fingers into her dripping sex, I twist as I pull them out, my eyes trained on her face as she lifts her body up to curl over my head.

"Holy shit, holy —" Her words die out on a silent scream as I plunge my fingers back in, crooking them up and feeling for the soft, spongy spot...there.

The clench and release of her pussy around my fingers is followed immediately by a flood of moisture coating my tongue. I'm pretty sure I'm gonna have a bald patch given how hard she's gripping my hair, but I don't give a flying fuck. Tori moans her way through the most spectacular orgasm I've ever had the pleasure of witnessing on a woman.

When she finally lets go and falls back on the bed, her chest heaving and legs shaking as I lower them from my shoulders, I stand up, ignoring the ache from being on my knees. Any shred of pain was worth it just to experience Tori unraveling like that. Stepping out of my pants, condom in hand, I take in the sight of her sprawled out on my bed, curves for fucking days, all flushed pink with satisfaction.

Her eyes slowly blink open as I'm pushing down my boxer briefs, and they zero in on my throbbing cock. Licking those perfectly plump lips, she looks up at me.

"I was right. You really are going to ruin me, aren't you?"

"Happy to be of service."

I roll over as I wake, my hands already reaching for Tori. Morning sex is not to be missed if you ask me. A good one-night stand can absolutely include sleepy sex and shower sex before you say goodbye forever.

But instead of finding the luscious body that kept me up most of the night, bewitching me with her every move, I find only the cold sheets of an empty bed.

My surroundings come into sharp focus as my brain registers the fact that I'm alone.

Guess that's a *no* to the morning sex.

Why am I so disappointed?

Chapter Four

Tori

2 months later

"Muffins, Willow. Someone left a basket of muffins on my front porch."

I fold another one of Cooper's T-shirts before sliding it into the drawer of his dresser.

"Were they good muffins?"

"Yeah. Delicious."

Willow lets out a huff. "Then what's the problem? You moved to Dogwood Cove to be closer to your parents. You've been welcomed by everyone from the mayor, who happens to be your landlord, to the old guy running the hardware store, to some crazy lady wearing a weird hat. Now someone's dropped off muffins, and you're complaining? Welcome to small-town life, T. Everyone knows your name and your business, but everyone wants to help you out as well."

Well, when she puts it like that, I guess I do feel like an idiot. "It's just weird. No one would ever do this in the city."

"Because no one bothers to get to know their neighbours in Vancouver. It's pointless with how big most apartment buildings are."

"That's not fair, I knew my neighbours," I protest weakly.

I swear I can hear Willow roll her eyes over the phone as I pick up a pair of Cooper's shorts, noticing a hole in them and putting them in the discard pile.

"That's because you're *you*. You want everyone to like you, and to feel like you belong wherever you are. But what you've always missed is that it's not up to everyone else to decide whether you belong, it's up to you. When you finally find the place where you can relax and just be yourself, then you'll fit in and belong, wherever the hell you are."

Tears prick my eyes. Willow's the best kind of friend. The kind who will hold you when you break, but not let you get away with being a self-deprecating idiot.

"I miss you."

A soft sigh comes down the line. "I miss you, too. Good thing it's just a short ferry ride between us. I'll come over the weekend after next if you want. Help finish unpacking since Lord knows your living room is probably stacked full of boxes."

I wince at that all too accurate statement. "Thanks, Willow."

"Thank me with one of your mystery muffins."

I hang up the phone a few minutes later, and once Cooper's clothes are finally put away, I go in search of the kid himself. At almost eight years old, he's pretty independent, and the second we moved into the house and he discovered the tree house out back, he took off, declaring it his space.

"Coop? Let's head into town and get some groceries, bud. Mom needs tea and you need cereal if we're gonna survive tomorrow morning."

His dirty blonde head pokes out of the window of the tree house, his latest comic book in hand. "Can I get Honey Nut Cheerios?"

My smile is automatic. How I got so lucky with him, I don't know. "Sure can. But only if you pick some fruit to go with it."

He grimaces. That's the one challenge Cooper and I have — getting him to realize there's more to eat than just sugary cereal and peanut butter sandwiches. Vegetables might as well be a dirty word in his mind, and even fruit is a struggle.

"Apples."

"Deal."

Once he's buckled into the back seat of the car, and I've run back inside to grab the cloth shopping bags, we head out for the quick drive to the Grab N Go. According to Ethan Monroe, town mayor and my landlord as Willow pointed out, it's the only grocery store in Dogwood Cove. I'll have to head to Westport soon for a bigger stock up shop, but for now, we'll grab the essentials here.

I'm so happy with my choice to move here instead of Westport, where my parents have been for the last decade. It's a nice city, don't get me wrong. But the second I saw the town square here in Dogwood Cove, with an honest-to-goodness white gazebo in the middle, I knew this was where I wanted Cooper and I to live. It's small-town without being redneck, quaint and friendly without being oppressive. And when we toured the elementary school, the principal assured me there were tons of kids Cooper's age.

Sure enough, when we drive past the school where Cooper will start next week, the playground is full of kids outside on their recess break. "You ready for school, bud?" I ask, my eyes checking his reaction in the back seat.

He's always been outgoing and friendly, but I can't imagine how he feels starting over in a new school with just a couple of months left in the school year. I debated waiting until the summer, but the city started feeling claustrophobic.

Probably had something to do with my ex deciding he was ready for the family life a few years too late for *our* family. Not that I'd ever actually wanted to marry Tim and settle down with him, heck no. He was never Mr. Right, just Mr. Right Now. Still, when those two pink lines showed up a few weeks into our dating, I figured he would at least want to be a part of our son's life.

I was wrong.

"Yeah, I guess. You said I can join the chess club, right?"

That makes my lips tilt up. A couple of years ago, my kid, at the ripe old age of five and a half, walked into the house after kindergarten and announced he was going to be a competitive chess player. And could I please take him with his piggy bank to the store to buy a chess set so he could practice?

To be fair, he's got mad skills. Beats me every damn time. When the principal, Mr. Corser, confirmed there was in fact a chess club at the school, Cooper's eyes lit up and his satisfied nod was all I needed to know he'd be fine here.

He's always been happiest on the island. When we'd come to visit my parents, the pure joy I'd see on his face running along the beach or through the field of the small hobby farm next to their house was enough to fill my cup to the point that I could handle months on end in the smoggy, dirty, busy city.

We pull into the parking lot of the Grab N Go just in time to see a couple walk out hand in hand. And it's a damn good thing the car is already turned off. Because my heart leaps into my throat, turns around a few times before flopping over dead, then jumping back up, restarted with a thousand jolts of freaking-the-heck-out. They walk past our car, and it's only when they're close enough for me to make out details, like the glasses the man is wearing, that I start breathing normally again.

Not Sawyer. Someone who looks a hell of a lot like my smokin' hot one-nighter, pun intended. But it's not him.

"Mom?"

Coop's voice penetrates the fog of panic that may or may not have overcome me at the barest thought of seeing the man who rocked my world two months ago.

"Yeah, bud?" I manage to croak out, diverting thoughts away from the source of inspiration for most — okay, all — of my self-love sessions lately, and on to the tasks at hand.

Groceries. Cooper. Unpacking.

Not fantasizing over a one-night stand that will most definitely be staying in the realm of fantasies, and not reality.

"Are we gonna go in?" my kid asks pointedly, and I fight back the blush that always wants to creep over my face and body way too easily. A curse of having Irish heritage. I didn't get the cute red hair or freckles, just the annoying ability to blush at every little thing.

"Yep. Let's go. Apples, Cheerios, tea, and broccoli."

"Eww. I don't eat trees."

"But they're cute little trees," I reply cheerfully. This is an ongoing conversation Coop and I have. I've tried everything to get him to eat a vegetable. Cover it in butter, cheese sauce, bake it, roast it, fry it, raw with dip, salad, anything and everything. But the only way I get anything green into him is blended into a smoothie or snuck into spaghetti sauce. And I can't eat spaghetti every night.

We head into the store and make our way up and down the aisles. To my immense shock, Cooper chooses the apples he wants *and* agrees to a basket of overpriced berries. I bite my tongue over the cost, aching to tell him to wait a few months until the nearby farms are bursting with fresh local berries. But if he's willing to eat million-dollar strawberries? He can have them.

We pass down the aisle with cleaning supplies and pet supplies, and Cooper comes to a stop. "Mom, can we get a dog?"

My normal response, the one I've given the last five times he's asked, bubbles up, then fizzles out just as fast. Because we're not in the city where we don't even have a backyard anymore. Which means that's not a reason to say no. Is there a reason?

"We can talk about it," I say, hoping that's enough of an answer for him to not push the matter right now. All I want to do is get the groceries home, make some dinner he may or may not eat, and then pour a large glass of wine before staring at the unpacked boxes Willow called me out on. Okay, maybe it will be a mug of wine, not a glass since those are in the boxes I have yet to open.

Not that I'm going to unpack them. Just stare at them.

"Okay. But like, really talk? Or me talk and you just make random noises that you think sound like you're talking but really is just you avoiding things."

That makes me wince. When the hell did seven-year-olds get so damn smart? "Real talk. Promise. I'll use words and everything." Thankfully, that satisfies him and he turns the corner out of the damn dog aisle, leaving me to grab a bottle of laundry soap and hurry after him.

A few hours later, after dinner, dishes, and bedtime, with not one but three chapters of the book we're reading together, I carefully close the door to Cooper's bedroom. It's the only room that's fully unpacked and set up in the whole house.

Wine in hand, I eye the stack of boxes in the living room for a minute, slowly sipping the Viognier that was recommended to me at the store. It's from a local winery that's been open a couple of years, and it's flipping delicious. But it's not helping me find the ambition to unpack a box. No matter how much those boxes are judging me.

"We've only been here a few days," I mutter under my breath, glaring at the boxes. It's totally normal to not be unpacked in less than a week. I refuse to feel guilty about choosing to spend time with Cooper instead of finding the bath towels.

There's nothing wrong with using a beach towel after a shower. Nothing at all.

My eyes drift over to my computer instead. Or as I've taken to thinking of it in my head, the other inanimate object that likes to judge me.

So what if I haven't been able to write a decent sentence in months. The scene I wrote the day after my night with Sawyer was some of the hottest stuff I've ever put on paper. It had nothing to do with the book I'm on a deadline for, but it was hot.

I just haven't been able to write a damn thing since. And my editor is not pleased.

"That's Tomorrow Tori's problem," I announce to the room full of judgmental objects before pivoting on my foot and going out the front door. The house came with the most adorable porch, complete with a swing. Settling onto it, I drape the blanket over my feet and sip my wine, looking out at the quiet neighbourhood, feeling peace settle into my bones.

This is exactly where I'm meant to be. Moving here was absolutely the fresh start Cooper and I needed. The start of something amazing.

Chapter Five

Sawyer

"Beatle!" I lift my glass to toast my brother Jude as he maneuvers around the tables in Hastings Bar, his girlfriend Lily on his arm. His grimace is not unexpected. For the life of me, I cannot understand why my brothers don't appreciate the unique nicknames I give them. I put *effort* into thinking up those nicknames, and they choose to be aggravated instead of impressed.

Rude.

Lily sits down across from me, leaning over to give my baby sister, who's sitting next to me, a hug. She and Kat are best friends, which makes Lily like a second sister. Good thing Jude doesn't see her that way or their relationship would be majorly weird. Granted, she was the physical therapist assigned to help him rehab from an injury that ended his NHL career, so maybe they made it weird all on their own.

"How's my peanut?" Lily asks, rubbing Kat's stomach. Yeah, I'm about to be an uncle in a few months since Hunter knocked up my baby sister before they were even married. Fine, it was only a couple of months before they were married, but still.

"Keeping me up all night, pushing on my bladder." Kat's face twists into a pseudo frown. We all know she's not really upset at the parasite growing inside of her, but we indulge her complaints.

"As soon as Sawyer the second is born, I'll be sure to take him aside and remind him to apologize. He'll listen to his favourite uncle."

I take a sip of my beer and wait.

Three. Two. One.

"There's not a chance in hell my kid is going to be named Sawyer the second."

"Do you honestly think a newborn baby will understand a word you say?"

"Who said you'll be the favourite?"

There it is. Nothing I like better than riling up all of my siblings. And with everyone except my oldest brother Max and his fiancée Heidi present for tonight's beer and wings, I've got a captive audience. I spread my hands wide magnanimously.

"As the only Donnelly that's not tied down, it stands to reason I'll have the most time to dedicate to our newest family member. Thereby cementing my position as favourite uncle. And what the hell is wrong with the name Sawyer?"

Hunter, Kat's husband and father of the as-yet-unnamed baby, sets a fresh pitcher of beer down and a lemonade in front of Kat before sitting down himself and pushing the hair off his forehead. "What did I miss?"

"Sawyer being Sawyer, Jude being grumpy, and me trying to be a voice of reason," Kat answers helpfully. And okay, accurately.

Camilla, my twin brother Beckett's wife, who threatened bodily harm when I first tried calling her by her full name instead of Cam, leans over with a smirk. "Listen. I already share a name with the café, I don't mind sharing a name with my niece or nephew, and Cam could work for a boy or a girl."

Everyone groans at that, because Cam laying claim to Camille's café, which was named long before she moved to town, is a joke only she and Beck find funny at this point.

Beckett slugs me in the arm just as I open my mouth to give Cam heck. Instead, I glower at him. "Ow, dude."

He just cocks his head to the side. Goddamn it, having a twin who knows what you're thinking most of the time is seriously annoying.

The conversation moves on to Jude's hockey team and their playoff chances this year. The very fact they made it to the second round says a lot about his skills as a coach, and we're all gunning for them to win. I let the talk swirl around me, my eyes moving around the darkened space of Hastings Bar. This place has seen a lot from us Donnellys over the years. Dates, boys nights, family nights like tonight, and okay, fine, in years past, me on the prowl for a body to warm my bed.

The only problem is, Dogwood Cove isn't that big of a town. Meaning that I made my way through any eligible bed buddies a long time ago. And now, as I look at my siblings and how fucking happy they seem, wrapped around their significant others, getting sex on the reg, I'm annoyed because I'm a little jealous. Of the sex, of course, nothing else. But as soon as I even start thinking of sex, a beautiful blonde face upturned in ecstasy crosses my mind. I shake my head to clear it, the same way I have to every time I think of Tori.

No idea why I keep thinking of her. I mean, I'm the guy who has always said relationships are bullshit. The brother who stupidly tried to convince more than one of his siblings *not* to tie themselves down.

So what the fuck am I doing, sitting here alone, moping because I don't have a girl by my side, and thinking of a one-night stand? It's not like I want a girlfriend. Hell, no. But I'm also not loving this odd man out feeling.

"Oh hey, did you guys know Ethan finally rented out the old Quinlan house? Mila said she dropped off some muffins the other morning. It's a single mom; I think her son is around Violet's age, maybe a little older from what I've heard."

Kat's mention of our cousin Leo's kid brings a smile to my face. Vi's a riot. She was so shy when she and Leo first moved here, but over the last couple of years, she's really come out of her shell. Now, at six and a half, she's got all of us wrapped around her little fingers.

"We should see if the mom wants to come to book club," Lily injects, a mischievous glint in her eye. All of the guys chuckle. Except me.

When I turn to my twin, trying to hide my confusion, he leans in to mutter quietly, "Their book club reads super sexy romance books. The girls always come home tipsy and...let's just say, eager. Not gonna lie, I look forward to book club night."

Well, if that isn't some damn salt in the wound, I don't know what is. Still, in typical *me* style, I brush it off. "Geez, twinski, I didn't need the deets on your sex life with Cam. Keep that shit to yourself next time, you dirty boy."

I push back from the table. "I'm gonna order some food." Pointing finger guns at Kat, I wiggle my eyebrows. "Preggo, you need some more garlic cheese fries?"

Her face lights up. "Oooh, yes, you're my favourite brother. Thanks, Sawyer."

"See?" I say, spreading my hands with a grin. "Favourite brother means favourite uncle."

Someone throws a wadded-up napkin at me, probably Jude, the grump. I just let it bounce off me. Then, after taking their requests for food, I head to the bar and pass it on to the waitress.

"Hey, handsome," a voice purrs at the same time nails rake down my arm, making me shiver — and not in a good way.

Turning at the same time as I shift back slightly, I flash a smile at Carrie Lyons. She lives in Westport but often visits friends in Dogwood Cove. Nothing against the woman; we hooked up and it was not a terrible way to spend an evening. But she had this habit of raking her stupidly long and pointy nails down my back. And while I don't mind a little pain with my pleasure, that sensation was a hard no for me. Reminded me too much of needles.

I fucking hate needles.

"Carrie. Hi. How's it goin'?" I try to keep my voice neutral. Because from the tone of her voice, and the way she's leaning forward, making it almost impossible not to stare straight down her shirt unless I keep my eyes trained on her forehead, Carrie's got one thing on her mind.

A repeat.

And I don't do repeats.

But if Tori was the one asking...

Yeah, I wouldn't say no to another night with her in my arms, surrounded by her warmth, her fucking perfect pussy hugging my dick so tight I have to fight back my orgasm almost instantly. The sound of her sweet voice screaming my name as she climaxes ringing in my ears.

And now I'm fucking hard. In front of Carrie Lyons. Who's still looking at me like I'm a tasty snack she wants to eat.

Fuckity fuck fuck.

"You know, my friends are ready to head home, but I'm not." As if I didn't already know what she's aiming for, Carrie's suggestive tone is making it impossible to misunderstand.

I try to school my expression away from the grimace I want to give her. "Sorry, Carrie, I'm here with my fam-jam. Catching up, you know?" I stop myself before tacking on the words *another time* because there's not a chance in hell I want to leave that door open. I'm saved by the bell — or in this case, the appearance of some of the food I ordered for the table. Snatching it from the waitress with a grateful wink, I say, "Here, let me help." I glance over my shoulder to Carrie, who actually looks disappointed, making me feel a teeny tiny bit bad for dismissing her so thoroughly. "See ya, Carrie."

Then I beeline back to the table surrounded by my siblings. Setting the fries down in front of Kat with a flourish, I sink back into my chair. "Enjoy, parasite host."

Her mouth stuffed full of fries already, Kat glares at me. I know what's coming as soon as she swallows. "That's got to be the worst nickname you have *ever* come up with, and if you call me that again, I'll revoke your uncle status."

I just give her a massive grin. "You can't do that. It's biologically impossible."

"Fine. You won't be invited to the hospital after I give birth, so you'll have to wait, knowing everyone else meets the baby before you." She smiles triumphantly as my mouth falls open in horror, because that is a risk I'm not willing to take.

"Fine. You win this round." I lean over and steal a fry from her plate, earning another glare. But this time I just shrug.

Lily catches Kat's attention about something, and the spotlight from my aggressively emotional sister, thanks to pregnancy hormones, is off me. Not gonna lie, I sag in my seat a little. The woman has always been a powerhouse; she had to be with four older brothers. But now? Kat is a force to be reckoned with.

"Since when do you walk away from a beautiful woman at the bar?"

Beckett's amused whisper is low enough for only me to hear. Twisting in my seat, I make sure he sees my eye roll. "Listen, twinbro. Just because you're happily married and all that shit doesn't mean I want to be tied down."

He holds up his hands in defense. "Don't be a dick. I'm just saying, I've noticed you haven't really been hitting on anyone the last few weeks. Everything okay?"

It takes me by surprise a little that my brother's asking me about my hookup situation, but Beck and I went through a weird rough patch a while back. My fault, I realize, so I guess he's just trying really hard to make sure things are cool.

"Everything's fine, Becky-boo. Worry less about my dick getting some action and focus on making sure yours doesn't get bored with old married sex, okay?"

Of course, Cam had to hear that last bit, and her arm snakes out behind Beck's back to smack the back side of my head. "Shut the fuck up, Sawyer, don't diss married sex. It's fucking amazing."

Hunter and Kat lift their glasses. "Cheers to that."

I drop my head in my hands with a dramatic groan. "Stop, please, for the love of cheese fries and beer. No more married sex talk. My dick is gonna shrivel up in fear."

The assholes I apparently am stuck with for a family all just laugh at me. Listen, I'm happy *they're* happy, but does that mean

I have to put up with their lovey-dovey *relationships are great* bullshit all the time?

No thanks.

This calls for another drink.

CHAPTER SIX

Sawyer

"Donnelly, you're the perfect man for the job, and you know it."

Those words are what led me to this moment. Well, those words and the realization that these kinds of things look really good when you're waiting to hear about a promotion like I am. Which is why, when Chief said he needed a volunteer for career day at Dogwood Cove Elementary, I put on my best smile and said, "Sure, sounds fun."

Spoiler alert — it *is* fun. Kids are a fuckin' riot. Their questions had me fighting back a grin. One asked, "Does it hurt when you slide down the pole?" Which was just marginally less hilarious than another who asked, "Why is your hose so big?"

Oh kid, you have no idea.

Of course, the best question of all came from one nosy little girl who waved her hand frantically at the end of our session, only to have every adult turning bright red in the room when she said, "My mom has a calendar with you in it holding a puppy, but it looks like you're not wearing pants. Is that 'cause the puppy peed on you?"

I nodded very solemnly at that one. "Yup, that's exactly why."

After the Q&A, the kids all followed us outside to climb on the engine, playing with the sirens and lights, but not the *very big hose*, no matter how much they begged.

Honestly, the whole day was fun. And over too soon. The kids headed back to their classrooms to get their bags and do whatever it is kids do at the end of a school day. Then Sloan, who was the sucker that had to come with me, and I had the job of putting everything back on the rig.

Reid Corser, the principal, wandered over to thank us again and we got caught up in conversation about a local rock climbing area I've been wanting to check out. Next thing I know, the bell rings and kids come flooding out the doors of the school, most of them beelining straight over to the rig.

Sloan shoots me a glare. "Told you we shoulda left," he mutters. Guess someone isn't a fan of rug rats. I shrug, grinning at his discomfort.

"Too bad, dude, we're here until the kids are done. It's called community service."

With a long sigh that makes it clear I owe the man a beer, Sloan turns to the kids and greets them.

Reid's chuckle draws my attention back to him. "I get why you're here, you're a natural with them. But he doesn't seem to share the enthusiasm."

"Nah, but he's a probie, so he didn't have a choice." I smirk.

Reid looks confused, so I explain the nickname. "Probie because he's still on probation, new to the department. Except, Sloan volunteered with us for a while before getting hired, so he knows what he's doing."

Understanding shows on Reid's face as he shakes his head. "You and your nicknames."

I shrug. "Eh, that one's cheating, we call all new recruits 'probie.'"

The sound of a pained cry pulls both of our gazes to the playground, where a boy is slowly picking himself up from the ground.

"Uh-oh, Cooper's a new student here. Hope he's okay," Reid says, the two of us already hurrying over to the kid.

"Hey buddy, did you fall?" I ask, taking in his brave face and the way he's fighting back tears. He gives me a shaky nod and holds out his hand, the palm of which is pretty scraped up.

"Ouch, that looks sore, Coop. Is your mom here? We can take you inside and clean it up." Reid's voice is calm, and it's clear why he's in charge of all the kids. The dude is unfazed.

"She's not here yet," comes a soft whisper. But I catch his eyes bouncing over to the fire truck, and I have a moment of brilliance if I might say so myself.

"Hey Mr. Corser, could you bring Cooper over to the rig? We've got a first aid kit and can clean him up there."

I see the kid's face light up, and Reid does too. "Sounds good, Sawyer. Let's go Coop,"

It takes no time at all to clean the kid's hand and get him bandaged up, with a sticker of course. When it's all done I bend down in front of him. "Y'know, Coop, you were probably the bravest kid I've ever taken care of. It's totally okay to cry, heck I cry when I get hurt. But you handled everything really well. In fact, you were so brave, I feel like you're ready to join the super secret brave club."

Out of the corner of my eye I can see Reid quirking a brow at me, but making shit up to make people smile is kinda my specialty.

"What's that?" Cooper asks quietly.

"It's a super secret group of people who are really really brave. We've got a special handshake that we do when we see each other."

His eyes widen. "Can I learn it?"

I let my face go serious. "You think you can handle the responsibility of a secret handshake?"

The kid nods eagerly. "Yup I sure can."

On the fly I come up with a combination of movements, not too crazy but complicated enough that Cooper asks me to go through it a few times until he's got it down. We're just at the end of our latest round when a voice I never expected to hear again comes from across the parking lot.

"Cooper I'm here, I'm so sorry I'm late buddy!"

My head whips around faster than a cartoon road runner, and there she is. Hurrying towards us, in a t-shirt with a bunch of old ladies on it, her hair in a sloppy bun with loose strands flying around her, and a look of stress marring her prefect face.

I watch in disbelief as Tori, the angel of my fantasies, swoops Cooper up in a hug ignoring his protests.

"I was in a meeting with Carol and I lost track of time then I got turned around and I'm so sorry, Coop. So so sorry." Her eyes look up to Reid, and I shamelessly take advantage of the attention not being on me for once to just take her in.

She's not all dolled up like she was the night of the gala, but she's just as beautiful. Maybe even more so now that I see her in daylight, where I can make out the smattering of freckles across her nose and the natural flush on her cheeks.

"Sorry Mr. Corser, I swear I'm not usually late for pickup. I don't think I've ever been late in fact, always on time if not early. It won't happen again, I'm still figuring my way around town and - "

"Tori it's absolutely fine. It happens to everyone, and Coop here was getting some special attention from our local fire department after taking a tumble on the playground."

Finally her gaze flips over to me, those gorgeous eyes that are seared into my memory growing impossibly wider. I see recognition and shock written all over her face and feel my own features smoothing into a smile. But any ideas that might have been forming my head about a round two with Tori get tossed aside when she stands up and sticks her hand out.

"Tori Charles. Thanks for looking after my son, sorry if it kept you from anything important."

Not gonna lie, it stings a bit her pretending not to know who I am. After all, I'm nothing if not memorable. But my manners force me to play along.

"Not a problem, Tori. Name's Sawyer Donnelly, and there was nothing more important than getting to see how brave Coop was." I flash her a smile before turning back to Cooper. "See you around, little dude." Placing my hand out palm up, I wait a second before he gives me a grin and we go through our handshake again.

Then, with nothing more than a nod of my head to Reid and Tori, I turn to the rig and my partner. "Let's go, Sloan."

As we make our way through town back to the station, I try to wrap my head around what just happened. And the reality that my one-night stand now lives in my small town. I've never had a woman I hooked up with, well, hook *me* so thoroughly. But there's no avoiding the fact that I keep thinking about Tori, of our night together.

Maybe it's because she ducked out when I was asleep, which has honestly never happened before. Granted, I've only fallen asleep after fucking once or twice, but both times my partner was still there in the morning for some epic morning sex. But Tori ghosted me. *Ghosted me!*

I could chalk it up to that, to being miffed that she disappeared, but that would imply I wanted something more. And I never want something more.

So why the fucking hell can I not stop thinking about wanting *more Tori?*

And more importantly, what am I gonna do about it now that she's here?

CHAPTER SEVEN

Tori

There are moments when having a kid is a major inconvenience. And no, I'm not being the world's worst mom when I say that.

How would you feel after running into the star of your hottest fantasies, the man you walked out on after a night of the best sex of your life, because you got a call from the mom hosting your kid for a sleepover, saying he woke up with a stomachache? Oh, and let's not forget that you run into said hunky hottie hero while wearing your grubbiest Golden Girls T-shirt, the comfort shirt you wear when it's laundry day, along with a ratty sports bra. Also, your hair's a mess and you're running late to pick up your kid because of a meeting with your editor where, yet again, you had to explain why you wouldn't be meeting your deadline.

Yeah, not my best moment.

Which brings me to now, driving Cooper home from school, when I just wanted to be left alone to my internal freak-out. But my wonderful, amazing progeny wants to talk *nonstop* about the super cool firefighter who was at career day. The one who bandaged up his scraped hands, gave him a sticker, and taught him a secret handshake.

Listen, kid, I know Sawyer Donnelly is hot shit. I do. I know it for my own reasons. And now I know he's good with kids which, surprisingly, does *not* help the lady boner going on within me. Listening to my son go on about how he's just *sooo awesome* is not helping my freak-out over seeing him again. Not one bit.

Thankfully, I guess, by the time we get home, I've managed to give Coop enough head nods and mm-hmm's of acknowledgment that he doesn't seem to realize how badly I'm about to explode mentally. He skips into the house without a care in the world, and I slowly trail after him, doing the usual cleanup as we go. Shoes he cannot for the life of him remember to put on the rack get picked up. The abandoned lunch kit, that at least this time made it out of the backpack, is collected and taken to the kitchen. Remnants of his snack is tidied just in time for my stressed expression to soften as I watch him pick up his tablet with a hopeful look.

"Can I video call Tommy from the tree house?"

I nod, because there's no better way to get a few moments to myself than to let him talk to his closest friend from Vancouver for a while. "Of course. Say hi from me."

Once he's safely ensconced in the tree house, I beeline for the bottle of wine in the fridge. I don't give a flying fuck that it's not even four o'clock. Since the wine glasses are still not unpacked, I pour it into a mug. Thank God Willow's coming soon to help because if I was by myself, those boxes would still be stacked there six months from now.

I briefly consider calling her to talk about Sawyer, but instead, I sink down on a kitchen chair and let my gaze go unfocused as my thoughts turn inward.

Of all the small towns in the world, he had to live in this one? Why? Why, universe, why? My one moment of being wild — since becoming a mom, at least — and it has to come back and haunt me like this? Life is so flipping unfair.

And of course, I had to make matters worse by pretending not to know him. Then again, what else could I do? It's not like I was going to admit I knew him because he gave me multiple orgasms in one night, right in front of my kid and my kid's new principal.

Again, I say, not fair.

I haven't had a man-made orgasm in eight years. *Eight. Years.* Then Sawyer Donnelly comes along and wrecks me for all other men. I could've lived with that, simply used him as masturbation motivation for the next ten years, or until Cooper moves out and I can consider dating again, but *no*. Oh, no. The universe decides to ruin my new start by throwing the very epitome of temptation in my path.

Damn it.

My internal rant finishes about the same time my mug of wine is emptied, and I push up to stand. Time to get back on track. I'm a single mom, my kid needs me to function and make dinner and do bedtime. Then I've got to push out some words or Carol is going to have my head. There's no more time to be spent wondering how I'll manage living in the same town as Sawyer and not want to immediately find the nearest bed.

I go through the motions of making a pasta dish Cooper loves. It's one of the few things in which I can hide some veggies, as long as he isn't looking. He knows they're in there, but for some reason, if he doesn't see me put them in, and there's a tasty enough sauce masking the flavour, he'll eat them. Which means we have homemade cheesy spaghetti casserole at least once a week. Cooper comes in the back door just as I'm sliding the casserole dish into the oven and his eyes light up.

"Is that cheesy sgabetti?" he asks, and I hide my smile at his name for it. Memories of the first time he said *spaghetti* that way flash through my mind. He was maybe three years old, and it was the cutest thing. Even though he knows how to pronounce the word now, it's our little inside joke.

God, I love this kid. He's everything to me. He's my priority; his happiness and peace of mind with this move are paramount above anything else.

Which is exactly why hunky hottie heroes need to stay away. My energy is devoted to Cooper. Not the man who is probably the inspiration for that cheesy trope of heroines intentionally burning their food just so the fire department will come to their house.

"You know it, bud." I lift up my salad bowl and tease him with it. "And look at this beautiful bowl of fresh veggie goodness. You know you're just dying to try some."

The horrified look on his face as he backs up makes me laugh. Picking up a slice of cucumber, I slowly start to walk toward him.

"Mom. No. Eww."

"Come on, Coop. One itty-bitty slice."

He's fighting back a grin now, too; the routine of this familiar, even in its ridiculousness.

"No way."

The ringtone of my phone interrupts our game. "Saved by the bell, kid," I say, arching my brow as I pop the cucumber into my mouth and pick up my phone. "Oh. It's your dad."

I watch Cooper's face carefully, but don't see any reaction. He hasn't really shown one since learning his sperm donor was marrying someone and moving to Alberta.

I worry that someday, Tim's easy dismissal of his own child will hit Cooper. How could it not instill feelings of unworthiness, abandonment, and anger? I know I feel all of that, and he's not my biological father.

He's just the man who knocked me up.

I love my kid and don't regret having him — not for a single second. But do I secretly long for the perfect family with two parents, a cute little house, and multiple kids running around in chaos? Of course.

I never wanted that with Tim; he was a short-lived relationship that never would have gone further, even if those two pink lines hadn't shown up. But I'm also not going to lie to myself and try to say finding out his whole "I don't want a family" shtick only applied to us didn't hurt.

My finger taps the button to accept his call and I lift my phone to my ear. "Hi, Tim."

"Hey, Tor."

I hate that name. I've told him a million times not to call me Tor.

"We're about to eat dinner, so I don't have long. What's up?" My voice sounds flat to my ears, but hopefully not to Cooper.

"My parents want Cooper to be at the wedding. Mom said they would fly out with him, take him to the wedding, then fly him back."

I have to bite back my initial response. *His parents want him at the wedding. Not him.* What an asshole.

Tim's parents have been good to Cooper, there's no argument there. Even though their son dropped everything and ran, the second they somehow found out Tim had fathered a child, they showed up and haven't stopped showing up whenever I've needed something. We had an unspoken agreement to just not mention Tim in those early days, and they never questioned my having full custody, but his mom was the one to ask me to let Tim see his child.

"Why isn't your mom calling me about this?" I ask, trying to keep my voice quiet. But of course, Cooper hears me, and his head lifts up at mention of his nana.

"She told me to."

Of course, she did. Racquel Watson is no fool. She knows her son will never step up and be the dad Cooper deserves, but that doesn't stop her from trying to push him a little.

"I'll think about it," comes my curt reply.

"I wanna go see Nana," Cooper says, and just my luck, Tim hears him.

"See? Cooper wants to come."

I frown, not at Cooper, but at my idiot ex. "I will *consider* it, talk it over with Cooper, and then talk it over with your mother."

"Fine. Whatever."

God, was he always such an ass? Yeah, he was. "We've gotta go, Tim."

"'Kay. Bye." He hangs up without even asking to say hi to his son. It breaks my heart on Cooper's behalf, but my kid is looking at me with such hope in his eyes, I can't help but reach out to him and pull him in for a quick hug.

"Let's eat, and we can talk about you going with Nana and Pops to your dad's wedding."

Between dinner and dishes, Cooper convinces me he really wants to spend the weekend with his grandparents. He doesn't mention the wedding, and it's abundantly clear to me that his father is not the reason he wants to go.

We called Racquel and finalized the plans, all without any mention of the deadbeat. I must admit, while I'm sad for Cooper that his father is so useless, I am grateful to have the connection to his parents. With mine living here on the island, when we were in Vancouver, Racquel would often help with childcare if I was on a deadline.

And the prospect of a kid-free weekend to catch up on this overdue book is a good one.

When I finally make it into bed, my thoughts are still a jumbled up, tangled mess. After I thump my pillow for the fourth time, flipping back and forth from my side to my back, just trying to make my body relax into sleep, I give up and yield to my curiosity. Opening my phone in the dark room, a quick search lands me on the Dogwood Cove Fire Department website. There, on the main page, is a photo of some of the crew, and of course — because that's how my day has gone — Sawyer is front and center, that big, wide smile plastered all over his stupidly handsome face.

"Not fair. No single person should wield that much power — being good-looking, good in bed, and a good person."

Because after what I saw today, the handshake and the way he handled Cooper, there's little doubt Sawyer is a good guy. I'm sure he's also a player, a flirt, and a ladies' man, but today he was just a kindhearted man who is now my son's new hero.

Awesome.

There's little chance of stopping myself now that I'm staring at his face, so even with my guilt and embarrassment in full swing, I scroll through the website, stopping anywhere there's photos. When I come up with just one or two more photos of Sawyer in full gear, I switch my search.

BC Firefighters Calendar.

And right there, on the bio page for Mr. July, is the information that could have saved me a ton of embarrassment earlier today.

"Sawyer Donnelly, an eleven-year veteran of the Dogwood Cove Fire Department, is honoured to return as your Mr. July for a second year."

If only I hadn't been so determined to keep Sawyer where I thought he belonged, in my memory bank only, I might have known I was moving to the very town he lived in. If I had let myself look him up sooner, I could have been prepared instead of being caught unaware, like I was today.

Would it have changed anything? Probably not. I'd still be here, fantasizing over the man who likely thinks I'm a crazy stalker for moving to his town.

Muffling my groan as another wave of embarrassment hits me over *that* realization, I set my phone down and squeeze my eyes shut. God, what he must have thought at seeing me again. Well, at least I can be confident I've ruined any chance of him wanting to strike up anything more with me. Between the possibility of me being a crazy stalker combined with the single mom status that makes guys like Sawyer sprint in the other direction, there's not a chance he's going to ever want to acknowledge my existence again.

But lying here with my eyes shut, an image of Sawyer's photo from the calendar seared into my brain, I have to admit, there's no way I'll be able to forget him. And I know that every time I see him around town, which is bound to happen in a place as small as Dogwood Cove, no matter how hard I plan on trying to avoid the man, it'll be a reminder there are good guys in the world. Good guys who give good orgasms.

Getting up, I go to my closet and reach for a locked box on the top shelf. There's only one thing that will help me sleep at this point, when I'm still feeling frustrated. But a different kind of frustration, if you know what I mean.

Making my selection — a long black vibrator that hits in all the right spots, although not quite as well as Sawyer's dick did — I lock my bedroom door and settle back in bed. Taking a deep breath, I try to push thoughts of the firefighter out of my mind.

But as soon as the first vibration hits my clit, I fail, and when my trusty battery-operated boyfriend brings me to a quick and dirty climax only minutes later, there's no escaping the hushed word that falls from my lips.

"Sawyer."

CHAPTER EIGHT

Sawyer

How I let myself get suckered into running one of the BC Wildfire Fighter new recruit boot camps, I will never know.

I've volunteered my time to fighting wildfires for several years. It's how I met Derek and Boone, and there's no denying the importance of the work, especially as the fire situation worsens every year. But as I move up in rank in Dogwood Cove, my priority has been my home station and crew.

But the man who runs the entire wildfire training program reached out to me personally, saying he was short an instructor. The next thing I knew, I was hopping on a plane to the town in the BC interior where the boot camp is run a few times each year.

The weeklong training session was fun, but also tiring, hot, sweaty, and at times, a stark reminder of what can go wrong in this job if your mind isn't fully focused. Some of these recruits need to get their heads out of their asses and realize the fire doesn't give a shit about whatever drama you have going on at home. The fire will eat that drama for breakfast and use it to grow into an even bigger bastard that needs to be extinguished.

Deciding to tack on a couple of days in Vancouver to catch up with the boys was a given, as was coming to this bar tonight. I need a distraction, someone to help clear the smell of wood smoke out of my mind for a few hours.

But we've been at this nightclub for over an hour, and no one has caught my attention. Or maybe the better word is *held* my attention. There's plenty of ladies here tonight; I've taken a few out on the dance floor for a spin. Yes, I dance. Quite well, I might add. It's my backup weapon if the smirk ever fails. Not that it does, but you know. A man's gotta have options.

And this man had a younger sister that wanted to learn how to dance when she was younger, forcing all of her brothers to learn as well. Thanks, Kat.

Right now, I've got one hand resting lightly on the hip of a redhead who's grinding her ass back into my crotch. The music is pumping through my veins and I'm feeling loose from the couple of drinks I've already had. This girl could be fun, even if my dick isn't responding to her at all. Then she spins around and yanks my head down to ask if I want to buy her another drink, and her rank breath hits me, making me fight back a gag.

No, thanks. Besides, I'm not so sure I want a redhead tonight, anyway.

Now, a blonde...

Ah, for fuck's sake. No. I'm not here to think about the cute little angel that decided to take over *my* hometown, *and* my sanity.

I manage to get away from dragon breath without any issue, especially seeing as some other dude was obviously biding his time and wasted none of it swooping in to spin her back out on the dance floor. Now unencumbered, I wander over to Derek, who's leaning against a post, surveying the crowd.

"Swing and miss?" he asks, sipping on what I know is a Jack and Coke. He'll move on to beer after this, seeing as one drink is all he can handle. Why else would his nickname be Lightweight? The baseball analogy makes me grin. Derek's a die-hard Vancouver Tridents fan, and even with my brother being a former pro-hockey player, I find myself preferring the old ball game as well.

"Nah, didn't even take a swing. Not feelin' that one."

He just nods. "Cowboy already left with the girl he's been seeing."

"Cowboy's seeing a girl?" I ask incredulously, but Derek just shrugs.

"Guess so."

"Huh, weird. Are we still doing breakfast at the diner tomorrow?" I ask, draining my glass.

Derek fixes me with an incredulous *are you a dumbass* look, but I just smirk. "Are you seriously asking that?"

My shoulders lift and I can't help but needle the guy. "I mean, it's been a while. Maybe tastes have changed."

"Fuck off, asshole," he grumbles, glaring at me.

Nothing's changed. Derek's still just as obsessed with the diner we always hit for breakfast when I'm in town. Or maybe it's more accurate to say he's obsessed with the owner. A cute little thing who never gives him the time of day.

"I'm getting a beer. You want one?" I ask by way of an apology for giving him a hard time. Getting a nod, I make my way to the bar. Of course, being the city, it takes way too long to flag down a bartender. This is when I miss Hastings, the local bar in Dogwood Cove. Sure, it doesn't have the dance floor teeming with hot babes ready for a night of anonymous sex, but it does have good beer and good food, and you don't have to wait forever to order a drink.

Finally, two beers in hand, I return to Derek and hand over his drink. We stand there, enjoying our beers before a flash of blonde hair catches my attention. It's not Tori, but the blonde hair is enough to get some sort of reaction out of me.

"I'll see you tomorrow, man."

Derek gets my drift instantly, taking my beer with a chuckle. "Go get 'em, Loverboy."

I make my way over to the woman who caught my eye. She's pretty enough, and definitely dressed to kill in a skintight red dress that barely covers a juicy ass. And I can tell by the looks she and her friends are tossing out to various guys, she's looking for some fun.

I wait until she catches my eye, then I unleash the smirk. There it is — her eyes widen and a sultry smile covers her face.

Her moves get even more sensual, and it's like she's set off a fucking tractor beam, intending to pull me in.

My hand slides around her waist, high enough to be respectful, just in case I've read things wrong, but let's face it, I *never* read things wrong. "Hey, beautiful."

Her arms come up around my neck. "Hi."

We start to move, and for a short while I let myself sink into the allure of the moment. I'm dancing with another beautiful woman, and this one might just hold my attention long enough to make it worthwhile. I don't want to think about why the blonde hair is making a difference.

Next thing I know, her hands are running down my chest and she's grabbing onto my belt, pulling my pelvis in to meet hers. "You're hot," she titters, and my mouth curves into an automatic grin.

"Thanks, babe."

She pouts, and that's the first sign this chick might not be what I'm looking for. "Don't you think I'm hot?" Her hand drops and covers my junk. "We're just two hot people looking for a good time."

Seriously? Is she for real? That's got to be the cheesiest line I've ever heard, and I've heard — and used — some doozies. She starts to lead me off the dance floor, making it crystal clear she wants more.

But even *I* have standards, and hooking up in the bathroom of a nightclub is below them, even for me. I know I could change the plan; I could convince her to come back to my hotel room with zero effort. And I should be into this, but I'm starting to realize just how *not into this* I am.

I don't even know her fucking name, and while she might be blonde, she's not the *right* blonde. She doesn't fit next to my body like she was made to be there, and she definitely doesn't set my blood on fire like I want her to.

She's not Tori. And given how annoyed I am that she pretended we'd never met, I fucking hate that my goddamn head won't stop throwing the memories of our night together at me like mini grenades.

I drop my hands from her waist as I lean down to say in her ear, "Listen, babe, I'm sorry to change it up, but this isn't gonna happen." I know I'm an asshole. The worst kind to string a girl along — even a little — and then drop her like this. I feel like a fucking chump as I disentangle myself from her clutches and step back. I'm at the edge of the dance floor and stuff my hands into my pockets as I hope she doesn't freak.

She freaks.

Her jaw drops open. "Are you fucking kidding me right now?" Her voice is so shrill, even over the pounding beat of the music, it makes me cringe. But I simply nod.

"You're seriously turning *me* down?" Her hands are on her hips, her outrage and disbelief clear. And all I can do is fucking nod *again*.

"Sorry. I know it sounds shitty; it *is* shitty. But yeah. I just..." I shrug because what the fuck am I meant to say? I'm sure as shit not gonna admit to a stranger that I don't want her because

I can't stop thinking about a single mom who rocked my world once, and now she won't even admit to knowing my name.

She storms off, back to the dance floor, probably straight to her friends to bash me. I make a quick exit out the front and call an Uber, any plans of finding a hookup for the night completely abandoned.

Once I'm finally back in my hotel room, I strip, letting my clothes fall as I beeline for the bathroom and turn the shower on. Stepping under the steaming hot water, I get to work scrubbing every inch of my body, as if soap and water can clean away how fucked up I feel inside.

Because hooking up with that girl would've been a mistake. One I never used to hesitate to make. Random sex with a woman? I'm there. Can't remember her name? Oh well. But now, it seems a certain blonde has invaded my head and turned me against myself. And I don't fucking know what to do about it.

Goddamn it, if that woman being in the same town as me is gonna ruin my game and make it impossible for me to have sex with anyone else, I'm gonna have to move.

"Okay, what the hell is wrong with you? You're never this quiet."

I glance over my shoulder at my twin, not breaking my stride. I got back from Vancouver yesterday and let Beckett convince me to go for a hike today, but I didn't realize "hike" was synonymous with "inquisition."

"Whatever do you mean, twinski? Can't a guy just enjoy the beautiful scenery and the dulcet tones of his brother's heavy breathing, signifying just how out of shape he is now that he's got the ole ball and chain?"

Must. Deflect. The downside of having a twin is having someone who legit knows you better than yourself most days. And Beckett and I, despite being opposites in so many ways, are very much like that.

"Dude, fuck off with that." He sounds annoyed. "Cam's *not* a ball and chain and I'm *not* out of shape. You're the one speeding up the damn mountain like there's a pot of gold at the top."

"Pfft. Who wants gold? I'll take a pot of gummy bears, thank you very much."

"Stop changing the subject. What's going on in that head of yours?"

Beckett grabs my arm and drags me off the trail to a frustratingly convenient bench at one of the many lookouts that this particular path has. "You've been distracted for weeks, bro. At the studio opening, you looked like you'd seen a ghost, then at Mom and Dad's last week, you didn't say anything when Jude took the last slice of pie. You *never* pass up fighting for pie."

I turn my face to hide my wince because I was *pissed* when I realized I missed out on a second slice of Mom's apple pie. That shit is delicious. "I wasn't hungry."

"Bullshit."

Slumping against the back of the bench, I tip my head and stare at the treetops, the blue sky poking through the gaps in the branches. I love living on the West Coast, and spring days like today are the perfect example why. It's warm, but not hot. Sunny, but still crisp and fresh. Birds are chirping, there's a delightful breeze and...

"Sawyer. Seriously?"

And my twin is getting increasingly annoyed with my avoidance. Letting my head loll to the side, I smirk. "Listen. I'm just trying to have a nice time with my brother. I don't know what you're getting at, but everything's fine. I was thinking about a call we had the other night, that's why I missed Jude being a pie thief. And as for Cam's studio opening, maybe I did see a ghost. You ever think about that? Hmm? Dogwood Cove has been around long enough to gather a few spirits, maybe my keen eyes caught one of them drifting along Main Street." Yeah, if a ghost is a beautiful blonde, who at the time I thought I was imagining — but after recent events, it turns out, maybe I wasn't...

Beckett stares at me through his glasses. He's an accountant, which means he's nothing if not logical and fact based in his thinking. Which also means, unfortunately, he can sniff out bullshit a mile away. It's just a question of how hard he is going to push me to explain myself today.

I'm hoping not too hard, because I'm not ready to confess to anyone that I know the newest resident of Dogwood Cove.

Intimately.

Some things are better kept to myself for now. At least until I can figure out what the hell I'm going to do with these pesky *feelings* being stirred up inside of me with Tori suddenly appearing in my life.

Feelings. The *real* "F" word.

CHAPTER NINE

Tori

There's a zero percent chance I will admit to anyone the fact that I'm mildly disappointed I haven't seen Sawyer in ten days. Not that I'm counting or anything.

I feel bad for pretending not to know him that day at Cooper's school. After thinking — okay, overthinking — about it all, I realized I could've handled it better. Does my seven-year-old need to know Mommy had sex with the nice firefighter who bandaged his hand? Nope, definitely not. But could he know that Mommy met the firefighter when she was with Auntie Willow? Sure. His mind is innocent enough not to read anything into that.

But that's a moot point now, seeing as the man has all but disappeared from town. I saw a guy who looked a lot like him, only with a thick beard and a beautiful brunette on his arm, coming out of Camille's café the other day, but no sign of Sawyer.

I have it all planned out in my head. We'd see each other, I'd be looking cute this time, and apologize for my fumble at the school. We'd laugh about the coincidence of living in the same town now and move on with our lives like adults.

Adults who had really, *really* good sex.

Okay, thinking about really good sex while walking the aisles of the grocery store getting food for my kid's school lunches is a little inappropriate. Giving my head a little internal shake, I refocus my attention on my current mission: some way to get Coop to eat more than just cheese and crackers for lunch each day. Picking up a box of macaroni and cheese that claims to have a serving of vegetables in it, I'm lost in thought, wondering if I can fool him into at least trying it.

"What are you doing here?"

The frustrated tone of that deep voice I'll never forget startles me. Looking up — way up — since the man is considerably taller than me, I take in the scowl on his face with some surprise.

"Excuse me?" I say like an idiot, still trying to catch up to why Sawyer would have any reason to be annoyed with me.

He runs his hands through his already messy hair and my eyes follow the motion, remembering the time I was the one to rake my own fingers through those locks. "You're just... You're here. In Dogwood Cove. You're everywhere."

My jaw falls open. What the hell is wrong with this guy? "First of all, I live here now. I had no idea this is where you live when we hooked up, trust me. This isn't some sort of weird stalker situation. And second of all, this is only the second time since moving here that I've seen you, so what the heck is your problem?"

He lets out a huff and mutters something under his breath, the only words I catch being "out of my head." Now I'm starting to think I might want to keep my distance from Sawyer Donnelly, no matter how hot he is and how good the sex was. I get that it might seem odd to him, his one-night stand suddenly showing up in his town, but it's an innocent coincidence. And his reaction to me right now is just bizarre. If I didn't know any better, I'd say he's flustered. Which, for a guy who runs into burning buildings for a living, seems odd.

"Listen, this doesn't have to be awkward." I try to use my best soothing mom voice, because Sawyer's still looking fidgety, like he would rather be anywhere but here. "I'm sorry for pretending not to know you that day at the school, but maybe that's for the best. A fresh start, if you will. No one needs to know our past connection, and we can just move on." There, that sounded calm and rational, didn't it? Except, the fire that flashes through his brown eyes makes my breath stutter.

"Connection? That's what you're calling it?"

I try to swallow and have to force my body to respond. "Well, yeah. I guess?" Damn it, where's the soothing mom voice now? All it takes is a few words spoken in that low, rumbly voice of his to reduce me to a puddle. "Anyway. I honestly had no idea you lived here when we first met, I swear. What we had was only ever meant to be, you know..." I drop my voice to a whisper. "One night."

I must be hearing things, because why the hell would his breath catch when I say that?

"Right. One night."

I nod, and finally find the courage to meet his gaze. Big, *big* mistake. Because somehow, we've moved closer to each other, and those whiskey brown eyes are just as arresting as they were when he was hovering over top of me, plunging his perfect cock into my... Shit. No. Stop it, Tori.

But it's too late. I've never been good at hiding my feelings, and it's clear Sawyer can tell exactly where my thoughts were going. He leans in, and like a magnet is pulling us together, my body shifts toward him as well. My eyes flutter closed as I tilt my head up, ready for...

"Fine. I guess I'll see you around, then." A slight brush of cold air whisks past me as my eyes fly open just in time to see him round the corner of the aisle before my brain can even catch up to whatever the hell just happened. Was he going to kiss me, or was that my wishful thinking?

One thing is for sure. I'm not the only one affected by our reunion, I'm just not sure if either of us knows what to do about it.

After leaving the grocery store, experimental lunch foods acquired, I stow everything in my car and decide to take a few minutes to check out a couple of places in the town square I've been meaning to visit.

With an iced coffee and a cookie in hand, I walk out of The Nutty Muffin, resolute in my decision to bring Cooper and

Willow here when she visits for the weekend. We need to try one of the gooey cinnamon buns I saw in the display case.

Just down from the bakery is the bookstore I've had my sights set on for weeks. But I'm not going near precious books with coffee and cookie crumbs, so instead, I stroll over to the adorable gazebo in the middle of the grassy square. This place really is a Hallmark movie come to life.

Complete with way too many handsome men, I realize as I watch another couple. A beautiful blonde and a handsome police officer in uniform walk hand in hand down to a dance studio. The man drops a kiss to her lips, and it's so freaking swoony, it gives me all kinds of ideas for my book. A meet-cute where the cop responds to a false alarm at the woman's house, and she answers fresh from the shower, wrapped only in a towel. So. Perfect.

I open the notes app on my phone and jot a few things down in between sips of the perfect iced coffee. The moment is lost when an incoming call from my editor covers the screen.

"Hey, Carol," I answer, filled with trepidation. I know exactly what's coming.

"Victoria, my darling girl, where the ever-loving crap are the chapters you promised me?"

I wince. Those chapters I promised her on our last call, the very call that made me late to get Cooper and caused the unfortunate run-in with Sawyer, are still not finished. "Um, coming soon?"

Carol heaves a sigh over the phone. After working together for the last four years, she knows I'm normally good for deadlines. Which is probably the only thing saving me from her dropping me as a client. "I need them this weekend, or I'll have to push your final edit to next month."

That has me sitting up straight. "I'll have them done, I promise. We can't push back the dates, I'm already cutting it close."

"I know you are, which is why you better find some inspiration or a muse or whatever you need, and fast. I need those words in my inbox by Sunday night at the absolute latest. Deal?"

Mentally, I try to calculate how much work it'll be to get that done, especially seeing as Willow's arriving tomorrow night to help me unpack. But reality is facing me. "I'll get it done."

We end our call and I immediately stand up. Looking wistfully at the bookstore, I try to convince myself that I need to go straight home and open my laptop. But the pull of my idea of heaven is way too strong, and my feet carry me across the street and into the adorable store called Pages.

"Just a few minutes," I whisper to myself as I push open the door. The interior is whimsical and fun, yet perfectly organized, and I know I'm in trouble.

"Hello, welcome to Pages. I'm Paige." A woman wearing a knee-length skirt and cute blouse with a pair of tortoiseshell glasses walks over.

"I'm Tori, I just moved here with my son recently." My mouth curves upward in amusement. "I love that you named your store Pages."

She gives a brusque nod, but I see her answering soft smile. "Yes. Thank you, I enjoy a good play on words. May I help you locate some new reading material?"

Her formal speech patterns could come across as aloof, but I have a sixth sense for fellow bookworms. "Actually, yes, I'm a sucker for some paranormal romance. Do you have anything by Lacey Greystone?"

Paige's eyes light up. "Absolutely. Her latest just arrived yesterday." I let her lead me over to what I happily note is the largest section of the store under a hilarious sign that reads *Oxytocin Stimulants*. "Romance is my preferred genre, and I personally feel traditional bookstores do not do justice to the multibillion dollar industry that is romance books. That is why you'll find this area of my store to be significantly more stocked than others. You should have many options for paranormal romance reads."

I spin around in a circle, taking in the multiple shelves of books. "Now this is my kind of bookstore," I murmur. My fingers trail along the shelves of contemporary romance, stopping when I hit a familiar name. Mine. Well, my pen name. It's always a thrill to see my own books on a shelf, and to know my new hometown supports my career? Well, that's just amazing.

"Ah, are you also a Starla Barrows fan?" I glance over my shoulder at Paige, my cheeks colouring. I keep my writing life very separate from my personal life, so very few people know my alter ego.

"Yeah, you could say that," I answer evasively.

"My friends and I run a book club in town, focused on romance novels. We've been considering one of her books for our read next month. If you'd like to join us, you're welcome to."

"Oh, ah, yeah, that sounds fun," I say, completely taken aback. Do I admit who I am? I'm saved by Paige continuing.

"If you want to get a feel for the group, to see if the dynamic is a fit for you, our next meeting is this coming Tuesday evening, next door at Camille's café. If you haven't read our current book, that's fine, you're still welcome to join."

My head is still spinning from trying to decide whether I reveal my identity to Paige, so I simply nod. "Thanks. I'll have to figure out childcare for my son, but I'd like to try and join."

Paige waves off my comment. "If you're comfortable with it, we arrange for a babysitter to stay here at the store with any children. Several women drop their kids off. The babysitter reads to them, or they can read any books they wish from the shelves."

"That sounds awesome."

Through her glasses, I can sense Paige studying me. "You've only recently moved to Dogwood Cove and as such, I imagine have had limited opportunity to meet other like-minded individuals. I sense you are a fellow book lover, and given your enjoyment of romance novels, I do believe our book club would be an excellent fit for you."

"I think you're right," I say happily. "Thanks, Paige. I'll definitely try to stop by on Tuesday."

I walk out of Pages with the new Lacey Greystone book in hand, feeling excited, and yes — ready to get back to my own manuscript. Maybe this is exactly what I need to feel inspired again. A chance to be a reader, not just an author. A chance to connect with *other* romance readers and talk about books.

A chance to remind myself why I love romance novels so much. The hope for a happily ever after, even if the only one I'm ever going to get is between the pages of a book.

Chapter Ten

Tori

"And...done." I hit *send* with a massive sense of relief, the promised chapters on their way to Carol, at last.

Even though I stayed up way too late last night reading my new book, I still managed to get up early this morning and crank out some words before getting Cooper to school. Then, to my utter shock, a solution to a plot hole I was struggling with in my draft hit me on the walk home from dropping him off. I was able to write three more chapters in the hours he was gone. It's been a long time since I had a day that productive, and my writing mojo couldn't have come back at a better time.

Glancing at the clock, I realize I've got time to whip up some cookies before I need to leave to get Cooper. Putting on some music, I dance around the kitchen mixing up some monster cookies, his favourite. But just as I'm scooping the dough onto a tray, inspiration strikes.

"I am on *fire!*" I crow to my empty kitchen as ideas start swirling in my head. I grab a scrap of paper to jot down the basics, but it's not enough. Sliding the cookie tray into the oven, I dash back to my computer and open up the document, my fingers starting to fly.

The only downside to having my muse return to me at this moment in time is that I forget anything and everything else around me as I lose myself in the fictional world I'm creating. That is, until the smoke detector goes off with the loudest beep I've ever heard, and I turn in horror to see smoke wafting out of my oven.

"Shit, shit, shit, shit, shit!" I shout as I grab the fire extinguisher and carefully open the oven. Thankfully, there are no flames, but the cookies are now charred black piles of grossness. I dump the tray in the sink, turn off the oven, then turn my attention to that damn alarm. There's no button that I can see, so I try waving a towel at it, which does nothing. I open the kitchen window, turn on the hood fan over the stove, and climb up on a chair to see if I can detach the thing. I manage to get it pried off, but the freaking beeping is piercing my skull.

"Oh my God, shut up, you stupid thing! There's no fire, everything's fine, and I swear to God, if you connect to the damn fire department and that man shows up, I will smash you to smithereens."

Is it logical to talk to inanimate objects? Nope. But I'm doing it anyway because this alarm is making me crazy. As I frantically try to figure out how to shut it off, somehow — despite the shrill tone of the smoke detector — I hear my front door opening and a familiar but unexpected voice calling my name.

I finally find the damn button and manage to turn off the obnoxious and unnecessary beeping when Willow comes into the kitchen, a wide smirk on her face. "You know, if you wanted to get your man's attention, there are easier ways than burning down your house."

My glower does nothing except make her laugh. "Shut up, Wills, don't make me regret telling you he lives in town. And what the heck are you doing here, anyway? I thought you didn't get in till tonight?"

She shrugs and pushes off the wall to come and hug me. "I was able to get out of the office early, so I figured I'd surprise you."

Wrapped up in the arms of my best friend, my entire body feels lighter. "It's a good surprise. Coop is gonna lose it when we pick him up."

We break apart, and Willow surveys the charred remains of the cookies. "So, what gives? You're normally a pro in the kitchen."

I grin. Despite the mess I now have to clean up, and the potential for how much worse it could have been, I'm not mad at myself. "I got inspired and was writing."

Willow knows me well enough to just laugh. "Girl, when are you going to learn not to multitask when you're in the zone?"

It's my turn to shrug. "I honestly wasn't expecting to write more today; I already sent four chapters to Carol. But this idea came to me and..." I trail off. If anyone knows what I get like when I'm in the writing cave, it's Willow. She's come to my rescue many times when I'm on deadline but still need to do simple things, like feed my kid and do some laundry.

"And you lost all sense of space and time until your smoke detector snapped you back to reality?"

I nod. "Yeah, basically. So much for cookies." I stare disappointedly at the burnt mounds. "I wanted to surprise Cooper with them after school."

Willow drapes her arm over my shoulder as she joins me at the kitchen sink, looking at the pitiful charcoal pucks. "You're still a good mom, even if you burn cookies."

I hip check her, because if there's one thing guaranteed to make me cry, it's Willow reminding me I'm good enough for my kid. She's witnessed one too many breakdowns as Cooper was growing up, when I would doubt my ability to be a single parent, to give Coop everything he needs, to act as both a mom and dad for him. And it's simple statements from her like that one that send me straight to tears.

"Thanks, Wills."

"So. Moving on from the crispy cookies, what are we getting up to this weekend? Aside from dealing with the unintentional box fort you've got going on in your living room."

A short laugh escapes me. "You have no idea how grateful I am you're here to help with that."

Tossing her hair over her shoulder, Willow gives a smug smile. "You know I love to organize. Just call me Marie Kondo. We'll have this place sorted in a day. So, then what? I want to see this adorable town, and might I just say, on the drive in, I saw a couple of absolute hotties out for a run. If the firefighter doesn't float your boat, looks like there's plenty of options."

My insides warm at the very mention of Sawyer. "Trust me, it's not that he doesn't float my boat —" I pause, tilting my head at her "— which is a seriously bizarre statement, but anyway. Sawyer has made it pretty clear he's not thrilled I'm in town."

I fill her in on the strange grocery store encounter, which has her laughing so hard a tear rolls down her face. "Why is that so funny?" I ask, genuinely confused.

"Oh my sweet, sweet girl. Are you seriously so naive? His poor little man brain can't handle the fact that you're suddenly here when he likely never expected to see you again. But I highly doubt he's *upset* by that. If anything, a man like him is trying to rationalize the fact that he wants to hit it again, the 'it' being you, and trying to figure out the best way to do that."

I'm already shaking my head in denial before she even stops talking. "Nope, I doubt it. He looked, I don't know, confused when he saw me at the school, and I pretended not to know who he was. Then at the store it was like he couldn't believe he was seeing me again. Which is ridiculous, and he's going to have to get over it because I'm here to stay. It was weird, Willow."

Placing her hands on her hips, my best friend looks at me as if she's ready to prove me wrong. Which, knowing her, she is. "Okay. Here's what we're gonna do. Tomorrow, we unpack your house. Then we send my beloved nephew to his grandparents for the night, and you and I are going out to the bar I saw on my way here. It's a Saturday night, and I'm going to guess there's a good chance he might be there if he isn't working."

"I'm not looking for a relationship, Willow. We just moved here. My focus is on Cooper."

If eye rolls were an Olympic sport, Willow would win gold with the one she gives me. "Woman, are you or are you not a writer of extremely spicy romance novels?"

I nod slowly, fully aware of where she's going with this.

"And are you or are you not a single woman with needs that no vibrator can possibly handle as good as the real thing?"

An indelicate snort escapes me, but I nod again.

"And are you or are you not open to a no-strings-attached fling that would help satisfy those needs?"

Here's where I pause. "Willow, I don't —"

She interrupts me with a wave of her hand. "No excuses." Her face softens. "You're a good mom, Tori. You give everything you have to that kid, and because of you, he has an awesome life. There's nothing wrong with taking just a little bit of that time and energy and devoting it to yourself."

I know my resolve is crumbling, and I'll be texting my parents to see if they want Cooper for a sleepover tomorrow. But that doesn't stop me from pushing back, just a little. Because I'm not the only one who's guilty of prioritizing everything else over myself.

"Okay, I won't deny what you're saying is true. But can you admit that you also need to find some better work-life balance? Why are you in the office late so much these days?"

Willow doesn't even try to hide her exhaustion. And it only makes me worry more because normally, she's unreadable.

"Wills. What's going on? Is your uncle okay?"

Willow's uncle Mike is the owner of the Vancouver Tridents, one of two Canadian major league baseball teams.

"He's fine, it's just the usual work stuff, plus the drama with Rafe Montego having a kid no one knew about."

I study my best friend, looking for any hint as to what the issues could possibly be, but she's back to her usual poker face. "But everything's okay?"

"It will be. We're waiting to hear if he's going to retire after this season, that's all." She brushes imaginary lint off her pants and tilts her head to the door.

"When do we have to go and get Coop?"

I glance at my watch. "Now, I suppose."

Willow claps her hands together with genuine excitement. "Great, I miss that kid. Let's go."

A short while later, we're back home, kid in tow. Cooper takes one look at the burnt cookies still sitting in the sink and blinks up at me owlishly. "You tried to bake while you were writing, didn't you?"

I can't hold back a wince. "Yeah, stupid idea, I know."

But instead of being disappointed by the burnt cookies, Cooper's face lights up. "Did the firefighter come? The one from my school? I still remember the handshake and I haven't told anyone about it."

My heart softens just a little toward Sawyer. He might have acted ten different kinds of strange when he saw me at the Grab N Go, but there's no denying he was so good to Cooper that day at the school. "No, buddy, they didn't have to come. There was no actual fire, just stinky smoke and burnt cookies."

His face falls, but only for a second. "That's fine. Maybe we can go to the station someday and I can show him I remember the handshake."

My eyes dart over to Willow, who's barely containing her laughter at Coop's obvious interest in Sawyer. Somehow, in all of the mental chaos of trying to sort through my attraction to the damn man and his weird reaction to me being here, I didn't realize my kid was just as infatuated with him after just one interaction. As much as I was after my first time, it seems.

I guess once is all it takes for someone like Sawyer Donnelly to leave an impression.

Cooper wanders outside to the tree house, and Willow saunters over, propping her elbow up on my shoulder as we look out the window into the backyard.

"There are worse role models for your son than a local hero."

"You're not wrong, but does that local hero have any interest in being a role model to a seven-year-old who comes with a horny mom? I'm guessing the answer is no."

"Well, tomorrow night, if we find him at the bar, we'll figure out if he's up for a second round or not. If he isn't, I'm sure we'll find someone else to take care of the horny mom, and Cooper can find someone else to hero worship."

CHAPTER ELEVEN

Sawyer

I'm not proud of how I acted at the store on Thursday. In fact, Tori had every right to question my sanity. I barked at her, then I almost kissed her, for fuck's sake. And even if I don't want to admit how often I think about her, the way her eyes sparked when she challenged my dumbass behaviour was fucking hot.

It's messing with me, the fact that I can't get her out my head. I thought it was bad enough before when she was just a sexy memory, but then she messed with my mojo when I tried to hook up with someone else, and now it really does feel like she's everywhere.

Apparently, even at the bar when I'm just trying to have a chill night with my brothers.

"Fuck." I try to muffle my curse as the door to Hastings opens and the woman who's haunting my dreams — and apparently, my waking hours, too — walks in with none other than her brunette friend from the gala.

Jude gives me a hard look. "Are you okay?"

I nod brusquely, keeping my head turned away from the entrance. It's not that I'm mad she's here. She's got every right to be. I'm mad at myself for reacting like this. It's not like I haven't run into women I've hooked up with before, and it's never been an issue. Carrie and her determination to land a round two not included.

But Tori's different. And I really need to figure out how to handle that before anyone, especially my siblings, figures out that the newest resident of Dogwood Cove has me all tied up in knots.

And not the sexy kind of knots.

I force my attention back on to what Max and Jude are talking about, even though discussing injury stats in NHL players is not high on my list of fun topics.

"Hey, guys." Hunter, who I still haven't adjusted to calling my brother-in-law, drops down into the empty seat beside me and immediately pours himself a beer from the pitcher on the table. He takes several long swallows, and all focus shifts to him. Hunter's not normally one to chug down a beer.

"What's up with you?" Max asks, a frown creasing his forehead. Even though my gut reaction is to tease old man Maxy about getting wrinkles, I'm also curious about what might be bothering the guy who's normally so fucking happy it's annoying.

He takes another drink, then sets the beer down and looks up at us with a slight grimace. Even in the dim lighting of the bar, I can see his cheeks colour.

"You don't really want to know, it has to do with your sister."

The three of us groan. That's definitely the hardest part about being friends with the dude who's married to our baby sister. Obviously, we know they fuck. Her being pregnant is proof enough of what they get up to behind closed doors, but that doesn't mean we wanna hear about it.

"Ignore them. We can be adults." Beckett sits down across from me, setting the plate of nachos he was getting us in the middle of the table. "We'll just pretend it's not Kat you're talking about."

"Easier said than done, twinbro," I mutter, shooting a mock glare at Hunter. "In my mind, you guys sleep in separate bedrooms."

"How do you explain the baby?" Max says, stifling his own laughter.

"Immaculate conception." I lift my own glass and take a drink to hide my smile.

"You're a dumbass," Jude says, shaking his head. "Okay, Hunter, we can handle it. What's wrong?"

Hunter looks at each of us in turn. "Are you sure? I don't exactly have a lot of other guy friends to hang out with, but I don't want to make things weird."

I clap my hand on his shoulder, instantly realizing he needs some reassurance that we're cool. "Dude. You're our brother now. Just, maybe, skip any gory details?"

The look he gives is indescribable. "Gory details? What the fuck do you think we're doing?"

I shrug. "I don't ask questions I don't want the answers to."

Shaking his head, Hunter shifts in his seat. "Okay, well, no. Nothing like that. It's just, I always heard pregnancy hormones can mess with a woman's, you know...sex drive."

Pushing back from the table, I stand up. "Hold on. If we're talking about our pregnant sister's sex life, we need something stronger than beer."

"Sit the fuck down and shut up, Sawyer," Max barks at me. Glaring back at him, I slowly sit back down. "Go on, Hunter, ignore the asshole that can't handle talking about anything to do with commitment or relationships deeper than a wading pool."

Flashing me a somewhat apologetic look, I nod at Hunter to continue, folding my arms across my chest. Max may be right, but he can fuck right off with that attitude.

"I guess I never pictured a situation where it would be too much." Hunter's voice drops at the end, to the point I'm not entirely sure I understood. But judging by the smirks the others are fighting back, I heard right.

"You're saying you can't keep up?" Beckett's tone is teasing.

Jude snorts into his glass. "Our little sis has got some serious game. I'm impressed."

"Guys, you don't understand! It's constant. Every day, multiple times. She's insatiable." Hunter actually looks miserable, but the rest of us are trying not to laugh. "Fuck off, all of you. My dick is getting chafed."

That does it. We all bust out laughing, drawing attention from nearby tables, but none of us give a fuck. Even though it's our sister Hunter's talking about, it's fucking hilarious that he's in a *too much sex* situation. I honestly can't imagine that ever being a problem, but what do I know. Maybe pregnant women really are on another level.

Eventually, things settle, and I get up again to go for that round of shots I wanted earlier. As I'm waiting at the bar, a familiar voice comes at me from the side.

"Do you only associate with handsome men, or is tonight just my lucky night?"

I turn to face the brunette, scrambling to remember her name. She puts me out of my misery, sticking her hand out. "Willow. Tori's friend. We met at the firefighter's gala."

"I remember," I say with a cheeky smirk. "And to answer your questions, yes and no." I gesture to the table where my brothers are still seated. "They are some handsome fuckers, but they're my brothers and they're all taken. So no getting lucky for you."

Willow gives a sound of disappointment, but it's clear she's teasing. "That's sad, for me at least. But you, on the other hand, could have a much better ending to your night if you play your cards right."

I lean against the bar and fold my arms across my chest. "Are you playing matchmaker?"

"If I say yes, what will you do about it?" she fires back. I like this woman. She doesn't get to me like Tori does, but she's fun. And it's clear she's a good friend.

"If it were someone else, I'd tell you not to bother. But..." I intentionally let my words trail off. She's smart, she'll read between the lines. Sure enough, a triumphant smile crosses her face.

"I knew it." She picks up her glass of wine and starts to turn away before pausing and looking over her shoulder at me. "By the way, I get the feeling you're only looking for something casual, and that's fine. That's all she can handle right now. That doesn't mean I won't come back here and castrate you if you hurt her in any way. Got it?"

I nod. "Got it. And for the record, if I did anything to hurt a woman, they'd take care of the job for you." I jerk my head toward my brothers. Seeming satisfied, Willow walks off.

"That didn't go well," the deep voice of Dean, the bar owner, rumbles across at me. "Never known you not to seal the deal."

I flash him a magnetic grin. "Ah, my good man. That was not the woman for me."

He raises an eyebrow as he slides the tray of shots over to me. "Getting picky or something?"

I pretend to be affronted. "Deano. I have standards."

He just snorts. "Don't call me that unless you want me to sneak strawberries into the next round."

Now, I really am offended. "You know what that'll do to me, bro. Hives. Everywhere. Don't you dare."

His deep chuckle doesn't reassure me in the slightest. "Then don't be a shithead in my bar."

As he walks away, I call after him, "When have I ever?" This earns me a middle finger salute. Turning away, I head back to the table and set the tray of shots down. I'm just about to sit down myself when out of the corner of my eye, I spot a head of blonde hair heading toward the bathrooms.

"Enjoy, boys. Be right back."

I don't have a plan, hell, I don't even know if I should be doing this. But after talking to Willow, I'm starting to think that maybe I'm not the only one who's wondering what the hell is going on between me and Tori. This could be a stupid idea, but it's the only one I've got right now. And it might just give me the answer I need.

The door to the ladies' room opens, and there she is, wearing jeans that are painted on and a simple black shirt that hugs every curve. Her eyes are popping, thanks to some sort of makeup magic, and her lips are a deep pink that I instantly want to see wrapped around my dick.

"Sawyer!" she says, but I don't let her say another thing before cupping her head in my hands and dragging her in close. Her hands land on my chest, and my lips find hers, and then...

Then I'm lost.

If I thought kissing her would help get her out of my head or make me realize I'd built up a fantasy of her that can't possibly be real, I was fucking wrong.

Kissing Tori feels so good, it should be illegal. I've never had this. Never had this instant explosion of chemistry with just one touch. But the instant my hand connects with her softness, the instant my lips land on hers, something releases in my chest. And there's no stopping me from sliding my hands down her neck to her shoulders. She's clutching my shirt, our kiss turning desperate and messy. I spin us around so her back is to the wall, pressing her against it as I grab her hand in mine and slide it up above her head.

Her back arches, pressing those perfect tits into my chest as she moans into our kiss. Fuck, this woman, I can't get enough. And that should be fucking terrifying.

The sound of loud laughter from the main bar breaks through the spell she's weaving and I pull back. I'm not the only one breathing heavily, and the glaze that covers her beautiful chocolate and gold eyes tells me I'm definitely not alone in my shock.

"Tori…" I start, then stop. Because honestly? I'm speechless. I thought kissing her would get her out of my mind. I was wrong. Taking one step back, my hands fall away from her body and I instantly feel…wrong. Like I need to be touching her again. Which is crazy.

"There you are. Listen, Max is heading out and so am I. You ready to settle up?" Beckett's interruption is both a curse and a blessing.

"Not a doppelgänger."

My head whips back to Tori, who's looking between Beck and I, a bemused look on her face. "What?"

She pushes away from the wall and slips between us without answering. I guess I put it down to shock that I don't try to stop her.

"Sawyer?" My twin pulls my attention back. "Sorry if I cock-blocked."

I shake my head. "No. It's fine."

He gives me a look that says he thinks that's a pile of bullshit but doesn't push. Instead of chasing after Tori, who's grabbing her stuff and heading to the door, Willow in tow, I follow Beckett back to the table where my brothers are also getting ready to leave.

But the whole way through settling the tab, saying goodbye, and walking home, I'm not really present. I'm going through the motions, but my head is still stuck in that dark hallway, feeling her body against mine, taking in every sound, every smell, every touch of her.

And instead of finding answers to why I can't stop thinking about her, I'm left with another question.

What the hell was that?

One kiss really shouldn't have messed with me as much as it did. But after tossing and turning all night, constantly replaying that damn kiss, I dragged my ass out of bed bright and fucking early today to get a run in, hoping the brisk air would wake me up. It did, enough to make me function, but I still yawn as I fill my coffee mug and continue pulling together the gear I need for my shift starting this afternoon. I've just drained my first mug and am in the process of refilling it when my phone vibrates with an incoming message. And it's one I've been expecting for a couple of days.

D-MAN: What's the plan this year? Are we heading to the island to camp?

COWBOY: Depends on what weekend. Saria and I are going to the interior for wine tasting in a couple weeks.

My thumbs fly over the keyboard.

SAWYER: Who the fuck is Saria and why are you going wine tasting? You hate wine.

COWBOY: Dude did you hear nothing I said at breakfast when you were in town? I've been dating Saria for a month now. And I might hate wine, but I like regular sex, so I'll go and sip some fucking wine.

SAWYER: You're still with her? I thought she was just some random.

COWBOY: Fuck off bro, and watch yourself. I really like her.

My mind is blown. We've always been the same, Boone, Derek, and me. Not interested in anything serious with anyone. To realize that one of us is actually dating the same girl for over a month is making my head spin.

SAWYER: Sorry. You just took me by surprise.

COWBOY: Can't be single forever, bro. Someday we gotta grow up and find a woman who makes us better men.

D-MAN: Look at you. Regular pussy and you get all philosophical.

COWBOY: Better than staying a scared of commitment dumbass.

D-MAN: Okay let's focus boys. Lance's weekend, what's the plan?

COWBOY: Find somewhere to get drunk? Same as every year?

We're discussing the weekend where we remember our friend who lost his life because he was distracted by his girlfriend cheating on him while we were out fighting wildfires. At the same time Boone announces he's in a steady relationship. The irony is not lost on me.

None of us will ever forget that day almost ten years ago now. We were with Lance when the text came through while at base camp, some well-meaning friend back in his hometown thinking Lance should know his girl was out with another guy while he was fighting fires. Lance lost his shit. And then went out on the line, his emotions a mess.

A change in wind conditions can come with very little, if any, warning. But even so, on that day, the only one caught unaware was Lance. And for a guy who normally erred well on the side of caution with environmental shifts when fighting fires, to say his death was a shock is an understatement. As far as I can figure, the only thing different that day from any other was that Lance must have been really fucking distracted by the shit going on at home.

Ever since then, I swore I would never let anything distract me like that. I keep my career, my family, and my friends perfectly compartmentalized in my brain so I can focus on one at a time and not let anything interfere.

And there's never been space for anyone else. But one fiery blonde angel is forcing her way in, whether she means to or not. Last night was a bit like pouring a glass of water on a grease fire. Instead of dousing the heat, it only made the flames burn stronger.

Somehow, I've got to get her out of my head before things get any hotter.

Chapter Twelve

Tori

Taking a deep breath, I push open the door to Camille's café. The room is full of close to a dozen women, all chatting animatedly as they sip on cups of what must be tea or coffee.

When I left Cooper with my mom back at the house, I was full of excitement for tonight. But now, faced with a bunch of strange faces, I remember why I love my career: I don't have to interact with people all that often.

"Books. You're here because you all love books," I whisper under my breath, trying to calm my nerves. An introvert at heart, normally talking about romance books brings me to life. But this feels overwhelming.

"Tori, I'm pleased you were able to join us for tonight's gathering." I turn at the sound of Paige's voice. She's the only one I really know here, even though I think I've seen some of the other women around. Pretty sure I recognize the brunette standing behind the counter dishing out cookies, and there's another one

I'm sure I've seen at school. But Paige is the only one whose name I know.

"Hi. Yup, I'm here." God, could I possibly sound more awkward? That was embarrassing. I force my face to relax into what I hope is an honest-to-goodness smile. "Thanks for inviting me."

"Of course. May I presume you are unfamiliar with many of the attendees tonight?"

A new voice cuts in. "I think you can, Paige. Here, I'll take her around and introduce her to everyone. Tori, was it?" I look over at the woman I recognize from the school and nod. "I'm Abby. My husband is the principal at the elementary school, and my daughter is in grade five. I think I've seen you at pickup a few times."

I take her outstretched hand gratefully. "Right, I thought I recognized you, too."

Abby gives me a gentle smile that eases even more of my nerves. "C'mon, let's meet everyone." I let her lead me over to a group of three women, one who is very definitely pregnant and slightly familiar, somehow.

"And these are the Donnelly girls."

Shit. Donnelly? They're related to Sawyer. But that means I've slept with their... brother? Husband?

No... Ohmygod. The room starts to feel stifling, like I'm trapped in an absolute nightmare.

I realize Abby's still talking and I tune back in, hoping to hear something to reassure me as I pray my worst fear isn't about to come to life. I can't be the other woman. I'd have to move, just when Cooper's settling in, and...

"Well." Abby laughs. "I suppose for now, only Kat and Cam can claim the name, and technically Kat's not a Donnelly anymore. But I'm guessing you will be soon, right, Lily?" Pulling out her phone from her pocket, Abby frowns. "Oh shoot, I'm sorry to abandon you, Tori, but this is my babysitter. I'll leave you with the girls, you're in good hands."

Except, I'm not. She might as well have left me in a pit of vipers, depending on what comes next. The three stunning women are smiling at me, completely unaware of the danger I might pose. I already can't remember their names, thanks to my absolute panic that I might have fucked one of their husbands.

"I'm Kat. Tori, was it?" The pregnant lady rubs her rounded stomach. "Welcome to Dogwood Cove. How are you finding everything?"

"G-good," I stammer out, my heart still racing. How the hell do I find out how they're related to Sawyer without sounding like a total nut job? "There's a lot of nice people here."

Lame, Tori. Lame.

"Yeah, my family has lived here almost my entire life. My parents and my brothers all live in town, or at least close by, so if you see a bunch of guys who look sort of like me, that's who they are. And I'll apologize now for anything dumb they might do."

"Come on, Kat, the only dumb one is Sawyer. Don't give the rest of them a bad name," one of the other women teases. "I'm Cam, and I'm married to the dumb one's twin brother."

"Yeah, and Sawyer's the only single one, so maybe we should also be warning her away." This comes from the last woman of the trio, who's got a streak of purple hair artfully woven into a braid.

Oh, thank fuck. I normally save the swear words for my books, but this moment absolutely calls for one as relief washes over me. He's single. Suddenly, I feel like an absolute fool for jumping to the worst conclusion so quickly. *Save the drama for your writing, Tori.*

Purple hair keeps talking, and now that my pulse is slowing to normal, I pay closer attention. "I'm Lily, her best friend —" she jerks a thumb at Kat "— and I'm dating another one of her brothers."

"You seriously are all living, breathing, romance tropes," I murmur, earning myself another laugh from the three gorgeous women.

"It's disgusting, isn't it? Wait till you hear this — Beck and I only got married so I could access my inheritance." Cam grins.

"Jude and I started out fake dating," Lily pipes up.

We all turn as one to Kat, who raises her hands. "Don't look at me, Hunter and I were a perfectly normal, not at all fiction-inspired relationship."

It's Lily who snorts, I think. "Sure, having a crush on your sexy neighbour, then dating him in secret is totally normal."

"Listen. At least I don't have the whole asshole ex marrying a family member angle. That was straight out of a Starla Barrows book, and you know it."

I shouldn't have taken a sip of the water I brought with me, because it's all I can do not to choke on it. Kat looks concerned as she touches my shoulder.

"Are you okay?"

I nod vigorously. "Yup. Totally fine. Sorry." They read my books. These women, Sawyer's family, read my books.

"Y'know, you sort of look like her."

My head whips around to face Cam, who's looking at me intently. "Wh-what?"

"Starla Barrows. She's this romance author; we're reading one of her books next. I was scoping out her website the other day, and you look a lot like her."

Oh boy. In all the years I've been writing, I can honestly say, I've never been recognized by a reader. It's not that I keep my identity a secret, but for Cooper's sake, I've always tried to maintain some privacy. This scenario, where I either have to lie to people that I'm going to see on a regular basis around town or come clean about my alter ego, is one I feel wholly unprepared for. But the decision of whether or not to tell them is taken out of my hands.

"Oh my God, it is you, isn't it?" Kat looks up from her cell phone, excitement dancing in her eyes. "You're Starla Barrows. Holy crap!"

Other women have wandered over, thanks to Kat's not exactly quiet exclamation. I guess there's no hiding now.

"Yeah, I am." I muster up a smile, feeling the professional persona I try to exude slip over me like an uncomfortable coat. "But tonight's not about me or my books."

Unfortunately for me, Kat doesn't catch the subtext. Instead, she waves her hands dismissively. "I know, but this is so dang cool. A famous author, living in our town, joining our book club. Oh my God, did Paige know? Is that why you're here?"

"Did I know what?" Paige has a curious look on her face as she pushes her glasses up her nose.

Kat grabs her arm. "Know that Tori is Starla Barrows."

I give her credit, Paige manages to school her reaction pretty darn well. I honestly did not expect this kind of a reaction; I'm hardly a big deal of an author. I mean, sure, it's touching, but I just wanted to be able to relax tonight, be myself, and talk about books. Not *my* books.

"I was not aware of this information. And I apologize for my ignorance, truly, I should have known."

Poor Paige looks so upset with herself, I'm unable to take it any longer. "No, please don't feel bad. I'm truly flattered that you all actually read my books, but I didn't come here as an author, I came as a book lover. Tonight I just want to be Tori. Not Starla. Is that okay?"

Finally, I see comprehension dawn on their faces. Out of nowhere, Kat pulls me in for a hug, made slightly awkward by her large belly. "Of course, that's okay. If anyone understands the need to just be yourself, it's my family. My brother Jude is a retired NHL player, and he's always loved the fact that when he's here, he's just Jude Donnelly, not some famous athlete. I'm sorry, I didn't consider that you of course, want the same basic courtesy."

For the second time tonight, I feel relief. "Thank you. I'm sorry if I seem ungrateful, it really does mean a lot that you like my books."

Paige inclines her head toward me. "But you wish to keep your two identities separate. We can respect that. As Kat indicated, you deserve to have whatever privacy you desire. Tonight, you are a reader. Not an author." Shifting in closer, she touches my wrist. "But could we perhaps set a time in the near future to discuss a future engagement in which you would be willing to be present as our featured author?"

Well, I can't exactly blame her for that very reasonable request, so I simply nod. "Sure."

Paige steps away, an enigmatic expression on her face. "Wonderful. Well, please excuse me, I must ensure we stay on track with our itinerary for the evening."

I wait until she leaves before turning to the Donnelly ladies. "Itinerary?"

Lily smirks. "Yeah, Paige likes things organized. Even when the book club was just her and her close friends, they had discussion questions and a schedule. As more of us joined, we learned to just go with it. Honestly, she comes up with some fun questions."

I look down as an arm loops through my elbow. It's Kat again. "C'mon, you can sit over here with us."

Letting myself be towed along by Sawyer's younger sister, I sink down on the comfortable armchair she guides me to. Eventually, everyone finds a seat and settles in, our attention all going to Paige, who moves to stand in front of us.

"Thank you for coming, everyone. I trust you all read and enjoyed this month's selection. Discussion questions are being handed out now, and while you have a chance to read them over, I thought we could start with a quick poll. Based on chapter four of the book, where Fancy is giving Rex her first blow job, what is your preference. Spit or swallow?"

"What did she just say?" I whisper to myself, certain I misheard. But I wasn't quiet enough, I guess, as Cam leans over from beside me.

"Like Lily said. Paige comes up with some fun questions." She smirks. "Rumour has it her husband has a pierced dick. Now, I love my husband, and there is not a damn thing wrong with our sex life. But that kind of jewelry has always intrigued me."

"Do any of the boys have piercings?" That question comes from Lily and has Kat sputtering under her breath.

"Oh my God, you two, stop it. Those are my brothers you're talking about, and I do *not* need to be thinking about their penises."

It's a good thing we're at the back of the room, because Paige and someone else are still talking — I assume about the actual book. I should probably be paying attention to that discussion, but I find myself drawn to the women at my side. They remind me of Willow and I, with no filters and nothing but love and respect. I didn't expect to make friends my first time at this book club, but I won't deny I hoped to find someone I connected with.

There's just the small issue of the hot firefighter we have in common. The one *they* don't know that *I* already know.

As if she knows I'm thinking about him, Cam leans forward to whisper across mine and Kat's lap to Lily. "If any of them do, it would be Sawyer, I'm betting."

Nope, I think to myself, pressing my lips together. I can say with absolute certainty that man has zero piercings. Or tattoos.

"Nah, he's petrified of needles. Like, I'm talking screams like a baby when he needs vaccinations or anything." Kat gently pushes Cam back. "Now stop talking about my brothers and pay attention, or Tori's never going to want to sit with us at book club again!"

She couldn't be more wrong. It makes me so happy the way they welcomed me after the initial surprise of my pen name wore off. As someone who's no more than a fellow book-loving woman. As if I could truly be friends with them and be my own authentic self, instead of "author" me.

But if they found out my *other* secret... That I can't stop thinking about Kat's brother. Would that all change?

CHAPTER THIRTEEN

Sawyer

Thursday is laundry day. That's the only excuse I have for wearing ratty dark blue sweats and a hoodie that still has paint stains from when I was helping Max and Heidi repaint their apartment today.

Well, that and I figured I could be in and out of the hardware store quickly enough there was no point in changing out of the clothes I put on to tackle cleaning the gutters at my parents' house. Ever since my dad's accident twelve years ago, he hasn't been able to climb a ladder, so my brothers and I deal with all of those kinds of jobs for them.

But lady luck obviously has it out for me today as I round the corner of aisle three and come face to face with Tori.

How does she still manage to look so fucking beautiful every damn time I see her? You'd think my reaction would dim over time, like it does with every other woman, but instead, my attraction to her feels more intense.

Fuck, I'm in trouble.

"Sawyer!" Her eyes widen, her tongue darting out to moisten her lips. Such a small move shouldn't make my dick twitch. But apparently, the fucking traitor doesn't care about what it should or should not be doing.

She's wearing another T-shirt with an old lady on it; this one saying, "Picture it, Sicily 1922." At least this time I have some sort of an idea what it means, recognizing the iconic Golden Girls character. My lips tip up.

"Hey, Tori." Her lips part, and I swear, she leans into me ever so slightly. Or maybe I'm the one doing the leaning? It's kind of hard to tell, all I know is, I'm drawn to this woman.

"The other night. At the bar. That wasn't. I mean... Oh, good grief."

I stuff my hands in my pockets and let her start and stop a few times, my trademark smirk growing wider. I kinda like seeing her off-kilter, knowing it's being around me that does this to her. It feels like payback for when she first moved to town and I felt like I was going crazy. But now that I'm giving in to the fact that I need to get this woman in bed one more time, all these chance meetings feel like kismet.

"We kissed, Tori. And it was just as hot as it was the first time." I step in closer. "I have a feeling *everything* would be just as good." Her eyes flare wide, her sharp intake of air telling me with no uncertainty my words are hitting their mark.

I lean down to whisper in her ear.

"Picture it. Me and you, fucking again."

We end up at my apartment, and as soon as the door closes behind her, we're tearing at our clothes. I'm always down for sex, but this level of desperation, this deep need to feel her body against mine, is foreign to me.

I'm powerless to try and stop it.

So I don't. She's down to her bra and panties, and I'm kicking off my pants as our tongues hungrily dance. She wraps her arms around my neck, and I bend and lift her off the ground, finding the way to my bedroom by memory alone, all of my senses drunk on Tori.

We reach my room and I lower her to the bed, following right after her until she's stretched out underneath me.

"You with me?" I ask in the second I manage to wrench my lips away from her skin. Her fervent nod is consent enough for me. My hands skate down the side of her body, stopping at her hips. My lips follow, tracing a line down between her lace-covered breasts, intent on one thing and one thing only.

"Do you still taste as sweet as you do in my mind when I'm jerking off to the memory of you?" I whisper against the drenched fabric covering her pussy. She quivers in response, and I glance up with a smirk. "I bet you do, angel." I press a kiss to her mound before hooking my fingers in the sides of her panties and tugging them down. Leaning back in, I kiss the crease of where her hip meets her torso on one side, then the other.

"Please, Sawyer," she pants, and I swear my dick starts to leak. It's as if she's cast a spell over me, a spell where I am a slave to her every word, her every desire.

"You don't have to beg. I'm not leaving this spot until I feel you explode on my tongue." My next kiss lands right on the tip of her clit, already swelling with arousal. "Mmm. Even sweeter than I remember." Flattening my tongue, I press it firmly against her slit, then slide up so I can swirl around her clit. Following her moans and the subtle hints from her body, I work her up until she's writhing underneath me, her legs clamped tightly around my head. If I thought I was drunk on her before, it's nothing compared to now when I'm flooded with her taste.

"Come for me, angel. Now."

I've never been with anyone as responsive as Tori. The way her body bows beneath my touch, the intensity of her release, it's all a thousand times more powerful than anything I've experienced. I surge up, wrenching my bedside drawer open and grab a condom, rolling it down my already leaking dick. Once I'm covered, I grab Tori's hips and flip her over, lifting that round ass into the sky. My hand lands on the pale flesh in a gentle slap, and she shrieks out my name.

"You're mine right now, Tori. Mine to play with, mine to pleasure. Got it?"

She twists back to look at me, her blonde hair a mess around her flushed face. "Yes." My hand lands on the other cheek and her mouth falls open. "God, yes."

I give her a wicked grin. "My angel likes having her ass spanked, huh?" She squirms underneath me, but I just grip her tighter, smacking her pink ass again. "God, you're so fucking perfect." Unable to hold back any longer, I dip my fingers into her still-dripping pussy to make sure she's ready for me.

"More, Sawyer. Give me more."

My fingers are replaced by my dick in an instant, and I'm thrusting all the way inside until her ass is meeting my pelvis. Only then do I still, leaning forward to kiss her spine. "You good?" I whisper against her sweaty skin, and I feel her nod again.

Lifting back up, I pull out almost all the way, then slam back in.

"Fuck!" she cries out, her head dropping down. Placing my hand on her back, I guide her upper body down to change the angle and I slide out, then in again. "Sawyer," she says, a tremble in her voice. "It's so good."

"I know, angel. You feel like heaven. What are you doing to me?" The last part I mumble, mostly under my breath, not ready to answer that question.

Her hips start to rotate in time with my thrusts, small turns that make my eyes cross. Then I feel her walls tighten down on me. "Oh shit, Tori." I start to speed up, feeling my orgasm barreling toward me. Leaning back down, I wrap one arm around her body and zero in on her clit. Strumming it with my thumb, I kiss her shoulder, her back, anywhere I can reach. But I'm not ready for this to be over. Pulling out, ignoring her cry of protest,

I flip her over, hitching one of her legs up onto my shoulder and push back into her wet heat.

"There. Right there. Ohmygod, right there, don't stop!" Her voice gets higher and higher, and then she screams out my name, her back arching off the bed. There's no holding back, so with a roar, I come, thrusting into her over and over, making the bed creak beneath us until I feel completely drained, and yet, totally sated at the same time.

Tori's got a dreamy smile on her face, even with her eyes closed. Meanwhile, my arms are shaking so hard, part of me worries I might collapse onto her. Dropping my forehead down to meet hers, I press a soft kiss to her lips. "Woman, I don't know where you learned to do that swivel-clench thing, and I don't really want to know. But goddamn, that was next-level." Her light giggle makes me draw back so I can look at her. "You find my admiration funny?"

"No," she says with a smirk. "You could say my job requires me to do a lot of research."

What the fuck... I move to pull out, but she laughs and grabs my ass, holding me in place. "Oh my God, if you could see your face right now. I'm not a porn star, Sawyer. I write spicy romance novels. Writing sex scenes requires inspiration at times. That's all."

I start to laugh as well, because damn it, she had me going for a second. "Jesus, woman. Way to bury the lede." The vibrations from her giggles send zings straight to my dick, but even so, I can feel myself softening to the point of it becoming a problem if I don't deal with things. So, holding on to the condom, I pull out and climb off the bed. "Be right back."

After cleaning up, I head back into my room to see she's pulled the sheet up to cover her luscious body. Grabbing the bottom of it, I yank it down, making her squeak.

"Don't cover up around me, angel. If you're in my bed, I want to see every inch of your body." I jump onto the bed, making her tits bounce. My dick takes notice, and I look down at it, then back to her face, where amusement is dancing in her eyes.

"You make my recovery period nonexistent."

Tori snorts, then slaps her hand over her mouth. "Can we pretend I didn't just do that?"

I pull her hand down, grinning as I lean in and kiss her. "Nope." I try to give her some space, stretching out beside her on the bed, but what can I say, my love language is touch. My hand drifts out and starts to draw circles over the soft, rounded curve of her stomach. "Will you tell me more about your writing?" It strikes me in this moment, she's the first woman I've ever had sex with here, in my apartment. That fact is unnerving, but not nearly as much as I expected it would be.

"What do you want to know?" There's some trepidation in her voice, making me wonder if she thinks I'm going to judge her or something, but my mama didn't raise no fool.

"Have you always wanted to be a writer? Did you always want to write romance?"

Something akin to relief flashes over her face, confirming my earlier thought. I'm betting someone, maybe more than one, has given her a hard time for her career choice.

"Yes and yes. I've been writing stories since I was a child, even went so far as to get my degree in creative writing. And as for romance, I guess you could say I'm a sucker for a happy ending."

Warning bells are sounding off in my head, but like an idiot, I ignore them and just lean in to kiss her again. I can't seem to stop wanting to kiss her.

"And the dirty stuff?" I sense her tense under my lips, but just kiss her again, trailing down the column of her throat until I feel her relax. "Is there anything you've written about that you've wanted to try in real life?"

Shifting slightly, my mouth closes over one of her nipples and I suck it gently, releasing it with a pop as I wait for her to answer.

"I mean, sure." She sounds breathless, so I lift my head up to check, and her eyes are closed, her head tipped back slightly on my pillow. I lower my head back down and lick a circle around her other nipple. Her hands come up and grip my hair tightly, pulling me so I'm half sprawled over top of her. "Sawyer," she murmurs, her body twisting on the sheets.

"Does my dirty angel have a list?" I mumble against the pillow of her breast. Her fingers tighten their grip, and that's all the answer I need. But she confirms it with a sound that has my cock fully ready for round two. "Will you show me that list?" I lift myself up onto my elbow, my free hand gently squeezing her tits.

"I don't exactly have it written down," she replies, the words sounding breathless. "And don't ask me to remember everything on it while you're doing *that.*"

I grin. I'm a boob man, which means the way Tori gets turned on by me playing with hers is fucking hot. But I'm still intrigued by this list. I want to be the one to help her carry out the things on her list.

"I like lists." Bending down, I suck her nipple into my mouth again. "I like checking things off them." I give the same attention to the other one. "Maybe we should check something off your list."

Her hands come to my chest, and I feel her push against me. I let her move me until I'm on my back and she's swinging a leg over me.

"You want to do something from my list?" she asks, seduction heavy in her voice. I nod, trying not to seem like an overeager fool. But I'm a sucker for a woman taking charge every now and then. I see that hesitation in her eyes and run my hands up her thighs, around to her ass, and squeeze.

"I want anything you're willing to give me, angel." She bites her lip, and my thumb lifts to tug it out. "Tell me what you want."

She leans down, her hands coming to the pillow on either side of my head. Her naked pussy rubs along my dick that's growing harder by the second. I have no idea what she's going to say, but I'm here for it. All of it. Then she whispers, "I want to sit on your face while you eat my pussy."

Fuck. Yes.

Chapter Fourteen

Tori

Does it make me a terrible mom to resent the fact that I have to pick up my kid, and that means I can't have more filthy, hot sex?

If it does, well, so be it.

"I have to go, Sawyer." I hold back my giggle at the pout on his face. He really is stupid-level handsome. "I can't just *not* pick my kid up from school."

"That's not what I said, angel. I said, you need a backup plan for when you can't make it there in time. I mean, first it was work, now it's..." he trails off, a wicked glint coming to those deep brown eyes. "Research."

This time my laugh breaks free. "Research? Really?"

He nods, a solemn look coming over his face. "Yes. Clearly what we just did is excellent inspiration for your next bestseller."

I roll my eyes and make myself climb off the bed. As I search for my panties, I say, "Does that mean you expect me to write a firefighter romance?"

He hops out of my bed, completely comfortable in his naked glory, bends down and picks up my panties, letting them dangle from one finger as he crooks a grin. "I mean, as long as he's ridiculously hot and a god in bed. You gotta be accurate, after all."

Snatching my panties away, I pull them and my bra on, keeping my eyes averted from the walking, talking temptation that is Sawyer Donnelly. "I'll let you know."

Thank goodness, he finally grabs a pair of shorts and covers up, and damn it, I have to bite back a whimper when his cock goes away. The man has a perfect cock. God in bed? No lie there. Not that I'll let him know that, of course.

Walking out of his room, I make my way to the front door, where our clothes are strewn all over the floor. Dressing quickly, I wait for the post-hookup awkwardness to settle in. Clearly, Sawyer's unaffected as he leans against the wall next to the door, seeming totally relaxed and comfortable.

"Got plans this weekend?"

I consider what to say. The truth might seem obvious, but that opens doors I'm not sure I want to unlock. Mostly because setting myself up for disappointment is exactly the opposite of what I need this weekend. But then again, maybe he'll surprise me.

"I plan on getting drunk and cursing my son's father."

His eyes flare wide for a second before settling back into an easy gaze. "Curse, as in voodoo dolls and full moon spells, or curse, as in mentally damning him to hell?"

"Option two. No witchcraft, just booze." I don't know why, but something makes me want to keep talking. "Cooper's dad is getting married this weekend. Starting a life with a new family, since he didn't want the one he helped create."

If that doesn't scare Sawyer off, I don't know what will. He straightens up off the wall, his brows gathering together in a frown. "He's an asshole. Where's Cooper going?"

Glancing at my phone, I see I have enough time to give Sawyer the briefest of rundowns.

"Tim's parents are good people and they love their grandson. They begged to take him for the weekend, to go to the wedding and spend time with him." I lift my shoulders in a helpless shrug. "Just because his sperm donor is a waste of space and wants next to nothing to do with him doesn't mean I want to completely cut my son off from his family."

His frown eases, and Sawyer closes the small distance between us, surprising me by pulling me in against his warm, very naked chest for a hug. I slip my hands around his waist and relax into the hold.

"You're a good mom, Tori. A hell of a lot nicer than that prick deserves, but exactly what Cooper needs."

Tears threaten to build behind my eyes as I push back and force a small smile. "Thanks, but it doesn't really deserve praise. I'm just doing what I think is best and praying I don't mess it all up."

"Want some company?"

The question startles me, so I blurt out the first response that comes to my peculiar mind. "Messing up my kid? Nah, I can handle that all on my own."

His deep chuckle sends shivers down my spine. "No, goof. This weekend. Drinking and cursing the sperm donor. I'm off, thanks to some shift swaps, so if you want company, I make an excellent drinking buddy."

I suck in a breath. An entire weekend, kid-free, with my one — no, two — night stand? "I'm not looking for a relationship, Sawyer. Coop's my priority."

He moves in closer again, his breath tickling my ear. "I'm not offering a relationship, Tori. I'm offering a weekend of dirty sex."

And all of a sudden, I don't want to leave. I want to push this man to the floor and mount him like a cowgirl. My sense of responsibility is still stronger than my need for more sex, however, so I feebly press against his chest. He steps away, and I look up at him.

"Cooper's grandparents are picking him up after school tomorrow."

Sawyer's expression promises all kinds of dirty things. "I'll bring condoms and the booze of your choice." Leaning in, he pecks a kiss to my lips. "Go get your kid before I decide to start the weekend a day early."

Opening his door, I stumble out, still not entirely sure what just happened. I go to my car, drive to the school, pick up Cooper, and drive home. All on autopilot.

When he runs off to his room to get some game he wants us to play, I type out an SOS to Willow.

TORI: I had sex with Sawyer again. And he wants to spend the weekend. I AM FREAKING OUT.

The bubbles indicating she's replying show up instantly.

WILLOW: HOLY SHIT WOMAN! I knew he was into you. I knew it! My girl is getting LAID. Make sure you stretch. You haven't done marathon sex in a long time.

I snort at that.

TORI: More like ever. Oh my god, Willow. Is this a fling? Am I having a fling with a hot firefighter?

WILLOW: I think so you dirty girl.

WILLOW: Don't overthink it, T. You deserve this. Let that man take care of you.

TORI: I'm the president of the overthinkers anonymous club Wills. I don't know how to turn it off.

WILLOW: I bet orgasms will turn that part of your brain off.

WILLOW: Have fun this weekend. Be safe, but have fun. I gotta run, talk soon babes.

I put my phone down just as Cooper comes racing back into the room. "Found it, Mom."

He holds up the box triumphantly, and of course, it's the one game that he loves and I absolutely hate. Groaning inwardly, I school my expression. "Let's play."

I sit down on the couch and watch Cooper set up the game. There's nothing I wouldn't do for this kid, including play Monopoly. "You do realize, we might not be able to finish the game today, buddy, and you leave tomorrow with your grandparents." Crossing my fingers in my mind, I hope and pray he'll decide to play something else. But my darling child just blinks up at me and smiles.

"That's okay, Mom. It can just stay here until I get back. I trust you not to steal from the bank."

I can't hide my chuckle. "Yeah, you can trust me. Okay, but I get to be the dog."

Coop just rolls his eyes. "You say that like it's a surprise. You're always the dog and I'm always the car. Geez, Mom."

Well, he's got me there.

An hour later, I stand up from the couch, despite Cooper's protests. "Nope, it's time to pause, kid. Especially if you want to eat dinner tonight."

Flopping down on the floor dramatically, Cooper crosses his arms over his chest. "Depends. Are you gonna make me eat a vegetable?"

Leaning over, I wiggle my fingers and slowly move toward him. "Maybe."

He squirms away giggling, but I pounce anyway, tickling his sides until he says, "Mom, stop!"

Lifting my hands immediately, I back off, already anticipating his next move. Sure enough, Cooper launches himself in the air, making me stumble back with an *oof* as I catch him. "Dude, you're getting too big for this!"

Burrowing his head in my shoulder the way he used to when he was a baby, his words are muffled. "Nope, I'm not. Never too big for hugs, that's what you always say."

My arms squeeze him even tighter as my heart threatens to burst. "That's right. Never too big, even if you are a giant."

He wriggles to be let down and grins up at me. "I'm never gonna be a giant, Mom. You're too short."

That makes me laugh. "That's true. Okay, I'm gonna go cook, and you are going to hop in the shower. Deal?"

Coop huffs, but nods. "Fine."

I watch my son head down the hallway and let out a long sigh. "I'm not screwing him up," I whisper to myself, making my way into the kitchen. "Even if I have dirty sex with a firefighter, I'm not screwing up my kid."

With that thought firmly in mind, I quickly whip up a rice and chicken casserole, empty Cooper's lunch bag, and load the dishwasher.

Once dinner's done, Cooper and I pack his bag for the weekend before he suckers me into reading three chapters. Finally, his eyelids are drooping, and I steal one last goodnight kiss before sneaking out of his room and down the hall to my office.

For all my big talk with Sawyer about drinking and cursing Tim this weekend, I also planned on writing. A lot. Something tells me Sawyer has other plans for me. And if I have to choose between a weekend of writing about hot sex or a weekend of actually *having* hot sex...well. There's only one right answer.

Firing up my computer, I open my manuscript, resigning myself to a long night. But instead of immersing myself in the story, I find my thoughts wandering back to earlier today.

My list.

Sure, I've got one in my head. A list of romantic and intimate scenes I wish I could experience in real life but have resigned myself to only ever reading and writing about. But I've never, not once, put these ideas down on paper and actually considered they could happen to me. Until now. Until Sawyer made it clear he wants to, what did he say? *Check some things off my list.*

Opening a new document, I start to write.

1. *Toys and tongue — at the same time*

2. *Sex under the stars*

3. *Blindfolded sex*

4. *Make a sex tape*

5. *Be surprised with a romantic bubble bath*

6. *Explore the back door*

7. *Drive him wild with a strip tease*

8. *Use a cock ring*

9. *Be whisked away on a sexcation*

10. *Play with food in the bedroom*

When I finally stop, I review what I wrote down, snickering to myself at a few of them and feeling my pulse race at others. Would Sawyer ever wear a cock ring? Who the heck knows. Would I ever be bold enough for a sex tape? Probably not. And do I ever expect a man to take me on a sexcation? Definitely not in the cards for a single mom like me. But the other things... I can see those happening. Maybe even this weekend, if I can be brave enough to tell him what I wrote down.

Will I ever show the actual list to Sawyer or anyone, for that matter? Probably not. But it feels damn good to get it out. Freeing, liberating, and inspiring. Switching over to my manuscript, the words start to flow.

Chapter Fifteen

Tori

Saying goodbye to Cooper when his grandparents picked him up was an interesting experience, to say the least. There were the usual hugs, reminders to behave, and embarrassing him by gushing over how much I'd miss him. But as soon as they pulled out of the driveway, my brain went into overdrive running through the list of all the things I needed to do before Sawyer's arrival.

Shave my legs.

Moisturize.

Change the sheets.

Check the condom, lube, and toy stash.

Close all the drapes and blinds.

It's a little bit like what I imagine a setup for a porn shoot would be. Personal prep, supplies, environment. Considering number four on my bucket list, the thought makes me giggle. Before I know it, it's seven o'clock, and the knock I've been anticipating falls on my door.

I open it to see Sawyer standing there, a pizza box in one hand, a six-pack of cider in the other, and wearing a backpack. It's the last thing that makes my eyebrows raise as he winks at me and walks past, coming inside my house.

"Do I want to know what's in the backpack?" I ask.

He just flashes me a smirk that instantly makes wetness pool between my thighs. "My, what a dirty mind you have. If I'm staying for the weekend, I need a toothbrush."

That makes me laugh. "And a change of clothes?" I tease as I follow him into the kitchen.

Sawyer scoffs. "Not likely. I don't plan on us wearing clothes very much."

It's a fight not to laugh again. "Then what else is in there?"

His eyebrows raise and mischief dances over his face. "You'll find out later. Right now, we're gonna eat some pizza and get to know each other."

That surprises me even more than the backpack. He clearly sees that written all over my face, because he sets everything down on my kitchen table before turning to me, running his hands down my arms to take my hands in his. "We both know why I'm here, angel. But just because my primary goal is to make you forget that asshat ever existed, it doesn't mean we can't also enjoy each other's company outside of sex." He huffs out a laugh. "Although, to be fully transparent, that's the first time I've *ever* said that to a woman. You've bewitched me somehow." Shaking his head, he lets go of my hands and takes out two ciders from the case he brought in. "Not sure if you drink cider, but this is from a local place. It's strong, so if all we do tonight is the drink and curse portion of the weekend, it'll be effective."

I take the open beer and drink from the cool glass bottle. A hint of citrus flows down my throat along with the full-bodied apple taste. "It's good. Thank you." Setting it down, I lean back against the counter and study him. "I don't know if I've ever known someone so unapologetically candid about their intentions. It's refreshing."

Sawyer shrugs. "I've never hidden who I am from anyone. I'm not a relationship guy, Tori, and if I thought for a second that's what you wanted from me, I wouldn't be here. Leading someone on isn't my game. Never has been, never will be." He steps in closer, setting our beers down and cupping my chin, tilting it up slightly. "But I know you're not in a place for a relationship, either. You just need someone to fuck you senseless and show you that you're more than a mom. You're a beautiful woman with needs and I am more than happy to meet those needs."

He sees me.

That's the only thought in my head as I lift up on my toes to kiss him. His hands move to my ass, gripping it so tightly I wonder if I'll have little bruises from his fingers. I kind of hope I do. Then he's pushing his thick thigh between my legs, and there's no way I can stop myself from grinding down on it, seeking any sort of relief from the ache that's already starting to build from just one kiss.

"I thought we were gonna talk," I murmur cheekily against his lips, feeling his turn up in response. But my teasing backfires when he pulls back, and I have to bite back a whimper at the loss of his body against mine.

"You're right. Let's play twenty questions."

The only sign he's even remotely affected is the very prominent bulge beneath his joggers. A bulge I'm eyeing up as he opens the pizza box.

"You done ogling my dick, angel?"

My head whips up to see him staring at me, amusement warring with lust on his face. His ridiculously handsome face.

"I met your sisters," I fire back. Two can play at the teasing game. And maybe talking about his family will ease some of this insane tension. After all, I am hungry. *For more than just his cock.*

He holds out a plate with a slice of pizza on it and inclines his head toward my living room. Picking up my cider, I lead the way, sinking down on my couch. He sits in the opposite corner, angling his body to face me. "Whatever they told you is a lie."

"They said you're stupidly handsome but also warned me away from you."

When Sawyer chokes around his bite of pizza, I almost feel bad. Guess I could've waited for him to finish chewing.

"Okay, maybe not a lie after all," he replies, setting down his pizza and taking a drink from his cider. "I am stupidly handsome and you probably should stay away from me."

"And yet, here you are." Our gazes lock on each other as I take a sip from my own drink.

"Here I am."

"What if I don't want to stay away from you, I just want you to make me feel good." I'm basically confirming I want this man to fuck me six ways to Sunday. The temperature in the room feels like it's rapidly rising. So much for easing the tension. I force myself to break the connection and pick up my pizza. "Okay, questions. What's your favourite colour?"

"Brown."

I quirk my lips at that. "Brown? Really? Like, are we talking poop brown, or chocolate brown, or autumnal brown?"

He lifts one hand and strokes down the side of my face. "Deep brown. Molten chocolate, with flecks of gold that catch the light and make it sparkle."

Holy fuck. This man. "Bet you say that to all the brown-eyed girls you hook up with," I say, trying to keep some thread of sanity intact.

A flash of a frown crosses his face, but it's gone before I can fully register it. Then he's sitting back in his corner, acting completely unaffected. "What's yours?"

"Teal. But a light shade, like what you think of with tropical beaches and clear waters."

He nods and takes another bite of pizza. Is he seriously not struggling to hold back right now? Because I am having a hell of a time trying to focus on food with him just sitting there looking perfectly comfortable on my couch.

I move slightly, lifting one leg up to rest my knee against the back of the couch. There's no missing the way his eyes dip between my legs. Thank God I'm wearing dark leggings or he'd probably see the evidence of my arousal right there. "What's your favourite movie?"

It's his turn to move, and he almost mirrors my position, except his one leg is bent flat on the cushion of the couch, his foot resting on his other muscular quad. "*Top Gun.*"

"Do you 'feel the need...the need for speed'?" I say, ending on a giggle.

Sawyer just winks. "Everywhere but the bedroom, angel. Mach 3 or dead." He sets his plate and his drink down on the coffee table before taking mine from my hands and doing the same. "Are you done?"

I eye the half-finished slice of pizza, then cock my head at him. "Does it matter how I answer?"

His smirk is the only reply, and then he launches himself across the couch toward me. I let out a stupidly girlish squeal as he pushes me onto my back, grabs my hips, and yanks me down so I'm lying flat on the couch.

"I'm allergic to strawberries, terrified of needles, and like to spend as much time naked as I can. My family comes first, then my job. I love dogs more than cats, and don't tell anyone, but I wouldn't care about hockey if it wasn't for my brother playing it. I'd rather watch baseball. Feel like you know me well enough?"

All I can do is nod. His lips quirk up, but the fire in his eyes doesn't diminish in the slightest.

"Good. Because I'm ready for dessert."

My leggings and panties are peeled away from me faster than it takes me to process that last sentence, and then Sawyer's lifting my legs over his shoulders and dropping his head down. But instead of getting right into things the way I would have thought, he pauses and ever so lightly strokes a finger through the moisture that's already gathered between my legs.

"I've missed you." His whisper is so earnest, so adorable. It's kind of a surprise, though, because that sentiment feels a little too relationship-y for what we're doing. Then I prop myself up on my elbows, despite the awkward angle with my legs still being elevated on his shoulders. I look down to see him staring between my legs.

"Are you talking to my pussy?" I say, letting mock outrage colour my voice. He lifts his head with a wolfish grin.

"What can I say? It's a nice pussy, and I missed it."

It's all I can do not to shake with laughter. "Considering where you were not even forty-eight hours ago, that seems a touch dramatic."

Sawyer says nothing. Keeping his heated gaze locked on mine, he lowers his head and swipes his tongue along my length. "Do you want to call me dramatic, or do you want to lay back and let me worship you with my tongue and my fingers before I fill you with my cock and make you scream my name?"

Chapter Sixteen

Tori

This man is truly talented with his tongue. By the time I drift back to reality — after he sends me to the freaking stars — he's managed to carry me to my bedroom and is setting me down to stand as he starts lifting my shirt over my dazed head.

"You back with me, angel?" he says with an amused expression on his absurdly handsome face.

"Why do you call me that?" I ask, my eyes dropping to where he's pushing his pants down his hips.

He pauses mid-strip. "Because when I first saw you, the lights made your hair glow like a halo. You had this look to you, sweet but sinful, all at once. I knew you were an angel. A fallen one, maybe, but definitely an angel sent to tempt me."

I guess my jaw must drop, because he reaches over and pushes my chin up before doing that sexy thing only guys can do, pulling his shirt off with one arm.

"That, and nicknames are kinda my thing." He finishes stripping and then, there he is, in all his naked glory, his cock jutting out toward me. "Now. Have you thought any more about that list of yours?"

Why does this man always have me feeling like I'm playing catch-up? Oh, yeah. Because he's deliciously distracting and his brain seems to move at warp speed. "I may have written a few things down."

"And?" he asks. There's an edge of command to his voice that makes me shiver. "As the man who's gonna cross some stuff off that list, it would help to know what's on it."

Taking in a deep breath, I slip past him and go to my dresser where I hid the printed list last night. Pulling it out, I turn around and push the drawer closed with my body, holding the list up, pinched between my finger and my thumb.

His lips twitch. Then he plucks the paper out of my hand and starts to read. Maybe I should be more nervous about his reaction, but I'm decidedly not. After all, the lines are clear between us. This is sex, nothing more. If he decides my list is too scandalous, not that I think that's going to be his reaction at all, then no harm done. He can see himself out and the list will never see the light of day again.

Sawyer looks up at me and slowly starts to shake his head.

Oh, crap.

"I'm disappointed, Tori. We missed an opportunity to cross number one off not ten minutes ago. I'm a big fan of using toys. Guess you'll have to show me your collection before I eat your sweet pussy again." I choke out a laugh. But he's not done. "And

I noticed *fuck a hot firefighter* isn't on here. Is that because it's already been completed? Or an oversight on your part?"

I bite my lips together to stop from laughing even harder, but then his lips are on mine, and his teeth are tugging my mouth open.

"What was that?" he asks, laughter colouring his tone as well. His hands have made their way to my waist, and then the jerk starts to tickle me.

"Completed! Oh my God, stop! Please, Sawyer," I shriek. To give him credit, he instantly responds, his hands instead cupping my ass to lift me in the air. I wrap my legs around him and just hold on.

"Good answer. Now, back to this list. I'm down for any and all of them, but a few might need some prep time. And I don't know if I can wait any longer to fuck you. But after, we're gonna talk about this and come up with a game plan for the weekend. I'm thinking we can get at least three or four of those done. Sound okay with you?"

He's serious. Oh my God, he's serious. How Sawyer manages to be both incredibly funny and yes, sex-god level sexy is mind-boggling. In the same breath, he's talking about fucking me hard and fast, and then about completing my sex bucket list. All in such a casual, conversational tone, as if we're discussing the weather.

"Okay." A pitiful answer, thanks to the pathetic mess of lust-addled mush that is my brain right now. Good thing Sawyer seems more than willing to take control. Taking the few steps to cross the room to my bed, he crawls onto it, still holding me, before slowly lowering my back to the sheets. I've never had a sexual partner so physically strong and dominant, able to just move me around at their whim. It's seriously freaking hot. His hands snake around underneath me, and he makes quick work of undoing my bra before pulling it off and tossing it to the side.

"You're scary good at that." I say breathlessly as his head lowers to capture my nipple in his mouth.

He pulls off, letting his teeth graze the tip and I arch up, missing the warm contact of his mouth. "Is that a good thing or a bad thing?" His hands squeeze my breasts, kneading them together. He's straddling my legs, meaning his hard cock is just...lying there right above where I want it to be. If I wasn't basically pinned down by his body weight, I'd be squirming, trying to find relief.

"It's just an observation. Most men can't undo a bra even if they're staring at the clasps. You managed it one-handed while I'm on my back."

His hands still. "I've had a lot of practice." There's a question to his words. As if he's feeling me out, waiting for my reaction. If he thinks I'm surprised to hear he's not short on sexual experience, he's wrong.

"Put that practice to good use, then. I was promised worshipping and name-screaming." Feeling bold, I reach down and manage to get my fingers around his length. "Or option two is you let me see if I can make you scream out *my* name first."

"Hell yeah, angel." Sawyer moves so quickly, I can't help the giggle that escapes. He's stretched out on the bed next to me, starfish style, before he flashes me an impish grin. "Challenge accepted."

I rise up on my knees at his side and get a better grip on his cock. I've described men's junk many times in my books, but I can honestly say that, unlike my heroines, I've never been attracted to a penis. Until this one. This perfectly long, perfectly thick one, with its smooth mushroom tip that's starting to leak.

Dipping my head down, I lap up the moisture, taking the time to swirl my tongue along the underside of the crown before running it down his length. His dick jumps in my hand and his hands come to tangle in my hair.

"Damn, Tori," he groans. "Your mouth is heaven."

I wrap my lips around the tip, then open and take as much of him as I can into my mouth. The sounds he makes, the way his fingers tighten in my hair, I use all of it to guide my movements, enjoying this blow job more than I ever have before. And soon enough, I'm getting what I asked for when he shouts my name and pulls me off.

"Angel, you're too fucking good at that," he swears, rolling over and taking me with him until he's once again hovering over me. His body radiates heat, and when he rolls his hips, that dick I just had in my mouth hits a thousand sensitive nerve endings between my legs. Showing off his strength, Sawyer reaches over to the bedside table with one arm, all while still holding his body above mine. He shifts back, and using his teeth, tears open a condom packet. Only then does he sit back on his legs and roll it down his cock.

Moving back over me, he lifts one of my legs, turns and presses a strangely sweet kiss to the inside of my knee, then lines up with my entrance and achingly slowly pushes in. My body welcomes him eagerly, and we both groan with pleasure when he's fully seated inside of me.

"Your body was made for this. For me," he rumbles, dropping his forehead to meet mine as he pulls his hips back, then snaps forward again. "Look at how well you're taking my cock, angel. So perfect."

"Yes!" I cry out in response, my eyes fluttering closed. I feel his lips over mine, his tongue plunging into my mouth in time with the thrust of his hips. It's a symphony of sensation, the slap of our bodies coming together, the pinch of his grip on my hip, the moans and sighs we can't hold back.

Sawyer lifts his upper body away from mine, pulling my lower body up to meet the new angle and it hits just right. "Holy crap, Sawyer. *Ohmygod, right there.*" I hear the desperate whine to my voice, but there's no holding back my chanting of his name as I clutch at the pillow under my head.

"You're glorious. Look at you, Tori. Tell me you're close, angel. Tell me you're here with me."

"I'm there," I manage to whimper, and then I'm gone, shooting into the stratosphere, screaming out his name, just the way he predicted I would as my body shakes and shudders through its release. Sawyer's grunting, his movements becoming erratic, and then he's growling my name into my ear as his own climax sends a second wave of sensation through me.

Eventually, Sawyer climbs off the bed and disappears into the bathroom. But I can't bring myself to move. My bones still feel like jelly.

"I noticed you've got a big bathtub," he says as he drops back down on the mattress beside me. I look over at him, for once already knowing where he's going with that statement.

"I do."

"What exactly is a romantic bubble bath?"

Oh boy. How far do I take this? I decide to keep it simple — for now — and let him get creative.

"A bath where I'm not alone. Where there's someone else in it with me, someone focused on...me. My relaxation. My pleasure."

He bounces back up to sitting. "Well, now. That's one we can check off your list right the fuck now." Leaning over, he smacks a kiss to my lips. "Don't move, angel."

Watching his perfect ass jog into my bathroom has me grabbing a pillow to muffle my giggle of delight. I don't know how the heck I got to this place where a hot firefighter is making my sex bucket list dreams come true, but I'm not complaining.

A few minutes later, he opens the bathroom door, comes over without saying a word, scoops me up into his arms, and carries me into the steamy room. My eyes widen as he sets me down beside the tub. Candlelight flickers in the small space, and the aroma of my favourite bubble bath fills the air.

"How's this?" he asks, sounding oddly nervous, like my opinion truly matters. I lift my hand to run it through his hair before going on my toes to kiss his cheek.

"This is perfect."

His grin is so wide, so energetic, it has me smiling in response. Then he steps into the water and eases himself down into the bubbles before gesturing to me. "C'mon in."

I lower myself into the tub and lean back against his muscled chest. From somewhere behind him, he grabs a washcloth, and starts to slowly, gently wipe the soft wet fabric over my body. I let my eyes close and just soak in the moment.

"I've never done this."

Shifting slightly, so I can tilt my head back and look at him, I see him staring down at me. "Done what?"

"Spent this much time with a woman. With one woman. I've never wanted to."

Something in me makes me move to sit up and turn around, but his arm goes around my waist, holding me tightly in place. Settling back in, I let him share whatever he's going to say.

"Monogamy in moderation, that's always been my thing. One woman at a time, for one night only. Nothing more."

He's trying to sound full of bravado, but there's an underlying emotion I can't quite get a read on. Whether he's been hurt in the past, or never seen a healthy relationship, I don't know. But I find myself wanting to understand.

"Are your siblings all in relationships?"

He nods. "Yeah, and don't get me wrong I'm happy for them. It took a minute for me to realize my own issues with relationships didn't need to be theirs. Sometimes I'm even jealous of what they have. A partner, a person that's just always there. But it's not for me."

"Why not?" I press, but apparently, there's a limit to how much he wants to share. His face shifts into another one of his cocky smirks.

"Ah, now that's a story for another time. Or never. It's also a good story for never. Right now, I think we should cross off another item from your bucket list. Got any scarves?"

I let Sawyer distract me last night, and boy, did he distract me good. Multiple times. In multiple positions. And locations. We crossed off my romantic bubble bath item, and the blindfolded sex, which was weird for me, if I'm being honest. Not my kinda thing, even though I know lots of people get off on it.

Then he took me outside, and I rode his cock while he lounged on my deck chair, his hands twisted in my hair, holding me where he could kiss me senseless. The stars were out, but I can't say I noticed any of them, except for the stars he made me see.

I want to understand why I'm different. Why I'm the woman he'll break his one-night-only rule for. But I'm also terrified to know. Because I can tell Sawyer Donnelly is someone who could hurt me if I let him in.

Keeping it casual, keeping it a fling, is safer for my heart. And that means letting what he shared in my bathtub last night stay there.

"Okay. Here's what I'm thinking. As much as staying in bed all fucking day sounds like a good idea, we need to hydrate and refuel. So I'll go grab some food, let you do author shit, then I'll be back in an hour and you can explain exactly what's meant by *exploring the back door*, because I've got ideas." Sawyer waggles his eyebrows at me as he pulls a hoodie over his head.

The fact that he remembered my offhand comment at some point last night about needing to deal with some emails and write a newsletter for my readers is touching. And another thing I'm trying not to read into too much.

Turning away from him on the pretext of getting socks out of my dresser, I squash down the confusing feelings being stirred inside of me. He's here for sex, that's all. "Am I going to regret showing you that list?"

Strong arms wrap around me from behind, and I'm pulled back against a hard body. "Not if I can help it."

I let him turn me around slowly, then he takes my arms and loops them around his neck. "But if you're second-guessing anything you wrote down, hell, if you're second-guessing me sticking around this weekend, just say so. No harm, no foul, no feelings hurt."

He really needs to stop being so damn considerate. It's going to be even harder to keep strong boundaries if I start to fall for him. I paste what I hope is a convincingly blasé look on my face. "You'd really let someone else step in to help me with my list?"

His eyes darken. Is that *jealousy?* It can't be.

"As long as you're into what we've got going on, I am. I don't take it lightly, you sharing your list with me. But if you think another guy can help you complete things from it better than me, I'll make it my mission to prove you wrong."

That deep possessive note? I like that... A shiver runs up my spine. Then he lifts me into his arms and carries me back over to the bed.

"Starting now," he growls.

Well, okay then.

Chapter Seventeen

Sawyer

I slowly come awake because of something tickling my face. Blinking my eyes open, I realize it's blonde hair. I'm curled around Tori, her head resting on my arm, my face buried in her hair. We're naked, her warm, soft body pressed against mine. She's clutching my hand to her chest, our legs are tangled together, and we're so tightly connected, I can feel the soft rise and fall of her breath.

She's still asleep. And I'll be damned if it doesn't feel really fucking nice cuddling her like this.

I've never slept over at a woman's house two nights in a row. Hell, I've never spent a weekend with a woman just existing in each other's space, with the exception of my family. And there's nothing familial about this situation.

A part of me thinks I should be running for the hills or trying to find someone to conduct an exorcism. I must be possessed; that's the only explanation for why I have absolutely no desire to move from my very comfortable position, holding Tori in my arms.

But a larger part of me just feels good.

Her body shifts, and I know she's starting to wake up. Gently, I free my top hand from hers, and use it to run my fingers down her side, over the dip in her waist and the flare of her hip. She stretches, pressing her ass back into me with a soft moan.

"Morning, angel," I murmur in her ear as I lightly trace my fingers over the front of her thigh, getting closer to the soft thatch of curls that covers my destination but teasing by pulling away. Her hips start to move, and I know she's waking up more, and realizing what I'm up to.

"You're a tease, Sawyer Donnelly," she rasps, her voice thick with sleep. I let her wrap her fingers around my wrist and bring my hand to where we both want it to be. "If you're gonna wake me up, be nice about it."

I chuckle against her hair, but don't deny her any longer, sliding my fingers between her folds. She opens her hips to give me room, lifting one leg to rest on top of mine. My dick is already hard, but it's not about me right now.

Dipping into her wet heat, I swirl around the lips of her pussy, still keeping my touch light and teasing.

"Sawyer," she whines, twisting her head to look at me. Her eyes are hooded with desire. "Please."

I steal a kiss at the exact second I plunge two fingers into her, swallowing her moan, chasing it with my lips. We stay like that, kissing as I play with her, but as much as I can see myself staying right here all day, I've got other things planned. Curling my fingers, I find the spot that I learned over the last couple of days is guaranteed to make her fly, and I press into it.

Her cries are muffled by our mouths still being fused together, her hand gripping my wrist, holding it in place. I feel the flutter and then the tight clench of her walls around my fingers. We ride out her release together, and when she slumps back into my embrace, I kiss the top of her head and slip my fingers out from between her legs. She watches me as I suck the taste of her off them.

"Mmm. Forget coffee, all I need is the taste of you to wake me up in the morning," I tease. Easing back, I prop up on one elbow and look down at her. "I'm gonna make some breakfast, then I've got a surprise for you."

Tori's eyes light up. "I like surprises."

Grinning, I lean down and kiss the tip of her nose. "Good." Then I climb out of bed and dip into the bathroom. When I come back out after brushing my teeth and taking a piss, I'm still bare-ass naked. The first time I wandered around her house without any clothes on, Tori looked at me like I was crazy. By now, she's used to it, even if she hasn't joined me in naked time yet.

Heading into the kitchen, I open the fridge, pulling out ingredients to whip up an omelet. Minutes later, arms wrap around me and lips press a kiss to my back. "You're going to burn yourself if you cook naked."

I turn in her embrace, taking in my T-shirt she's wearing. "You got anything on underneath that, angel?"

Her eyes twinkle with mischief. "Feed me breakfast and then you can find out."

I kiss her, hard and fast, then take her hands and push her away from my body. "Be gone, distracting woman. Make yourself useful and get me some coffee."

Her laughter fills the room and I turn to the stove with a stupid smile on my face. This is fun. *She's fun.*

We eat breakfast, and I discover exactly what she's wearing — or rather, not wearing — underneath my T-shirt. Tori gets her second orgasm of the morning, sitting on the kitchen table as I drive my cock into her.

"I'm never going to be able to eat here with my son again without thinking of this," she gasps out with a laugh as I pull out of her.

"I'll help you sanitize everything, but I can't wipe away the memories." I smirk. She just groans and slaps at me feebly.

"That was ridiculously cheesy."

"I know, and I'm not sorry," I agree. I saunter down the hall and deal with the condom quickly before making a pit stop at my backpack and rejoining Tori in the kitchen. She takes in my stance, with my hands behind my back, and folds her arms over her chest.

"Whatcha got there?" she asks.

"When you invited me over —" I start, only to be interrupted by the blonde spitfire.

"You mean, when you invited yourself over."

I shrug. "Apples and oranges, baby. When we made plans for me to spend the weekend, you had two goals in mind. Remember what they were?"

Tori's fighting back a smile, trying to maintain her tough girl pose. Finally she huffs, "Yeah. Get drunk and curse my ex."

I nod slowly. "I'd say we accomplished the first last night." I wink, giving her a moment to remember the tequila shots we licked off each other's bodies. "But I didn't want you to think I forgot about the second." With a flourish, I reveal what's in my hands.

Tori reacts exactly the way I wanted her to, by doubling over with laughter. "Oh my God, is that a...is that a voodoo doll?" she wheezes, still clutching herself. I close the distance between us, my still very naked dick starting to halfway harden again. What can I say? Apparently, I'm insatiable around her. But I silently will it to stand down.

Cursing now, fucking later.

"Sure is, angel. I didn't know what the asshole sperm donor looked like, but it turns out you can just get generic voodoo dolls."

"Where the hell did you get that?" she asks, her face still full of mirth.

"The internet is a wonderful place." I hold it out to her, along with the small container of pins. "Would you like to do the honours?"

"You're ridiculous," she says, but she takes the items from me. "How does this work, exactly?"

"Pretty sure you just stab the thing and pretend you're stabbing him," I supply helpfully, earning an eye roll.

She hums softly under her breath, looking down at the doll. Flashing me a mischievous glance, she sets the container of pins down, opens it, and chooses one with a round, red, head. Inhaling dramatically, she raises her hand, then jabs it down in the doll's crotch area so violently I instinctively cover my own junk.

"Damn, girl, tell me how you *really* feel," I tease. Picking up another pin, I watch as Tori takes her time choosing where to stab the doll, then with another wicked grin, she sticks it right over the mouth area.

"He was terrible at oral."

Another pin, this time into each of the doll's hands. "A selfish lover."

A pin into his heart. "And a terrible father."

The doll falls from her hands, and she looks up at me, a feral glint to her eyes. "You're not selfish, or bad at oral."

I raise my eyebrows. "Nope and nope." Without warning, Tori launches herself at me, and it's only thanks to my quick reflexes kicking in that I catch her midair, her legs wrapping around me and squeezing tightly as she devours my mouth with her kiss.

Who knew cursing someone could be hot as fuck foreplay.

They say all good things must come to an end, and I'm living that reality right now. After I fucked her from behind as she leaned over the kitchen counter, we made it to the bathroom before she dropped to her knees in the shower. I returned the favour — twice — in her bed, and only then did we finally realize the time and the fact her kid will be back in a couple of hours, grandparents in tow.

Getting dressed was the last thing I wanted to do, but here we are, standing at her front door.

"Thank you," she says, leaning against the wall next to the door. There's a peaceful expression on her face that's so damn beautiful, it takes my breath away. "This weekend was more than I expected, but exactly what I needed."

I'm not loving how tangled up I feel hearing her say that. Part of me wants to cheer and high-five myself, the other part is panicking that things are veering a little too much into relationship territory.

Opting for cocky humour, I deflect those pesky feelings. "No need to thank me, angel. It's not like I didn't have a fucking fantastic weekend myself." Yeah, so fantastic I don't want to leave. And that's mildly terrifying.

Tori steps toward me, placing her hands on my shoulders and tilting her head to the side. Nervous energy radiates from her, and I weirdly want to take her in my arms and erase all of it. But that would be stupid.

"We could do this again, if you want."

My body freezes at her words.

"Just casual, I mean. I know you don't do relationships, and you said it yourself, I'm not looking for one. But you make me feel really good, Sawyer. I'd be open to feeling good again. That's all."

I force myself to relax. A casual fling, friends with benefits type thing? I could try that. After all, my friends don't distract me when I'm at work, so this doesn't have to be any different.

You're not fucking your friends, a not-so-helpful voice in my head points out. Maybe so, but there's no denying the chemistry between Tori and me. If this works as a way for us both to get dynamite sex on the reg, what's the harm?

No feelings, just fucking.

Cupping her chin in my hand, I give her a heated look. "Count me in."

Relief and excitement dance over her face before she schools it into something more serious. "Good. But one thing. If we're doing this, we're only being intimate with each other. That's a deal-breaker for me."

"Not a problem." My answer comes swiftly. She doesn't need to know that won't be an issue since I can't even think about another woman right now. "But that means all your orgasms belong to me."

Her eyes widen. "Excuse me?"

"You heard me." I drop my voice down to a low whisper. "All your orgasms are *mine*."

"What if you're not here and I'm horny?" she asks and I get a fucking semi just from hearing her say it.

"Doesn't matter. No toys, no fingers, nothing if I'm not here with you."

The little whimper that escapes her as I bite down gently on the skin where her neck meets her shoulder makes me seriously regret the fact that I need to leave right now. But if I don't go, we'll end up fucking again, and I know she's got a lot to do before her son comes home. That's the only thing that works to make me step back, pick up my backpack, and open her front door.

"Say hi to Coop for me," I say with a wink, making myself act as if I'm not fighting a raging hard-on at the thought of owning every single one of her orgasms.

I walk out the door and down the path to my truck, chancing a quick look over my shoulder after dumping my backpack in the back seat. She's still standing there, a dazed look on her beautiful face.

And I'll be damned if it doesn't feel good knowing I put it there.

Chapter Eighteen

Tori

"Mom, look! It's Sawyer. Can we stop, please?" Cooper's excited voice comes from the back seat of my car as we slow down at a four-way stop just before the fire station. My heart speeds up as I look for Sawyer, skipping a beat when I see his tall body climbing down from a fire truck. I want to stop, to see him again, but is that weird? To show up with my kid just a few days after spending the weekend naked with him?

We've kept in contact by texting occasionally, but we haven't seen each other since he left my house Sunday morning.

I certainly have thought about him — a lot. Especially at night, when I want to open up my box of toys but then remember I can't.

No toys, no fingers, nothing if I'm not here with you.

Even now, I shiver slightly, remembering the growl of his voice when he said that.

The honk from the car behind me startles me, and I realize Cooper is still talking.

"I never got to show him that I remember the handshake. Please, Mom? Please?"

Making a split-second decision, I turn the corner, into the parking lot next to the station. "Okay, but if he's busy, we stay out of his way and leave, got it?"

"Got it!" Coop's bouncing in his seat but waiting for me to turn off the engine before opening his door. I take advantage of him remembering our rule for a minute as I check myself in the tiny rearview mirror. Not that there's anything I can do about my appearance, but hey, can't blame a girl for trying.

"Mom, let's go!" Coop sounds impatient, and I don't blame him... Sawyer's got a magnetic pull to him. I noticed it the night we first met, and every time since. Something just draws me to him. And my son, apparently. I turn off the engine and Cooper's unbuckled instantly, opening his door, clambering out, and shifting from one foot to the other as I slowly get out.

As soon as I lock the car, he grabs my hand and starts dragging me across the parking lot. His enthusiasm is cute, but also a little concerning to my mama bear heart. Can Sawyer live up to the hero worship currently written all over Cooper's face? I silently pray that he can, because my kid has been disappointed by men in his life too many times. Okay, mostly by one man in particular, but of anyone, his father should have been someone Coop could count on, and he most definitely cannot.

When I asked Cooper how the weekend of his father's wedding went, all I got was a shrug and "it was fun to hang out with Nana and Pops." Not a single mention of his sperm donor, the wedding, or anything else. The therapist I used to see said I shouldn't push him to talk too much about his dad, I should follow his lead and focus more on making sure he sees me as a safe space to talk about anything. Which is why I've never said a disparaging thing about Tim in front of Cooper. The man might be a waste of space, and not deserve a second of my kid's time, but he is his father. And I never wanted to close the door on that relationship. Not until Cooper's old enough to decide for himself.

All of which makes me acutely aware that Sawyer has no clue the impact he had on my son with just that one interaction at the school. But I know. Sawyer made him feel seen, special, and important. Even though they only spoke for a few minutes, he did more in that time than Cooper's father had in years.

And now, as I watch Cooper speed over to where Sawyer and a few other firefighters are standing around with buckets and brushes, making it clear they're about to clean the trucks, I have to fight away the ache in my chest that wishes things were different between Sawyer and me.

Thankfully, the second Sawyer turns around and sees Cooper, his face lights up. I watch carefully as I approach them, and see Sawyer drop into a squat and hold his hand out. Cooper obviously knows what's going on, because their hands start to move in some intricate handshake that has my kid laughing delightedly as Sawyer grins back.

I reach them just as Sawyer straightens up, his eyes landing on mine and flashing with something intense that makes me gulp.

"Well, hi there. This is a nice surprise, what brings you here?" He winks and my goddamn knees quiver.

"I wanted to show you I remember the handshake. I kept asking Mom to bring me here but she was always busy writing her kissing books," Cooper answers helpfully.

I can see Sawyer fighting back a laugh as he lifts his hand for a high five. "I'm impressed, Coopzilla, you've got a great memory."

"Coopzilla?" Cooper tilts his head to the side, confused.

Sawyer just shrugs. "I give everyone nicknames. And your shirt inspired me." He gestures to the image of Godzilla on Cooper's T-shirt.

Cooper beams. "I love Godzilla. Mom won't watch the movies with me, but my grandpa and I have seen three of them."

"Dude, I love Godzilla! Oh man, he's the best monster."

The look on Cooper's face is pure amazement, and I know I'm never going to hear the end of this. If Sawyer was trying to cement his place as Coop's favourite person, he just succeeded.

"Can I see the fire truck?" Cooper asks, already starting to move toward the giant red engine, and I put my hand on his shoulder to hold him back.

"Hold on, kiddo, remember we said if Sawyer's busy we won't stay. Maybe you need to ask if he even has time for us to be here. We don't want to distract him."

But Sawyer's grabbing Cooper's hand and leading him over to the truck. "Nah, it's cool. If the alarm goes, we'll have to move fast, but right now is good." He looks over his shoulder at me and winks. "We can even spray the hose if your mom doesn't mind getting a little wet."

My cheeks flush. Good thing Coop's attention is solely focused on the fire truck. I stand back and let them have their moment, taking a few photos when Sawyer lets Cooper sit in the front seat and turn on the lights and sirens for a second or two. My heart is brimming with happiness, but it's tinged with worry.

I don't know exactly how to classify whatever is going on between Sawyer and me. But I know it's meant to be casual. Yet, the way my son is looking up at him, as if he hung the moon, I worry Sawyer's getting tangled up in my life.

"Do you ever get scared when you have to fight a fire?" Cooper asks, taking Sawyer's outstretched hand to help him climb down from the cab of the truck.

Once again, Sawyer surprises me, because instead of dismissing the question with some sort of cocky attitude, he adopts a serious expression and squats down again so he's at Cooper's level. "You bet I do. Fires can be really scary because they can be super unpredictable. You never really know what's gonna happen when you go to fight a fire. But I've got a great team with me, and we're all highly trained. We trust each other and our equipment. I get scared, but I also know I've got a really important job to do. And that helps me face my fear."

"I want to do something with animals when I grow up," Cooper says confidently. "Maybe work at a zoo or something."

"That's super cool. I love animals."

I take in their casual conversation, my heart warming. The ease with which Sawyer interacts with Cooper is exactly what I hoped for, even as it surprises me just how close they seem to be after meeting only two times. But that's Sawyer, I guess. You can't help but like the man, whether you're a kid idolizing a hero, or a woman daydreaming about a man. Then Sawyer gives a hard pull on the hose reel and turns to me with mischief written all over his face.

"Do you think your mom wants to handle my hose?" he asks, his tone of voice casual even as I choke on air.

"No, but I do!" comes Cooper's enthusiastic reply, his obliviousness to Sawyer's innuendos a relief.

I give them both a stern glare. "I don't want to get wet, boys. Not today, at least." My words hit their intended mark as Sawyer coughs to cover up his own laugh.

For several minutes, I watch as Sawyer lets Cooper spray the hose at the other truck his teammates are washing. When they're done, he shows Cooper how to reel the hose back in, the two of them laughing and joking with each other as well as the other firefighters the entire time.

Patting Coop on the head once they're finished, Sawyer says, "Hey Coopzilla, why don't you head inside with my friend Castro, and he can grab you some of the stuff we have for open house days. I'll be in soon with your mom."

"Okay," Cooper says, happily following after the other firefighter.

"Not gonna lie, angel, it's painful being this close to you and not touching you."

The rumble of his voice comes from closer than I expected, and my head whips around from where I was watching Cooper enter the station to see Sawyer leaning casually against the side of the fire engine.

"Thank you for this, for taking the time with him."

It's not what I want to say. Heck no, I want to tell him I'm struggling to keep my hands off him as well. That I want to kiss him senseless for being so good to my kid, that I want him to come to my house when Cooper's at school tomorrow and make me scream his name again.

But I can't say that. Not here, where his coworkers are around, scrubbing the other fire truck, hopefully oblivious to the ridiculous amount of lust I'm certain is radiating out of me. Thank God Sawyer seems to be on the same wavelength, because instead of flirting any more, he folds his arms across his chest and gives me a softer smile.

"He's a good kid, Tori. A great one. You've done an awesome job with him, I can tell, even after only hanging out with him a couple of times. He's smart and curious."

His compliment hits me hard, but in the best possible way. "Thank you," I murmur. "He makes it easy. Most of the time." Our eyes connect. "You handled his question about being scared really well. It's not always easy answering kids' questions; they have zero filter but they also can sense a bullshit answer a mile away."

Sawyer nods slowly. "Everything I said was true. I love my job, and I never underestimate the risk or the importance of it. It's my priority, because if I don't take it seriously, if I'm not focused, that's when stuff goes wrong."

The subtext in his message is clear. This is why he doesn't do relationships. Just like he said over the weekend, he can't afford any distractions at work. Now, I'm confused. Is he trying to say even our casual sex agreement is too much of a distraction?

Pushing off from the truck, Sawyer makes to move past me. "But what I didn't say is that my job can be summed up in one sentence. I go in hot, and I don't stop until everything is very *wet*." With one wicked wink, and a subtle brush of his hand against my side, he walks toward the station. "Let's go find the little dude and make sure the guys hooked him up right."

And just like that, Sawyer Donnelly walks away, yet again, leaving me a puddle of lust — and confusion.

Chapter Nineteen

Sawyer

"That was one hot mama who came to visit today."

The force of the glare I turn on Castro as we're packing up at the end of our shift could melt the pavement, but the piece of shit just stands there, unaffected. "Don't be a dick, Castro," I growl.

He scoffs. "Acknowledging a woman's beauty is hardly me being a dick. But if you're laying claim, I'll back off. Are you tryin' to get in her pants?"

I start to see red, but Sloan's hand on my shoulder holds me back. "Hey Castro, get your ass in the kitchen, you were on dinner cleanup duty and the place is a mess. You know Cap won't let you leave till it's done," he says to his fellow probie.

Thankfully, Castro hustles out of the bunk room without another word, but now I'm left with Sloan, the other guys already gone. And this motherfucker is looking at me like he knows something.

"What?"

"He's got a point, Sawyer. Anyone with eyes could see you flirting with her earlier."

I shrug off his hand. "Fuck off, probie. We're just friends. You were there, you saw, I helped her kid when I did the career day thing."

"I also saw you look at her like you'd seen a ghost, despite her acting as if you'd never met. So don't tell me nothing's goin' on."

This time my glare has the intended affect, as Sloan lifts his hands and steps back. "Listen, I'm not trying to cause shit or make you pissed. But do you remember what you told me when I first started?"

"Probably the same thing I tell everyone," I grumble.

"Probably," he agrees. "You said to never let anything take my focus away from the job. You said from the second I walk through the doors of the station to start my shift to the second I leave at the end, my attention had to be here, on my crew and the job, and nowhere else. You said *no distractions*."

I clench my fists. "Yeah?"

"You sure as shit looked distracted while Tori and her kid were here."

Fuck.

"But," he continues as if he hasn't just made my stomach drop. "The second she left and we got that medical call, you were back to business. Until Castro's dumbass remark just now, I'd almost forgotten they even visited, or that you were a lovestruck idiot with hearts in your eyes."

"I did not have hearts in my eyes," I protest, tossing a dirty shirt at him. He catches it easily and throws it right back.

"Are you forgetting I majored in psych at university? Dude, there's a way a man looks at a woman when he's seen her naked...and wants to see her naked again. That's how you looked at her."

"You're seeing things."

Like the truth. Damn it.

Sloan just shrugs. "Whatever you want to tell yourself, man. I'm just gonna say this before I get out of here. She seems cool, you seemed happy to see her and the kid, and it didn't affect your ability to do the job."

He saunters to the door of the bunk room without a backward glance.

"Your nickname is gonna be 'Shrink' when you're no longer a probie," I yell after him, earning a middle finger salute.

Is my usual running route one that goes past Dogwood Cove Elementary just before the bell rings to start the school day?

No.

Did I actually take the time to style my hair and pick out a decent running outfit today instead of grabbing a DCFD ball cap and whatever clothes I grab first?

Maybe.

Am I intentionally slowing down, my eyes searching for a particular head of blonde hair, as I jog along the sidewalk opposite the school?

Yeah.

When I woke up this morning, my first day off since the weekend, she was the first thing I thought of. Which should probably be a red flag, but I'm pretending to be colour blind, I guess.

Sloan's words haven't left me all week. His observation of my behaviour when Tori and Cooper were visiting — that I was oblivious to anything else — shook me more than I wanted to admit. But as he said, once they left, I was back to normal. I didn't think of Tori for the rest of my shifts.

Which only reinforces one thing in my mind. Me and Tori will only ever be friends who fuck. That's all. No feelings, no commitment or responsibility to each other. If I can compartmentalize fucking random women, and I can compartmentalize my friends, there's no reason I can't compartmentalize fucking the same woman who happens to be a friend.

I run past the school without sighting Tori or Cooper. Which is probably for the best. Shaking my head, I turn down the street that will take me to the gravel path that runs along the beach. It's gonna be a long run today; I need to clear my fucking head of the hot blonde who's making me rethink all my rules.

No, that's not right. I'm not rethinking them. I'm...bending them? I just need to reinforce the *friends* part of what Tori and I are doing.

When I eventually get home, I take a quick shower before texting my mom. She's watching my cousin's kid this weekend while Leo takes his wife Serena away for a baby-making getaway. That's not what they're calling it, of course, but we're not dumb. The entire family knows they plan on spending the weekend fucking as much as possible. I promised Violet, their daughter, that I'd hang out with her at some point, partly to give my mom a break but also just because she's a cool kid.

Which gives me an idea. A way to focus on the friends side of things with Tori, plus help Cooper meet some kids in town. Sure, Vi's a little younger than him, but not by much, so it should be fun. Once I've got stuff confirmed with Mom, I open another message window.

SAWYER: Hey angel. What are you and Coopzilla up to this weekend?

TORI: No plans yet, except he's got a playdate with a kid from school tomorrow. Why?

SAWYER: Come with me and my cousin's kid to Westport on Sunday? We're hitting the LEGO store.

I see the dotted message bubble show up, but no message comes through for several seconds. *C'mon angel, don't overthink this.*

TORI: You want to spend your Sunday with me... AND my kid?"

I grin. Yup, I do.

SAWYER: And Violet. She's younger than Sawyer and kinda shy, but I think it'll be cool. Who doesn't love LEGO?

SAWYER: Besides. We're friends aren't we? Friends hang out.

TORI: I thought we were the other kind of friends...

SAWYER: Why can't we be both? I like hanging out with you and Cooper. So let's do more of that.

SAWYER: We can do more of the OTHER kind of hanging out when the kids aren't around...

TORI: Okay. Sure, we'll come.

SAWYER: Yeah... you will. When Coops in school. *wink emoji*

TORI: *facepalm emoji* I walked into that one.

TORI: You know he's at school right now... right?

SAWYER: Are you booty callin' me angel?

TORI: That depends on if you're saying yes or not.

SAWYER: Be there in a few.

When I honk my horn outside Tori's house Sunday morning, I look in the rearview mirror at Violet, who's strapped into her seat. "You good, kiddo? I promise, Cooper's a cool dude."

She just nods, which is normal for her. She's a quiet kid, but I'm hoping she has fun today. Tori and Cooper reach the truck, and I hop out to open the door for them. "Hey guys, glad you could join us."

"Hi Sawyer! I'm so excited, Mom said I could open my piggy bank and bring some money to buy a big set today." Cooper scrambles into the back of the truck. "Hi. I'm Cooper," he says excitedly to Violet, who gives him a small smile and a quiet "hi" back.

"That's Violet. She's super smart and super artistic. If you're lucky, she'll draw you something. I have a unicorn on my fridge at home that is so realistic, I keep thinking it's gonna come to life," I say, watching Coop buckle himself in. I close the door, then pause a beat before opening Tori's. "Hey, angel. How's your weekend going so far?" I give her a wink.

She bites her lip. "Lots of laundry to do."

I laugh under my breath as she climbs into the truck, and I close the door before jogging around to my side. When I showed up at her house on Friday, I was greeted by a lace-covered angel holding a jar of honey.

Let's just say, things got a little sticky. In more ways than one.

I climb into my truck, and after double-checking everyone's buckled, we head out. The drive to Westport isn't long, but it's long enough for Violet to come out of her shell as soon as she finds out Cooper's a fellow animal lover.

"Mom, did you hear that? There's an adoption fair happening next weekend. Can we go? Please?" Cooper leans forward. "Violet told me all about it. There's gonna be a bouncy castle, too. Even if we just go to look. Please?"

Tori shifts in her seat to look back at him. "Coop, a dog is a lot of work. Who's going to feed it, clean up the poop, and walk it every day?"

A quick glance in the rearview mirror has me catching Cooper with his hands clasped in a prayer pose. "Please, Mom. Please? I'll help. I promise. I'll feed it, and clean up the poop, and we can walk it to school every day. Please!"

It's obvious this is a long-running conversation, so I wisely stay out of it. But out of the corner of my eye, I see Tori relax against the seat, and it's obvious she's close to giving in.

"We can go and look. No promises, because *if* we get a dog, it's got to be the right dog for our family."

Cooper cheers, then turns and gives a startled Violet a high five. "Thanks, Mom. Hey Sawyer, you wanna come with us?"

Now I grin. "Thanks for the invite, Coopzilla. I was already planning to be there, so I'm sure we'll see each other."

"Awesome," Coop says happily. "I love Dogwood Cove."

He doesn't notice his mom's hand drift up to cover her mouth, but I do, and I know it's because she's so damn happy he said that. I sneak my hand across the center console to squeeze her thigh briefly, flashing her an understanding smile. She covers my hand with hers and squeezes back, and something about sharing this moment feels really good.

When we get to the LEGO store, the kids dash off to different sections, whirling around like hurricanes of excitement. Tori and I stand off to the side for a few minutes just watching them.

We're close enough that our hands brush, and I grab on to her pinkie. Cooper runs up, and I drop it quickly.

"Sawyer, look at this one!"

I crouch down and take the large box he's holding. "Woah, that's super cool, little dude." It's a full fire station set, and something flip-flops in my chest that he picked this out. "I would've loved to have this as a kid."

"You could get it now, I'll help you build it."

"Cooper, I don't think Sawyer wants to buy a LEGO set," Tori interjects, but I give her a mock frown.

"Excuse you, but I happen to love LEGO." I stand up and reach out my hand to Cooper. He jumps to it, and we go through our handshake. "Thanks, Coopzilla. I think we better help Vi choose which one she wants, then we can find yours."

We grab some lunch after finishing up at the LEGO store, then head home. The drive back to Dogwood Cove is full of chatter from the kids in the back seat, but silence from Tori. When I pull into their driveway, I climb out to walk them to the door. To my surprise, Cooper doesn't go for a handshake, instead, flinging his arms around my waist and hugging me tightly.

"Hey bud, thanks for coming with us today."

"You won't forget me when you go to build the fire station, will you?" he asks, the words muffled. But the hope shining from his eyes when he lifts his head is obvious, and I know there's not a chance in hell I want to disappoint the kid.

"You bet I won't. I'm gonna need your help, for sure."

"Cool. Bye, Sawyer." He releases me, and with one more wave to Violet sitting in the truck, he bounds inside his house.

"He really likes you."

I look over at Tori, who's adopted a serious expression. "I like him, too."

"Don't... Just..." She lets out a huff.

"Just say it, angel. Whatever's on your mind, I want you to say it."

She gulps and takes in a deep breath. "He's got some serious hero worship going on with you, and if you can't handle that, just tell me so we can work it out. That kid has been let down by the one man who should've always been there for him too many times, and I'll be damned if I allow him to be let down by another, no matter what's going on between me and you."

Her mama bear attitude is kinda sexy, but I keep that thought to myself. Because I hear every word she's saying, and the ones she's not. And I don't know how to respond. Can I promise I'll always be here for her and her son? Part of me wants to, but part of me is scared.

Because that feels a hell of a lot like a commitment I'm not in any position to make.

CHAPTER TWENTY

Tori

"Get up, Mom! It's time to go look at the dogs!"

I let out an *oomph* as seventy pounds of kid lands on top of me.

"Cooper, buddy, I love you, but it is too dang early," I groan, looking at my phone that shows it's not even seven. "The adoption fair doesn't start for hours."

"But I'm awake now," he says in that matter-of-fact way that is sometimes adorable and sometimes — like now — really, really annoying.

I fix him with a glare. "Well, I wasn't, until you jumped on me."

He looks sheepish. "I'm excited. I know you said it's only a *maybe* that we get a dog, but I'm really excited."

Well, shoot. I push myself up to sit and drag him in for a hug. "I know you are. I'm sorry I'm a grumpasaurus in the morning."

"You need tea. I can make it for you," he says, giving me what I know is his best suck-up smile. "I'm real responsible."

"*Really* responsible," I correct gently as he bounces off my bed. "And I know you are, Coop, that's why it's a definite maybe on the dog. *If* we meet the right one."

His entire face lights up, and I'm filled with so much love for this kid, my kid, I feel like I might burst.

"Thanks, Mom! I'll be back with your tea," he hollers as he runs down the hall to the kitchen.

Dropping back onto my pillow, I pull the blanket up over my head and try to recover some of the cozy sleepy feeling I had before I was rudely awakened. But it's a lost cause, something I realized early on, being a single mom. Once the kid is up, I'm up.

I toss back the covers and swing my legs over the side of my bed, yawning as I arch my back and stretch. Ever since Sawyer and I started hooking up, I've been feeling muscles that I never used to. Sex with him is a full-on athletic endeavour, and I'm definitely into it. Being with him, I feel alive in a way I never have before. I feel sexy and powerful bringing a man like him to his literal knees. During our sex marathon weekend, he asked me to explain what I meant by "explore the back door," and the care and consideration he showed by listening to me stammer embarrassingly about my desire to experiment with anal was pretty incredible for a casual hookup kind of guy. But it isn't all that surprising to me, not anymore. He's made it clear we're just friends with benefits, but that hasn't stopped him from sending me text messages almost daily, some funny, some just checking in. He's living up to the friends side of things, until we're alone, and then all the benefits come out to play.

And the best part is, he's so engaged with Cooper, I don't feel like I'm neglecting my kid or my job as his mom at all. I've avoided relationships in the past because I never wanted Cooper to feel like he came second to anyone in my life. Thanks partly to Sawyer's shift work and partly to his connection with Coop, that's not even an issue in my mind.

The other day he texted me, asking if Coop could come over after school to start working on the fire station LEGO set. The way my kid's eyes lit up when I relayed the message was everything. I took him to Sawyer's apartment and was promptly shooed away by them both. I headed back home and took a long bubble bath, and tried not to obsess over how good Sawyer is with my son. And how devastated Cooper would be if things changed and Sawyer wasn't around anymore.

But that fear has lingered, like a ball of lead in my gut. I'm pretty sure casual flings aren't meant to hang out with your kid; that's a surefire way to complicate things. I know the more time they spend together, the more my kid is going to fall for Sawyer, and the more hurt he'll be if Sawyer ever decides he's done with the added complication of his fuck buddy having a kid.

"Here you go," Cooper says, his face a mask of concentration as he slowly walks into my room carrying a mug. He sets it down gently before grinning up at me. "I'm gonna go get dressed." Then he's gone again, and I'm left staring at a three-quarters full cup of very milky tea, tears building in my eyes as I wonder when my kid got so grown up and how I'm ever going to protect him from all the hurt in the world.

I can't. I know I can't. But goddamn it if I don't want to.

I drink the tea, which honestly tastes like tea-flavoured milk that got warmed up, but hey, it's the thought that counts. Then I get dressed. By the time I get to the kitchen, Coop's dressed and pulling some cereal down from the shelf for breakfast. We go about our usual morning routine, eating and cleaning up. To give the kid credit, he doesn't go on and on about a dog; instead, I have to try and keep up while he chatters about some video game update he's excited about.

"I want to play baseball."

I blink a few times to catch up with the sudden switch in subjects. "Okay, I think the season has probably already started, but we can look into it. Why baseball?"

Cooper looks down at his cereal bowl. "Sawyer said it's his favourite sport."

Oh boy. "Hey Coop, I know you really like Sawyer," I start, unsure of what exactly I need to say, but all too aware I need to say something.

"I know he's just a friend, Mom, but he's cool, and I'm old enough now that if you wanted to hang out with him, I'm okay with that. Like, date him, I mean."

A short laugh escapes me, because when the heck did my seven-year-old learn about dating? "Coop, I'm not going to date Sawyer."

"Why not?" He frowns.

"Because..." I trail off, at a loss for words again. "Because Sawyer and I are just friends. He's not looking for anything more, and neither am I."

Cooper stirs the leftover milk in his bowl, and I hold my breath, waiting to see how he'll respond. Who knew my kid would try to be a matchmaker?

"Okay." He hops up, takes his bowl and spoon to the dishwasher, then looks out at his tree house. "I'm gonna go read in the tree house till it's time to go, okay?"

Without waiting for my answer, he grabs the comic book he's reading and heads out the door.

What is with the men in my life leaving me completely flustered and spun upside down?

A couple of hours later, we walk up to the town square in the middle of Dogwood Cove. Hanging from the top of the gazebo is a large banner that reads "Dogwood Cove Animal Shelter Adoption Fair," and there's a lot of people spread out across the grassy area. Many are standing beside pens that hold a variety of dogs. Off to the side, I think I see a turtle slowly crawling around its own area, and there's even someone walking around with a lizard on their arm.

"No lizards, bud. Not happening," I say, touching Cooper's arm. "Only critters with fur or feathers are welcome in my house."

He narrows his eyes thoughtfully. "Does that mean I can get a bird *and* a dog?"

"No!" I reply quickly, and he laughs.

"I know, Mom. Birds are weird, anyway. But look at that guy." I let him drag me over to a pen with a black dog standing there, tail wagging patiently.

We make our way around most of the pens, Cooper getting excited over every dog, and me wondering how the heck I'm going to make a decision about any of them. Then the voice that never fails to give me shivers reaches us.

"There's my two favourite people," Sawyer says, seconds before draping an arm over my shoulder and ruffling Cooper's hair.

"Sawyer! Look at this dog, isn't he awesome?" Coop says, pointing at the beagle in front of us.

"He is, but beagles are escape artists and noisy. I'm not so sure your mom wants to deal with that while you're at school."

I mouth the words *thank you* to Sawyer as Cooper bounces on to the next dog. His arm falls away as we walk, and I mentally kick myself for how much I miss the feel of it.

"He finally wore you down, huh?"

I glance over at my kid, who's looking at a yapping Chihuahua with a perplexed look on his face. "I haven't committed to anything, but..."

Sawyer just chuckles knowingly.

Cooper makes his way over to us. "That one had crazy eyes. Hey, I'm hungry, can we get something to eat?"

Clapping his hands together, Sawyer makes a rumbling sound. "Mmm, do you know what's the perfect food to eat at a pet adoption festival, Coopzilla?"

Coop shakes his head.

"Hot dogs!" Sawyer starts to laugh, and after a second, Coop's eyes widen. Then the two of them are giggling together like that's the funniest thing they've ever heard. Eventually, their laughter settles down and two pairs of hopeful eyes are trained on me.

"Sure, let's go find some food," I reply. Coop cheers, then dashes off toward the food trucks we walked past earlier with Sawyer and I following behind at a more normal pace.

"You look good, angel. Good enough to eat." Sawyer's deep rumble is quiet as a whisper, but I hear it loud and clear.

Glancing down at myself, I chuckle. "So, you're attracted to weekend-mom chic?" I tease, chancing a look over at him.

The intensity with which he's looking back at me makes my steps falter.

"Guess I am."

Thankfully, we reach Cooper's side at that moment, saving me from melting any further. Under the heat of Sawyer's...well...Sawyerness.

"Hey bud, did you decide what to eat? Still want a hot dog?"

Cooper looks somewhat shyly over at Sawyer. "I dunno if I can eat a hot dog when I'm here to adopt a dog."

I make a sound without even meaning to and he quickly amends his words.

"*Hoping* to adopt a dog."

I nod but also flash him a wink, because I'm fully aware that even if we don't get a dog today, it's inevitable we will soon.

"All good, little dude. I'll be honest, I'm not a huge hot dog fan, unless I'm at a baseball game. Then it's like the law that you have to eat a hot dog." Sawyer's easy laugh rings out over the crowd. I've never known someone so relaxed, so comfortable in their skin. It's...well, it's addicting.

"My aunt Willow works for a baseball team," Cooper says. "This summer she promised to take me to a game."

"Make sure you eat a hot dog for me when you're there." Sawyer ruffles the hair on Coop's head.

"Or you could come with us, right, Mom? Aunt Willow said we could bring friends."

The expression on Sawyer's face is priceless and sweet. "Thanks, little dude."

I notice he doesn't promise anything, for which I'm equal parts grateful and sad. There's no escaping my reality anymore. My son isn't the only one falling for Sawyer Donnelly. I am, too.

"Hey, Tori!" I look over to see Cam waving at me as she walks up with Sawyer's twin. I wave back, and we come to a stop until they catch up. Sawyer and Beckett do that man hug thing. I go to introduce Cooper, but Sawyer beats me to it.

"This is Coopzilla, coolest kid in town." He tilts his head to the side and winks at Cooper. "Well, he's tied with Violet for that title."

Cooper just beams. Beckett reaches out for a high five. "My name's Beckett. Are you really named after a monster or is that Sawyer's doing?"

"You can call me Cooper, or Coop, or Coopzilla."

The adults all chuckle.

"Good to meet you, Cooper, I'm Cam" Cam says. "Are you here to get a pet?"

"Hopefully, but it's gotta be the right dog for us," Cooper answers sagely, his eyes darting over to me. I give him a reassuring nod.

"What about you?" I ask, and Beckett laughs.

"Nah, we're just here to check things out. No pets for us."

"Want to grab some lunch with us?" I offer, but Sawyer's hand whips out and covers my mouth.

"Don't invite them, Becky-boo takes *forever* to choose what to eat, and I'm starving."

I pull his hand down just in time to see Beckett looking at the two of us strangely.

"We already ate, so you're saved from the torture of Beckett's food truck analysis." Cam tugs on Beckett's hand, giving us a wave. "We were just heading home but wanted to say hi first."

"See you later, guys," Sawyer says cheerfully as his brother and sister-in-law head off. "*Phew*, dodged that bullet. Let me tell you, having an accountant for a brother means you're subjected to a lot of spreadsheets." He shudders.

"Spreadsheets about food trucks?" I ask, mirth lacing my tone. Sawyer just nods. Then, turning, he drops into a crouch in front of Cooper. "Hey, Coop. I got a follow-up hot dog question for you."

Cooper looks at Sawyer with absolute adoration in his eyes. "What?"

"Do you, or do you not agree that a hot dog is a sandwich."

I choke on the water I've just taken a sip of at his question, delivered with such seriousness, it's hard to reconcile the tone with the ridiculous nature of what he asked.

Cooper seems to consider it carefully, as I hold back my laughter — and my horror that anyone in their right mind would consider a hot dog a sandwich.

"I dunno. I mean, it sort of is, because it's bread with stuff inside. But also, it's not, because the shape is all wrong."

Attaboy Coop, I mentally cheer, then pause because no way am I getting in the middle of this insanity. I should've known better because the next thing I know, two pairs of eyes are looking at me.

"Mom? What do you think?"

"I think..." I start, then stop, shaking my head at the situation. "I think, at best, I would consider a hot dog part of the sandwich family. It's not a true sandwich in my opinion, but it's maybe sandwich-adjacent."

Cooper nods quickly, even though I'm fairly sure he doesn't know what adjacent means, but then darts his gaze toward Sawyer, who's folded his arms across his chest and is studying me intently.

"Hmm. Sandwich family. Okay, I guess I can accept that answer." He flashes me a grin before placing a hand on Cooper's shoulder and turning him slightly. "Now, how do you feel about tacos?"

Later that night, Coop and I go through his bedtime routine. "I'm sad we didn't find a dog today, Mom. All those dogs need a home," he says as he climbs under the covers.

I stroke the hair back from his face. "I know, buddy, we'll find one soon. But those dogs today need a different kind of home than what we can give them."

He turns on his side, nodding as he yawns. "But hanging out with Sawyer was fun."

My hand stills. "It was," I say quietly.

"You smile a lot when he's around."

"He's a pretty fun guy." Cooper nods, then yawns. I lean over and kiss his forehead, smoothing his blanket over him. "Goodnight, Coop. I love you."

"Love you, too, Mom."

Once I shut his bedroom door, I lean against the wall beside it and let my eyes close.

Sawyer makes me smile. He makes me and my son happy.

That doesn't mean he'll ever be something more than just the man who makes us smile.

CHAPTER TWENTY-ONE

Sawyer

"You've been MIA lately, what's going on?"

Max's tone is neutral, but I still pause mid-bicep curl for a second.

"Nothing," I say casually, resuming my reps.

"Bullshit," Jude coughs under his breath. We're in Westport, at the gym in the arena where his hockey team plays. Normally, I would work out in Dogwood Cove, but coming here meant Max and Jude could join in, and it's been a while since the four of us hung out.

"Not bullshit. I'm busy living life." I set the weight down and pick up a large medicine ball, inclining my head to the open space next to the weight rack. Jude follows me over, and we drop to the mats and start a set of crunches with a medicine ball toss.

"Something's definitely up. You haven't been whining about having no one to go to the bars with or ribbing us about our relationships." My oldest brother's helpful assessment of the last few weeks has me grinding my teeth together. Why the fuck do I have insightful brothers? Why can't I have oblivious idiots who are consumed with their own shit and stay out of mine?

I let out an *oomph* as Jude chucks the damn medicine ball at me with some extra force. "Can't a guy just enjoy a few chill weeks without it becoming a national emergency?"

"Not when the guy is Sawyer Donnelly, manwhore extraordinaire, destroyer of panties and hearts across the province."

I shoot a glare at Jude, ignoring the pang of hurt I feel at his words. Not that they're untrue, or at least they were accurate at one time, but it's never fun having my sins laid out for me like that.

"Does it have something to do with Tori? You guys seemed awfully cozy at the adoption fair the other day. For what it's worth, she seems nice," Beckett adds, all casual, as if he isn't digging into my brain and uncovering shit I don't want uncovered.

"We're just friends," I reply automatically.

"Looked like it could be more than that."

Goddamn Beckett and his ability to read me like a fucking book.

"It's not." I scramble to stand up and make my way over to the treadmill, climbing on and immediately setting a punishing pace.

"And now he's partaking in the Donnelly men tradition of trying to outrun reality." Max's wry voice comes from beside me as he leans against the handrail of the machine next to mine. Dropping his voice a little quieter, he says, "Seriously bro, is everything alright? You have to admit, you're different these days. Is it this woman? Tori?"

I ignore him for a couple of minutes, focusing on my breathing and the rhythmic sound of my feet hitting the treadmill. But of all of us, Max is the one who will wait it out the longest.

Eventually, I hit the button to slow down to a more reasonable pace, and glance over at him. "I'm fine, Maxy, seriously. I'm not dating anyone, I just haven't been interested in hitting the bars lately, so there was no need to ask any of you to go out. Not like you'd say yes, anyway. You three are boring fuckers these days."

Max raises one eyebrow. "Boring? You want to rethink that statement?"

I huff out a laugh. "Relax, old man. I love your women, they're my bonus sisters. But yeah, you guys are boring now."

Max slaps his hand on the rail of my treadmill, shaking his head. "Someday, you're gonna realize what you consider boring is actually really fucking nice. Having someone you can count on, someone there at the end of every day, someone who makes you happier than you've ever been? That's not a bad thing, and it's definitely not boring."

He saunters off, leaving me to my run — and my thoughts. Because when he was talking, telling me how nice it was to have someone?

I kept picturing Tori.

The next morning, my last day off before I head back to work, I've just climbed out of the shower when my phone pings with a message.

TORI: Remember the other day when you did that thing with me against the wall…

I chuckle to myself, already liking where this is going. Friends who fuck. That's what we are, and this is the perfect example of that fact.

SAWYER: You mean the time you gave me claw marks that still haven't fully disappeared from my back?

TORI: Focus.

TORI: But yes.

SAWYER: Yes I absolutely remember.

TORI: Okay, so, have you ever tried that with the woman's legs on your shoulders?

Holy shit. My mind is drawing a mental picture that is so fucking hot, my dick is hard underneath my towel, tenting it in a big way. I don't have a fucking clue how the acrobatics that are gonna be required will work, but I'm down to try.

SAWYER: I mean, I haven't but… if you need to work-shop the idea I'm game.

TORI: Yes please.

SAWYER: Be there in ten. Be naked.

I make it to Tori's house in seven minutes, and when I try the front door, it's unlocked. I let myself in, closing and locking it behind me, but she's nowhere to be seen.

"Angel?" I call out, kicking my shoes off and pulling my sweater over my head.

"In the bedroom." I hear her voice from down the hall and take off in that direction, unbuckling my pants and hopping around to get them off as I go. There'll be a trail of clothes to clean up when we're done, but I don't want to waste time. I hit the bedroom just in time to see her strut out of the bathroom, fully nude.

"Look at you, listening to instructions," I purr with a smirk, stalking over to her and grabbing her waist, yanking her in for a kiss.

Her hands land on my shoulders, then slide up to thread through my hair, gripping it tightly. Just having her warm, naked body pressed against mine feels so damn good. *Happier than I've ever been...*

I pull back, taking in the flush on her cheeks with no small amount of pride for being the one to put it there. I affect her just as much as she affects me, and that's fucking powerful.

"So. How do you propose we do this?"

Tori shakes her head slightly as if coming out of a daze. "Um, well, honestly, I don't know if it's even possible. I was just getting bored of the same old sex positions and wanted to see if I could write something new for this couple."

I place my hand on my chest and pretend to look insulted. "Bored? Of sex? I'm hurt."

Tori's eyes roll as she fights a grin. "Stop it, you know perfectly well I'm not referring to us."

Folding my arms across my chest and ignoring my cock bobbing around, I stay strong. "Nope, you implied sex was boring, and I'm the only one you're having sex with, so clearly, that was a commentary on my performance." Snapping forward with no warning, I grab her around the hips and toss her over my shoulder, slapping her ass as she shrieks. "Now I've got to prove you wrong, angel. It might take a while, but I won't leave until you're satisfied."

I can feel her laughter vibrating through her body, draped over mine, as I climb onto her bed on my knees. Only then do I lay her down, being sure to run my hands over as much of her soft skin as I can before pushing her legs wide open.

My head drops down and I suck her clit into my mouth, hard.

"Sawyer!" she shouts, her back arching and hips twisting away from my assault. But my arms are banded across her thighs, making it impossible for her to get away from me. She's pinned down, and when her hands twist in my hair again, it's obvious she's not pushing me away, she's holding me in place.

I don't hold back, licking and sucking, letting my teeth graze over the sensitive hood of her clit, then plunging my stiffened tongue into her heat. Over and over, changing up my motions every few seconds.

Moments later, she's pulsating through her orgasm. With one final swipe of my tongue through her juices, I lift my head and release her legs. Her chest is heaving as she cracks her eyes open, her blonde hair a wild halo around her.

"Still feel bored?"

Her throaty chuckle is full of affection. "Sawyer, I haven't been *bored* for a single second with you."

I push up off the bed and hold my hand out. Taking it, she lets me pull her up to stand. "That's more like it. Now let's try this crazy idea of yours."

Tori's face lights up. "Okay. I think it could be amazing if it works, like, hit my G-spot, free fall amazing. But I don't know if it's even possible. How will I hold myself up?"

My shoulders lift. "You can't. You'll just have to trust me."

Something passes over her face at the same time a weird feeling flips through me.

"I do trust you, Sawyer."

There's a second of silence. And another. Then, before it can get too heavy and throw me out of the zone, I lean over and snag a condom from her bedside drawer, rolling it on before stalking over to where she's leaning against the wall.

"Okay, so," she starts nervously. She bites her lip, then gingerly places her hands on my shoulders. "Do you lift me first, penetrate, then move my legs? Or move my legs, then penetrate?" She sounds flustered, and that's no good.

Leaning in, I press a soft kiss to her lips as I tuck a piece of hair behind her ear. "First, you relax, angel. It's just me and you. Nothing to be nervous about. We're gonna have some fun, like we always do."

Her forehead dips to meet mine as she exhales with a shaky laugh. "You're right. I don't know why I got all weird there."

That's better.

"All good. Now, here's how it's going to go. I'm going to lift you and brace you against the wall. Then we move your legs up while I hold you, and then it's party time."

Her giggle sounds lighter, more normal. "Alright. Don't drop me."

"Never."

That same weird feeling flips through me once more, but I shake it off — again.

Lifting her in my arms, she goes to wrap her legs around my waist, then stops. "Guess I don't need to do that," she says, and I shake my head with an answering grin.

We manage to maneuver one of her legs up, and let me just say, it's a good thing Tori is bendy as fuck. She grimaces slightly and I freeze. "Is that okay?" I ask, and she nods.

"Yeah, it's a little unsettling. But I think once my other leg is up and I can maybe rest them against your body, it'll work," she says gamely.

But as we try to get her other leg up, it all goes really fucking wrong. My grip on Tori slips, and somehow as I shift back slightly to readjust, her leg that isn't already in position moves, and I end up with a knee to the groin.

"Shit!" I shout, my instinct being to double over at the burst of intense agony, except I'm still holding Tori. I manage to set her down before dropping to the floor, trying to breathe slowly.

"Oh my God, Sawyer, I'm so sorry. Are you okay? Crap, what can I do? Do you need ice?"

The panic in her voice is clear, but I'm a little too focused on my pain to really respond beyond shaking my head.

Listen — guys will get it. A knee to the nuts? *Not. Fun.*

"I'm okay. Just need a minute," I manage to get out once I stop feeling like I want to puke from the pain. Tori stays beside me, her hand lightly rubbing my back. Eventually, I manage to rise up on my knees and turn to her.

"I'm sorry, angel. I slipped, and I promised I wouldn't drop you —" I start, but her lips are against mine, interrupting me.

"And you didn't. I just broke your penis," she says morosely.

I chuckle, and wince, because even though I know that's not possible, it kinda feels that way. We both look down at my now-soft dick, and I let out a little groan. "Not broken, but probably out of action for a bit."

Tori stands and then reaches her hands out to me. "Come on, up you go."

I let her help me stand and hobble over to the bed before flopping back onto it. "I think you need to change your scene. That position is definitely not a good idea. Give me some recovery time and we can brainstorm some other ideas."

Tori settles on her side next to me, resting her hand on my chest. "I'm sorry, Sawyer."

I lift her hand and kiss the palm. "Angel, don't apologize." Then, I smirk. "But you definitely can't say sex with me is boring."

Chapter Twenty-Two

Sawyer

"You did *what?*" Kat asks, her voice incredulous.

"I invited Tori and Cooper to family dinner." I set down the bottles of wine I bought on the way over. "Why do you sound horrified?"

"Not horrified, shocked. Surprised. In disbelief."

I look at my pregnant sister with confusion. "Why? I invited a friend to dinner. Is that seriously a big deal?"

Kat moves around the kitchen counter to stand next to me. "You invited a *female* friend and her kid to dinner. Yeah, it's a big deal. You've never invited anyone to family dinner. I mean, don't get me wrong, Tori's amazing, but..." She grabs my arm. "Oh my God, are you dating her?"

"Shh," I peel her hand off and glare at her. "Don't be crazy. I don't date. We're friends."

Why the hell does my family insist on seeing something that doesn't exist? They know how I feel about relationships. They can't just let it go and accept that I have a friend who happens to be a woman?

A woman I'm fucking every chance I can get. A woman I can't seem to stop thinking about. But that doesn't mean anything. Or does it? Shit, now they've got me overthinking things.

"Just friends," Kat says enigmatically, a bizarre expression on her face. "We'll see." She walks off, her hands resting on her belly.

My mom bustles in from the garage where she was getting something she needed for dinner, and I'm glad she missed that annoying conversation. "Hi honey. Oh, is that the wine? You're a doll." She lifts the three bottles in turn before choosing one and looking at me. "How about you open that and pour some."

"Sure." I make quick work of removing the cork and pour a glass for her first. "You're okay that I invited Tori and her kid for dinner, right?" I might be poking the hornet's nest, but one thing Kat said did stick out. I haven't ever invited someone to dinner, and the last thing I need is my mother getting the wrong idea.

Mom gives me a look. "Of course, I'm fine with it. The more the merrier, that's always been my attitude. I think it's lovely you thought to include her, and I'm looking forward to meeting them both."

There's a lot unsaid in her words, and I'm no fool. "Mom. We're just friends." Except, this time when I say it, the words don't land as solidly as they should.

"Mm-hmm." She gives an innocent-looking smile. "Hand me the pepper, please."

I pass it over just as the doorbell rings. Seeing as my siblings don't bother with it, they just walk in, it's gotta be Tori and Cooper.

I make my way to the front door, dodging Kat, who's trying to beat me there, and pull it open with a wide grin. "Welcome to Casa De Donnelly!"

I go through my handshake with Cooper, then move to pull Tori in for a hug, catching myself at the last second when I see the wide look of surprise on her face.

"Hi," she says softly as I step to the side and she walks past me.

God, I want to kiss her. I can't, not in front of everyone, but I want to.

I make the introductions and set Cooper up to play happily with the giant bin of LEGOs my mom saved from when all of us boys were kids. When I find Tori again, she's in the middle of the cluster of my brothers' partners, all of them giggling over something.

"What are they gabbing about?" I ask Jude, dropping onto the couch beside him.

"I heard something about books and tuned out," he grumbles.

The grin that feels permanently etched on my face whenever Tori's around widens. "Ahh. They must know who she is."

Jude raises his eyebrows. "What?"

I incline my head toward the women. "Tori's a romance author. She writes some seriously spicy shit. I'm betting that's what they're talking about."

"And you know this *how*, exactly?" he asks wryly.

Nope, not answering that. "I'm gonna get a beer." I stand up, ignoring my brother. But I don't miss his gruff chuckle as I walk away.

Beer in hand, I grab a glass of wine for Tori, and head over to the group of women.

"Where's my drink?" Cam says, arching a brow.

"You've got a husband that can get yours. Besides, I only have two hands." I hand Tori the glass of wine with a wink. "You doing okay? They aren't telling you too many horrible stories about me, are they?"

"Just the embarrassing ones," Kat pipes up.

"Of which there are plenty." Lily giggles. I point my finger at her.

"Listen, just because you're with Jude now doesn't mean I don't still see you as another little sister. Which means you're not immune to my retaliation, Lily pad."

She rolls her eyes, but then the door opens, and Max and Heidi walk in. It's not often they can make it to dinner, given both their schedules as doctors at Westport General Hospital, so everyone stops what they're doing to say hi.

I don't miss Max's face when he's introduced to Tori, or the look he flashes my way, but I sure as hell don't dwell on it, either.

Pretty soon, Heidi's joined the rest of the women in a conversation that seems to have moved on from books to some pregnancy photoshoot Kat and Hunter have planned. I make my way into the kitchen just in time to see my mom and Beckett set the final platter of food on the large kitchen island where we'll dish out dinner.

"That smells amazing, Mom," I say, my mouth already watering. "Oh, but can you hold off on the cilantro in the pasta salad? Tori doesn't like it."

Mom's hand freezes above the dish in question. "Of course, thanks for letting me know." She puts it in a separate bowl instead, setting it beside the salad. "Can you call everyone in?"

Dinner at our house has always been chaotic, but with the addition of a husband, girlfriend, wife, and fiancée, it's madness. My mom reigns over it all with an undoubtedly satisfied smile. She's loving watching our family expand, and I know she holds out hope I'll be adding to it soon, as well. Let's face it, that's probably the reason she was so pleased when I told her I invited Tori and Cooper tonight.

Watching them settle in at the table, Cooper happily ensconced on the other side of Tori with Hunter next to him, I do have to reluctantly admit, it feels right having them here. But like, in a *I'm glad I invited them* kind of way, nothing more... I think.

But as Tori talks animatedly with my dad, for probably the first time ever, I let myself imagine what would be different if Tori wasn't just a friend. If she was someone special. And the thing is? The only difference I can come up with is that I'd be able to hold her hand and kiss her without my family freaking the fuck out.

That realization has me shifting in my seat and then lifting my arm to drape it casually across the back of Tori's chair. I feel her body freeze when my fingers drift along the back of her neck, but I don't acknowledge it, forcing myself to carry on my conversation with Max and Heidi.

Fuck, it feels good to touch her.

After we've demolished the mountain of food my mom made, everyone migrates back to the living room. But Cooper's noticeably yawning as he carries his plate to the kitchen where Beckett and Cam are helping with the dishes.

"I think I better get him home," Tori says softly.

Mom touches her shoulder. "He's a wonderful boy, Tori. I'm so glad you both joined us, and you're welcome back any time."

"I'll walk you and Coopzilla out," I offer. We gather up their stuff, everyone says goodbye, and then I walk them to their car parked at the end of the driveway. Once Cooper's buckled in the back seat, I lead Tori around the back of her car, pausing to glance up at the house before dipping down and kissing her.

It's too short, too chaste, and I want so much more. But now's not the time. Not with her kid and my family right here. Instead, I walk her around to her door, hold it open, then crouch down to look at Coop in the back seat, then back to her.

"Goodnight, you two. Drive safe."

"Night, Sawyer," Cooper says sleepily. "Your family is cool for a bunch of grown-ups."

I chuckle. "Thanks, little dude, they thought you were cool, too."

He nods, his eyes already drooping shut. I turn to Tori, resting my hand on her thigh. "Goodnight, angel."

"Goodnight," she murmurs, her eyes searching mine. "Tonight was fun."

I squeeze her leg, then stand up. "See you soon." I wink, then close her door, standing there until they back out of the driveway and head down the street. Only then do I go back inside to face the firing squad.

Sure enough, all of my siblings are looking at the front door as I walk in, some with smirks and some with stupid knowing looks, even though they'd be wrong, no matter what they're thinking. My dad is studiously looking at a magazine and Mom is nowhere in sight.

"What?" I say, staring at each of them, daring them to say something. But smartly, no one does. "I'm gonna head out, too. I need to go to the station for a meeting early tomorrow morning." I gather my stuff, say goodbye to my dad, and give a reluctant wave to my siblings.

Then, I move to the front door, Mom following me. That alone isn't too unusual, but to my total shock, my mother, all five-foot-whatever of her, reaches up on her tiptoes to cuff me around the side of the head. Glaring at me as she sinks back down, she places her hands firmly on her hips, and says, "Listen to me, Sawyer Donnelly. You need to pull your head out of your ass and realize what you have right in front of you before someone else comes along and takes it away."

After that, she holds open the door and gestures for me to leave. Behind her, I can see the rest of my family barely holding it together, as if they're all in on some big secret I've been left out of.

I stumble out the door and down to my truck, drive home on autopilot, and let myself inside my apartment. Only then do I say the words I've been holding in since leaving my childhood home.

"What the fuck do I do now?"

Chapter Twenty-Three

Sawyer

"Donnelly, come on in."

I enter the chief's office at Dogwood Cove Fire Department and shake his hand. "Thank you, sir." Sitting down across from him, I rub my palms along my pants surreptitiously.

I've worked with this man for years, watching him move up in rank from when I started and he was my battalion chief until now. He steeples his hands and looks at me, his face unreadable.

"You've been with the department a long time, Donnelly. What is it now, ten years?"

"Twelve, sir."

He nods. "And you've done well for yourself. I know you've dedicated a lot of time to the wildfire service, and I always see you at community events. Your crewmates think highly of you, and you've proved your worth as a member of our department. You know you were short listed for a promotion to captain earlier this year. We had some delays in reaching our final decision, but I'm pleased to inform you that you are the successful candidate."

I exhale a shaky laugh, pride pumping through my veins. "Thank you, sir. That's fantastic news, I'm honoured to have been chosen."

I'm treated to one of Chief's rare smiles. "You've earned it. Your commitment to the department and the town doesn't go unnoticed, nor does your focus and dedication to the job. You've stepped up as interim captain and proved you're the right man for the job."

"Again, thank you," I say, because it feels damn good to know my hard work over the years at the department has been noticed. "I love this town, this department, and my crew. I look forward to leading them in my new role."

Chief stands and puts out his hand again. I rise and shake it. "Good. Sorry to drag you in here just for this short meeting, but protocol is what it is, and I had to tell you in person before we make the official announcement." He moves around his desk and I follow him to the doorway. "You're due back on shift tomorrow, is that right?"

"Yes, sir," I confirm. "I've got two night shifts, then another stretch off because of some shift swaps."

"Okay. Well, now that O'Doul has moved, we need to get you in place as the official shift captain for your team as soon as possible. So, we'll tell the crew, and you'll step into the role when you come in for those night shifts. We'll have to discuss those swaps with HR to make sure there's coverage, of course."

"Sounds good to me." My mind is already racing, thinking about the new responsibilities I'll have as captain. I'll be in charge of my team each shift, no longer just doing the grunt work as someone else barks out the orders; now I'll be the one in charge.

We make our way down to Sue-Ann's office, the head of our human resources, and Chief leaves me with her after slapping my back and giving me one more "congratulations." The next half hour is spent going through my scheduled swaps and vacations, ensuring there's coverage for my new position.

Finally, I duck out of the station, managing to avoid my colleagues. I don't know if I could hide the news from them right now, and the first person I want to tell is Tori.

Not my mom, not my brothers, not even Boone or Derek.

Tori.

I wait for that indisputable fact to wig me out, send me off the deep end into panic, but it never does. It settles inside of me like another piece of the puzzle fitting into place — the one I'm building without even knowing what the picture is.

As soon as I'm home, I whip out my phone.

SAWYER: Guess what angel, you're no longer fucking a hot firefighter.

TORI: Umm, I don't know how to respond to that...

SAWYER: You're fucking a hot firefighter CAPTAIN. That's right baby. The promotion is mine.

TORI: Sawyer that's fantastic! Congratulations.

SAWYER: Thanks. You know what would be a really great way to celebrate?

TORI: What?

SAWYER: Eating my favourite dessert.

TORI: I don't even know what your favourite is... But if I can buy it or make it I will!

SAWYER: It's your pussy.

TORI: OMG.

SAWYER: Sweet as candy, angel. Sweet as candy.

TORI: You're ridiculous. Tomorrow?

Well, that sucks. I was completely prepared to go over there right now. My excitement deflates a little.

SAWYER: Sure... You're busy today?

TORI: Yeah, deadlines from my editor and then I have to get Cooper early from school for a dentist appointment.

Right. She has commitments and responsibilities, and I'm just a hookup buddy. I've got no right to her time, except whatever she chooses to give me. Damn. No lie, the reality of that leaves a sour taste in my mouth.

SAWYER: Gotcha. Okay tomorrow.

TORI: Talk later, Sawyer. And congrats again!

I stare at the phone screen for a few more minutes. Why do I feel so let down by the fact she's rightfully prioritizing her work and her kid over me? That's what she *should* do, so why does it feel so damn shitty?

Standing up, I stuff my phone in my pocket, slide on some shoes, and grab my keys. Shaking off as much of my disappointment as I can over not getting to celebrate with Tori, I decide to make Beckett take me for lunch instead. I head out on foot toward the center of town, and when I reach Beckett's office, I take the stairs two at a time up to the floor where he works.

I push open the glass doors to the accounting firm and flash a broad smile at the administrative assistant, Colleen. She's well used to me showing up, so doesn't pause in her phone call, just waves me on back. I take that to mean Beck isn't in a meeting and make my way to his office.

"Beckster, we're going to lunch, you're paying," I announce, sweeping through his door.

He frowns up at me from his computer. "Today? I can't, we just got a contract for that new cidery and I've got to prepare my analysis report by the end of the week."

I perch on the corner of his desk. "Too bad, twinski, I just got promoted to beta team captain and I need to celebrate."

Beck relaxes back in his chair. "Dude, that's awesome. Congratulations." Straightening back up, he pushes his glasses up his nose. "But I still can't go out to lunch. Sorry, man."

I pout, but he just shakes his head.

"Really? You're gonna leave me hanging like that?"

"Yes, I am. Somehow, I think you'll survive," he replies wryly.

I stand up, giving him my very best unhappy sigh. "Fine. I'll find someone else to celebrate with."

"Probably Tori," he mutters half under his breath.

"What did you say?"

My twin has the decency to look chagrined. "Nothing. I gotta get back to work. See you later."

His fingers start to fly over his keyboard, and I frown at his dismissal of me. But it's obvious he's not going to join me, so I walk out, leaving him to his damn spreadsheets.

Colleen is off her call when I reach the front. "Don't suppose you want to join me for lunch?" I say, half-teasing. She just gives me her typical eye roll that I get every time I try to charm the older woman.

"Not today, Sawyer Donnelly."

Shaking my head and flashing her a wink, I leave and head home to grab my truck. I make my way to my parents' house, only to find their driveway empty and no one home when I unlock the front door.

"Well, shit, is everyone determined to avoid me or something?" I grumble as I climb back into my truck. This fucking sucks, being alone with no one to celebrate my promotion.

Max's words from the gym the other week choose my moment of weakness to come back to me.

"Having someone there at the end of the day is not a bad thing..."

Damn it if he isn't right. Instead of going home to an empty apartment, I want to be going home to someone who's waiting for me. Someone to share the good news and bad. Someone to just be happy with.

I ignore the first knock on my apartment door later that night. But then it happens again, and I hear a familiar voice calling out.

"Open up, Sawyer. We see your truck outside."

Fucking brothers. I drag my ass off the couch, beer in hand, and take my sweet time going to open the door.

"Can I help you?" I ask facetiously, and Jude just arches his brow at me.

"What's got you all pissy?"

I move to let them in, belatedly taking in the bags of food and drink, along with the box of poker chips. "I don't need an intervention, you're wasting your time."

I've got my back to them, but I'm pretty sure it's Max who chuckles. "Sure. We'll go with that."

Hunter moves to stand beside me, a beer now in his hand, too. He inclines it toward mine. "We heard you got your promotion, congratulations!"

"How come Beckett was the one to text us and not you?" Max asks.

I sit back down on the couch and take a drink. "I dunno, I figured you guys were working."

"Since when does that stop you? You're pouting like a little kid, Sawyer." Jude's hand cuffs the back of my head and I glare at him.

Rationally, I know he's right. I was disappointed earlier when I couldn't celebrate my promotion with anyone. Especially not the one person I really wanted to be with, and that disappointment multiplied when my brother and my parents were also unavailable. It drove home the fact that everyone in my life...has someone.

And I'm left with no one.

Beckett's been silent this whole time, setting up the poker chips, even though history shows we rarely actually play a game on these nights. "We're proud of you, Sawyer. I never doubted for a second you'd get the promotion, but I know it was hell waiting this long."

I finally relax into the couch. "Yeah, well, thanks. It feels good to have it confirmed, you know?"

"Are we here to talk about his promotion or..." Hunter whispers loudly to Max.

I roll my eyes. "If you're here to talk about Tori, save your breath."

"Oh, so you've pulled your head out of your ass and realized you, Mr. Never Gonna Do A Relationship, are, in fact, *in* a relationship?" Jude asks mildly, eyeing me over his bottle of beer.

My mouth opens to refute his statement, but nothing comes out.

"Woah." Max leans forward, placing his elbows on his knees. "Wait, Sawyer. What's going on in your head?"

It takes me a minute to figure out what to say. "I might be starting to realize that being with someone romantically isn't the end of the world." Hunter and Beckett high-five, and Max just settles back with a knowing smirk.

"So, it's more than just friends between you?"

I nod. There's no point in hiding it. "We met back in February when I was on the mainland for the calendar gala."

"By 'met' you mean you hooked up." Jude's blunt assessment hits hard.

"Yes. Because that's what I do. Or did," I start, feeling my face heat up. I'm not used to being in the hot seat. "Then she moved here, and we decided to just, I dunno. Keep having fun."

"Then fun turned to feelings?" Beckett adds, and the last bit of defensive tension I was holding melts away.

"Yeah."

The guys are all silent for a moment. I know I said it was annoying having insightful, in touch with their feelings brothers, but right now, I'm grateful for their woke asses. Because it's one thing to admit I have feelings for Tori.

It's a whole other thing to try and figure out what to do.

Lifting my head, I look at each of them in turn. "I don't know how to do this. How to be with someone for more than just sex."

Max's hand lands on my shoulder. "Brother, you're already doing it. You brought her to family dinner, you're spending time with her and her kid, you're in a relationship. The only thing that changes is you stop trying to hide it, and you call it what it is."

Exhaling a laugh, I lean my head back. "You make it sound so easy."

"Not easy," Beckett says quietly. "But worth it."

Chapter Twenty-Four

Tori

The second I open my front door, Sawyer pushes me back inside, slamming the door closed with his foot. His mouth is on mine, plundering me with his kiss. There's a new intensity to him; something's changed. But I don't have time to dwell on that as my pants are ripped down my legs and he drops to his knees in front of me. His tongue works magic all over me, and in an embarrassingly short amount of time, I'm pulling at his hair and screaming his name as I soak his face with my release.

He stands up, unbuckles his jeans, and notches his rock-hard dick at my entrance, then freezes. "Shit. Condom," he growls.

"I trust you. I have an IUD and there hasn't been anyone else in years."

Sawyer's eyes glow as he slides into me with a low groan. "Fuck yes, Tori. You feel so damn good, angel. You're made for me." He pulls out, then slams back in, harder this time.

"Again," I moan, my eyes fluttering closed. The feel of his hand wrapping around the front of my throat has them flying open.

"Eyes open. See me. See *us*," he rumbles, each sentence punctuated by a thrust of his hips. His hand tightens just slightly, enough to cut off some of my air and *good God*, why didn't I put this on my bucket list?

"Mine. You're mine. Mine." Sawyer starts chanting, his hand dropping from my neck to grab one of my legs, lifting it to wrap around his waist. I pull his head to meet mine, kissing him sloppily as I gasp and grunt with every push of his cock inside of me.

"So good, Sawyer," I moan in between kisses. We lace our fingers together and he raises one hand up over my head, dropping his head to kiss and suck down the column of my neck. "I'm close. Oh God, right there. Yes!" Anyone who says multiple O's are not real has never had sex with Sawyer Donnelly. As he tilts his hips up to hit me just a little bit differently, I feel my release careening through me, pushing me to the edge of ecstasy.

"Ohhh, fuck yes," I shout, and then I'm free-falling, shuddering through a spectacular orgasm.

When I come back to earth, my heart is still racing, but I can feel Sawyer softening inside of me. His chest is also heaving as he presses one more kiss to my collarbone, then slowly slides out.

"Stay there," he whispers softly before tucking his dick inside his jeans and hurrying down to the bathroom. He returns with a towel and helps me clean up. There's a wildly possessive glint in his eyes that makes me want to drag him down the hall to my bedroom and never let him leave. Something tells me he might not fight me on that too hard…

"I can honestly say, that's the first time we've had sex when we're both basically still dressed." I giggle, pulling my leggings up.

Sawyer winks. "Probably won't be the last time. You make it hard for me to keep my hands off you."

I give him a grin. "I'm not complaining."

We move over to the couch, and he pulls me sideways into his lap. Lifting my legs to lean against the couch, I settle in against his chest, feeling the steady rise and fall of his breath as his hand drifts through my hair. All of a sudden, I remember why he came over today.

"Oh! Congratulations on your promotion. I made you something." I move to stand up, but his arm around me tightens.

"In a minute. Just stay here with me right now."

The new intensity from before has been replaced with a new softness, giving me a little bit of emotional whiplash.

"You want to cuddle?" I say, half-teasing, half-hopeful. He's always affectionate when it's just the two of us, but as I let myself relax back into his embrace, there's no denying something's changed.

"So what if I do," he challenges, kissing the top of my head. I twist my neck to look up at him, and he meets me for a proper kiss, soft and sweet.

"Again, not complaining." I smile against his lips. I lay back down against his shoulder, forcing myself to enjoy the quiet moment with him and not overanalyze what might be running through his head.

But Sawyer doesn't keep me wondering for very long.

"I like you," he blurts out, his body tightening up under me.

"I like you, too," I reply softly, unsure where he's going with this. He shifts my body so that I'm straddling him and we're facing each other. An uncharacteristically serious expression is on his face.

"No, I mean, I really like you." I see his Adam's apple bob up and down as he swallows. "This was meant to stay casual, just fun, but it's more than that for me. I want more." He sucks in a breath. "If you do."

My jaw falls open in shock. With a gentle touch, he uses his finger to push it closed.

"Say something, even if it's just to let me down and tell me to get lost," he pleads. But yet again, he's rendered me speechless. Yes, me, the author, is without words to describe how I feel, hearing him echo what's been building inside of my heart for weeks now.

I kiss him, instead.

I pour everything into the kiss. All my hope, all my fear, all my desire. And he meets me with every press of his lips, every touch of his hands caressing my body, holding me tighter into him.

He pulls back, a wide grin on his face. "Does this mean you're okay with being more than friends who fuck?"

"As long as you still fuck me."

He stands up, lifting me with him, and strides down the hall to my bedroom. "As if I could ever stop. You're mine now, angel."

Even though my deadline with Carol is looming and I should be writing, I let Sawyer keep me in bed for most of the day. He claimed he needed to practice "having sex as a boyfriend, not just a hookup," and who was I to argue that?

Now we're standing outside Cooper's school, waiting for him to get out so I can hopefully give my son the best surprise of his young life. When I told Sawyer about the puppy I met at the shelter this morning, he begged to come with us so he could witness Cooper's reaction.

"He's gonna freak," Sawyer says, his around my waist. I swear he's almost as excited as I expect Coop to be.

"I know, this puppy is just so perfect," I sigh happily. The bell rings, and he drops his arm. We agreed to keep the PDA low until I've had a chance to talk to Cooper. Not that I think he'll mind, but my kid deserves that courtesy.

Cooper comes out of the school, waving goodbye to his friends. When he sees Sawyer standing next to me, his eyes light up and he runs the distance separating us. His hand shoots out, and the two of them go through their ridiculous handshake routine.

"Hey Mom, Sawyer! I didn't know you'd be here today!" My kid is basically vibrating with excitement as we walk over to my car. "Are you coming over? Are we going to the LEGO store? What's going on?"

"Slow down, kid, I'll explain in a minute." I laugh as he tosses his backpack in the back seat and climbs in. Once we're all buckled in, I turn to Sawyer, who's got a giant grin on his face, then twist farther to face Cooper.

"I got a call from the animal shelter yesterday," I start, and Coop audibly gasps. "They had two puppies transferred in from another shelter, and before they move them to foster homes, they reached out to see if we wanted to meet them. I stopped by first thing this morning after I dropped you off, and I think —"

"We're gettin' a puppy?" Cooper yells, and Sawyer and I both laugh.

"It looks that way, as long as you like her," I say, my eyes starting to tear up. Who knew granting my kid's number one wish would be so emotional? Sawyer's hand sneaks across to mine, and he gives me a squeeze. It feels right that he's here with us for this.

"Let's go! Why aren't you driving?" Coop gestures impatiently. "I need to meet her!"

I turn forward, brushing away the tears, and turn the car on, pulling slowly out of the parking lot while Sawyer and Cooper talk about his day, giving me space to pull myself together.

And an hour later, the three of us walk out of the Dogwood Cove Animal Shelter, Cooper holding a surprisingly calm black and brown bundle of fur in his arms.

"Are you okay with her name?" I ask as we get her settled in a crate on the seat next to him.

"Chloe? Yeah, it's cool. I don't want to confuse her," he answers seriously, his eyes glued to his puppy. "Are you sure she's okay in there? It doesn't feel like prison?"

I do a better job than Sawyer at hiding my laugh and shoot him a glare over the roof of the car. "I'm sure, buddy. She's crate trained, that means she likes it in there. It makes her feel safe."

He sighs, still sounding worried, but eventually nods. "Okay but let's get home fast."

"You got it."

When we reach the house, Sawyer helps us get all of the puppy stuff inside. After making sure Chloe does her business in the backyard, I let Cooper bring her inside, and the two of them run around the house, his giggles making my heart feel ready to burst.

"I wish I didn't have to go to work," Sawyer says, walking up behind me and wrapping his arms around my waist as Cooper and Chloe explore his bedroom. "This is probably the cutest damn thing I've ever seen."

I lean back against his chest. "Are you going to give the dog a nickname?"

The vibrations of his chuckle pulse through me. "Maybe."

Cooper and Chloe come racing back into the kitchen, the puppy skidding on the floor. Sawyer steps back from me, and it seems Coop didn't notice how close we were.

"Hey Coopzilla, I gotta head to work," Sawyer says, and the genuine regret in his voice warms me.

Cooper frowns, but only for a split second, his new puppy apparently beating out his affections for Sawyer at the moment. "That sucks. But okay. Come back when you're not working. I finished the fire truck set."

They go through their handshake, then Cooper throws his arms around Sawyer for a hug.

"See ya, Sawyer." He picks up Chloe, throwing her half over his shoulder as he walks back to his bedroom, whispering something to the puppy that I can't make out.

Outside on the front steps, Sawyer draws me in for another hug, sweetly kissing my forehead, then my lips. "Thank you for letting me join you two today, it was seriously awesome."

I squeeze him a little tighter, not wanting our time today to end; it's all been so magical.

"There's a fundraiser for the fire department next month. My mom would probably babysit Cooper if needed," he starts, drawing back slightly so he can look in my eyes. "I've always gone by myself, but this year...I really want to take you."

My lips tip up. "Like, as your date?" I ask.

His thumb comes up to stroke my cheek lightly. "As my girlfriend."

I let out a happy sigh, then think about the meager contents of my closet. "I have nothing to wear."

"What about the dress from the calendar gala?"

Shaking my head, I reply, "That was Willow's, I was just borrowing it. I'm not exactly a fancy dress kind of girl."

"You would look beautiful in a sack," he says, kissing me firmly. "But if we need to go shopping, that's fine. I'll even come in the dressing room and help zip you up." He winks before kissing me again and then stepping back.

"Goodbye, Sawyer," I say, my voice tinged with laughter. He waits until he reaches his truck to reply.

"Goodbye, girlfriend." Then he climbs in the truck cab and drives off, leaving me with my heart melting into a puddle, right there on my front steps.

Gah, that man. For someone who claims to have never been in a relationship, he sure is winning the swoony boyfriend award right out of the gate.

Chapter Twenty-Five

Sawyer

This boyfriend stuff is easy.

When I picked Tori up today to take her shopping, I gave her a long, slow kiss right there on her front steps for anyone to see. Not that we were hiding it all that much before, but this time was different. She's mine and I get to claim her in public. Case in point, here we are at the mall in Westport, her hand is laced with mine, and it feels so damn natural.

Why have I been so scared of this? Work hasn't changed; my night shifts went smoothly, despite being busy ones. I was just as focused and in control as ever. Sure, when the guys were talking about the upcoming Summer Solstice Festival, I instantly pictured taking Tori and Cooper to it, but as soon as the alarm bells went off, I was all business.

Lying on my bunk in between calls last night, I tried to catch a nap, but my mind instead wandered to Lance. I've always blamed his relationship for being what led to his death. But maybe it wasn't the relationship, but the end of it that was the problem. I mean, what person wouldn't be affected by news that while they're out fighting fires, trying to save people's homes, their partner is screwing around on them. Because the truth I've conveniently ignored for so many years is that Lance was an incredible firefighter up until the end. He was dedicated, and a guy many looked up to. All while holding down a serious relationship. Hell, I remember him talking that summer about proposing to his girl.

It was her infidelity that distracted him, not his love.

Realizing that was like the final piece to the damn puzzle sliding into place. And suddenly, the picture became clear.

Me, Tori, and Cooper. Happy. Together. For a long fucking time.

Now, I might not be experienced in relationships, but even I know it's a bad idea to go from casual sex to full-on commitment, so I'm keeping that to myself for now.

"What do you think of red?" Tori pulls me to a stop outside of a store, and I instantly know which dress she's talking about.

"You make any colour look good, but that? That is a dress designed to bring grown men to their knees," I say lowly into her ear. I love how reactive she is to my words as I feel her body shiver.

"So I should try it on, then?"

I simply drag her into the store as a response. A salesperson sees us and comes over, and I point to the dress in question. "She'll try that one, please."

"Sawyer, you sound like a caveman," Tori whispers, then her lips land on my cheek. "I kinda like it."

My lips twitch up as we follow the older woman to the changerooms. She hands Tori the dress and gestures to a stool for me. "You can wait here."

The message is clear, no funny business. I give her my most winning smile and sit down like a good boy. "Thank you," I say cheerfully as Tori fights back a laugh. She's no doubt thinking about the last store, where I most definitely did not sit on a stool outside.

How was I meant to hold back when she opened the door wearing a scrap of fabric that had me instantly getting hard? I pushed her into the stall and kissed her silly until the sound of the salesperson clearing their throat had me stepping back. Tori's face was flaming, but I just walked out of there and told them the dress didn't fit.

It did...but the only person who gets to see that much of my woman's skin is me.

Tori mouths the word *stay* and disappears into the room. When she finally opens the door again, the fucking world stops turning.

"Holy shit, angel." I stand up slowly. I can hear my pulse pounding in my ears as I take in the vision in front of me. The deep red fabric hugs every curve as one side goes up high to cross over her shoulder in a wide swath, but when she turns, I see that it splits into two skinny straps that drape across her back. It hits her just below the knees, and let me say, I never realized how

fucking sexy that length of a dress could be. I always figured the
shorter, the better, but this? This dress with a small slit up one
thigh? Fuck, yes.

"Do you like it?" she murmurs.

"It'll be hard to keep my hands off you all night," I answer
hoarsely. "You're the most stunning woman I've ever seen."

She slowly walks over to me, resting one hand lightly on my
chest as she lifts up to kiss my lips. My hands are fisted at my
sides so that I don't embarrass her again by pushing her into the
changeroom and show her just how much I *like this dress.*

Lowering back down, she peeks over my shoulder. "I'll take
it, thank you."

Yeah, that's how oblivious I am in the presence of my woman
wearing this dress. I didn't even realize the salesperson was
standing right behind us. Tori heads back into the dressing
room, and I sink back down on the stool, hoping my hard-on
isn't too obvious.

"There's a reason we call that dress the showstopper," the
salesperson says, and I can hear the amusement in her tone.
"Your partner is a lucky woman to have a man look at her the
way you do. That's true love."

I don't even bother correcting her as she walks away. Hell, I'm
not so sure she isn't right. I could love Tori. Pretty damn easily,
if I'm being honest.

The woman who's stealing my heart emerges from the
changeroom, completely unaware of the transformation she's
evoking inside of me. I guess I'm still staring at her with some-

thing akin to awe on my face because she looks confused as she walks over to me.

"Everything okay?"

I nod, taking the dress from her hands. "Absolutely amazing, actually."

I ignore her protests as I pay for the dress, winking at the salesperson, then taking Tori's hand to lead her out of the store.

"Sawyer Donnelly, just because we're dating now doesn't mean you get to pay for everything."

I pull her over to an alcove just outside the store. "Listen to me, angel. That dress? That's a gift for *me*. You wearing it to the fundraiser while there as my girlfriend. That's all I ask in return. Because being with you is an honour. A privilege I don't take for granted. So let me do this. Please."

Her hand cups my face. "You're a charmer, Sawyer. An irresistible charmer."

I cover her hand with mine. "As long as you know I mean every word. No games. This is me and you."

She nods. I lean down and kiss her, taking my time without a care about the fact we're in the middle of a mall with people walking past. I need her to know I'm in this for real now. We break apart, and I take her hand in mine again, lifting it up to press a kiss to her knuckles. Then we walk through the mall, desire sparking between us so strong, I swear it's like a live current of electricity.

We pass by a gourmet candy store, and I see Tori look inside as she makes a small sound. I stop walking and she looks back at me.

"What?"

I gesture to the store. "You wanna go in there?"

She laughs lightly. "We don't have to, we came here for a dress."

"And now we're at a candy store. I happen to love candy, and I know you've got a massive sweet tooth. So let's go in."

Her eyes light up. "Really? Okay."

This place is incredible. The walls are lined with giant clear bins of every candy imaginable. There's a rack of weird candies from around the world; random stuff I've never heard of. Tori slowly wanders around the whole place, her eyes big with wonder. I chuckle to myself, loving her excitement over something as simple as a candy store.

Grabbing one of the clear bags, I start putting some stuff in that looks good when I come to a bin with what look like candy LEGO bricks.

I immediately get a second bag and scoop a bunch in.

"What are those?" Tori asks, leaning against my arm.

I hold up the bag. "Candy LEGO. I thought Coopzilla might like them."

She looks up at me, her expression indescribable. Something passes between us, and I kiss her forehead. A few minutes later, we make our way to the cashier to pay for our haul, and Tori comes to a stop in front of a display of long, spiral rainbow lollipops. She stares at them for a minute before giggling and picking one.

She must see the question on my face because she leans in and whispers, "I just had an idea for an inexperienced heroine who's learning how to give blow jobs on one of these. Lot more fun than a banana." She winks.

I choke out a laugh, my mind immediately seeing the scene she's describing. "What's the equivalent for your hero? There's gotta be something here for the dude to learn how to eat pussy."

"Shh! Keep your voice down." She swats at me, but I see the wheels of her romance author mind turning. She slowly turns in a circle, then takes off toward the wall of international treats. When I catch up to her, she's lifting a package of cookies, of all things.

"Oreos?" I ask, and she nods sagely.

"Sure. You pull it open and lick all the creamy goodness inside."

I grab the package from her and stride back to the cash register, setting the cookies next to my bag of candy and the bricks I'm getting for Cooper. I don't even look at Tori as I pay, pick up my bag, and step aside so she can check out. But when I see that damn lollipop with her candy, I have to stifle a groan.

Once we're outside of the store, I grab her hand and make a beeline for the exit. "I never knew going to the mall could be an exercise in self-restraint. But if I don't get you naked in a very short amount of time, we're gonna be adding *sex in a public place* to your bucket list *and* checking it off, all at the same time."

Her laugh follows me as I basically drag her to my truck, opening the back door to put our bags inside, and climbing in before gesturing impatiently at her. "Hurry up, woman," I growl.

Now, I'm not admitting to breaking the speed limit on the drive back to Dogwood Cove, but I might have been pushing it. We reach Tori's house in record time, and as soon as we're inside, our clothes are off and she's bending over the couch, crying out my name as I slam home inside of her, my hands holding her ass tightly.

I bring her to orgasm just like that but hold off on my own release. Pulling out, ignoring my angry cock, I spin her around and lift her up in my arms to carry her to her bedroom. I lay her down, and staring into my woman's eyes, I slide back in, slowly this time, stealing her gasp with a kiss.

"That's it, angel. You take me so damn well."

Her nails rake down my back as she meets me, thrust for thrust, her hips lifting in tempo with mine. The perfect synchronicity of our movements, the ease with which I read her body, knowing just what she needs — it takes simple sex and elevates it to a whole new level I could not imagine reaching with anyone but Tori.

And this time, when she crests over into another climax, I follow her, bellowing out her name.

A quiet yip brings us both back to reality in a flash.

"Oh my God, the puppy." She laughs, pushing at me. "Poor thing is probably traumatized."

I roll off her, draping my arm over my eyes. "She better get used to it, because I'm not gonna be cockblocked by a ball of fur," I tease.

Tori gets up and opens the door to Chloe's crate, and the puppy instantly runs around the room, sniffing everywhere. "I better take her outside to pee." She scoops up the puppy, then freezes. "Wait. I'm naked."

I jump up and grab a towel hanging on the back of her door, wrapping it around my waist. "Here, I'll take her."

Taking the wriggling puppy from her, I head to the back door and set her down on the grass outside. "It's a good thing you're cute," I murmur to the mutt as she wanders around, sniffing every damn blade of grass. "Come on, Chloe, I don't have all day." Finally, the puppy does her business and comes trotting back to me. But when I open the door to let her back inside, I can hear the click-clack of Tori's fingers on the keyboard.

Sure enough, I find her in her office, typing at an insanely fast speed. I lean in the doorway, still wearing nothing but a damn towel, and wait for her to notice. Except, she doesn't, her focus solely on the computer screen for several more minutes.

"So that's a no to round two before you have to get Coop?" I tease and she spins around in her chair, a sheepish look on her face. She's fully dressed, but her eyes instantly drop to the bulge I'm sporting under the towel.

"I'm sorry, I suddenly realized how I could fix a plot issue and..." Her voice trails off.

"And now you need to work." I walk over and kiss the top of her head. "I'll get out of your way, angel."

She tips her head back and looks at me. "How are you even real?"

I chuckle. "I dunno, but I promise you, I am." I give her a wink and drop another kiss to her lips before stepping back, loving the disappointed little whine she makes.

"Do you want me to go and grab Cooper from school so you can just power through?"

"You'd do that?" she asks softly.

"Of course, I would. Your work is important, and if you're having a breakthrough, you should focus on that. I can get him, we'll go to my mom's house and steal some cookies, then I'll drop him off around four so I have time to get ready for work."

Pushing back from her desk, Tori closes the short distance between us and flings her arms around my waist, hugging me so tightly its almost hard to breathe. "Thank you," she mumbles into my chest and I grin as I kiss her head.

"No problem. Doing my boyfriend duty."

She tilts her head up. "You're doing it really, really well today."

I kiss her again, even as I mentally high-five myself. "I aim to please. Now get to work, woman. I'm going to steal a quick shower, then head out." I slap her ass and push her back toward her desk, letting myself linger to watch her settle in for a minute.

Yeah, this whole boyfriend thing? *I got this.*

Chapter Twenty-Six

Tori

June starts off with days full of sunshine, making it clear summer is right around the corner. The last couple of weeks have been better than I could have hoped for. Sawyer's attentive, affectionate, and still as much fun as always. Cooper's been thrilled with how much time Sawyer has been spending at the house. Any worry I had about my son feeling like he was coming in second to my relationship has been proven pointless. Not only because of me, but because of Sawyer. He makes Coop a priority all the time, whether it's playing in the backyard with Chloe, tossing a baseball around, or building their LEGO sets.

We're still careful with how affectionate we are around him, and I haven't figured out a good way to tell Cooper that Sawyer and I are more than friends. I keep waiting for Sawyer to push me on that, but he hasn't yet, and I'm thankful. I know I need to tell Coop, but I need to do it the right way. I just haven't figured out how.

It all seems so easy, Sawyer fitting into our lives, like he was meant to be here all along. And I finally feel a balance between work, being a mom, and being a woman.

But that old saying about something being too good to be true keeps lingering in the back of my mind, casting an unwelcome shadow over my happiness.

Sawyer's at work for the next couple of days, and the house is unnaturally quiet without his bright energy filling it. Cooper's in the backyard with Chloe, trying to teach her to roll over, when the phone rings. It's Tim's mom, so I answer.

"Hi, Racquel."

"Hello Tori, how are you and my grandson doing?" Her warm voice makes me smile, even as the familiar pain hits me. How Cooper's father can come from someone so wonderful but be so heartless himself, I will never understand.

"We're great. Did you get my email with the photos of our new addition?" I ask, stirring the pasta sauce I've got bubbling away on the stove for dinner.

"I did. She looks adorable and Cooper seems thrilled."

We make small talk for a few more minutes. But with every second that passes without her either asking to speak to Cooper or getting to the point of her call, my stomach twists into more of a knot. Racquel might be a lovely woman, but she doesn't call me just to chat about the spring weather.

"Listen Tori, I want you to know I don't think I should be the one telling you this, but I'm very aware my son won't. And Cooper has a right to know."

Here it comes.

"Okay," I say, suddenly wishing Sawyer was here.

"Tim and Bonnie are having a baby."

I huff out my exhale. The news isn't such a surprise, but more of a disappointment. While I certainly hope he doesn't abandon this child like he did his first one, I'm also acutely aware that my son will soon have siblings in the world that he might never meet. "Right. Well, I guess that's what newlyweds do," I reply, but the words sound hollow, even to my own ears.

Racquel makes a sound, part derision, part sympathy. "I don't agree with how he handled things by taking off when Cooper was born. And I'm forever grateful you didn't cut us off from our grandson, even though you had every right to when Tim signed over his rights. Obviously it's not my decision, it's yours, but I believe despite my son's actions, Cooper deserves to know he's going to have a little brother or sister. And I hope when the time is right, you'll let me introduce the two of them."

I'm silent for a minute, trying to figure out an appropriate response. Tim's mother doesn't deserve my anger. She's only doing what she feels is best, and she's been nothing but understanding and accepting of every decision I make.

"Has Tim mentioned Cooper even once since the wedding?" I ask, not bothering to hide the harshness from my voice.

Her silence is all the answer I need. I exhale on a pained laugh. "Right. Why would he? In his mind, he doesn't have a son. He stopped having one the day he signed those papers when I was still in the hospital. Maybe it's time I stop hoping he'll be a decent human being and remember he already has a kid. Hopefully, he treats this new one better, because no child deserves to know their own father abandoned them."

The slamming of a door has me whirling around in panic to see Cooper racing through the backyard to his tree house, Chloe trying to keep up behind him. She plops down on her butt when he clambers up the ladder and she can't follow.

"Shit. Racquel, I have to go." I slam my phone down, quickly turn off the stove, then race out the back door without even bothering to put on shoes.

Climbing the ladder, I stop with just my head inside the tree house. Cooper is huddled in the corner, his knees drawn up to his chest, and he's picking at something on the floor.

"Hey, buddy. Can I come up?" I ask softly and wait for his small head nod.

I make my way into the tree house and sit down beside him, resisting the powerful urge to pull him into my lap and hug him to me. My heart is breaking for him, knowing he heard me say a truth I'd hoped he wouldn't realize for at least a few more years.

We sit there in silence for a few minutes, the only sound Chloe's soft whining from the bottom of the ladder.

"I'm sorry you had to hear that, Coop."

His sniffle breaks my heart even further, and I tentatively wrap one arm around his shoulder. He turns into me, burying his face in my chest, and I can feel the dampness from his tears seeping into my shirt.

"W-why doesn't he want to be my dad?" he whispers broken-ly, and I wish I knew how to answer.

"Sometimes," I start, then stop. Fuck, this is hard. "Some-times people aren't ready to be parents. I was, your dad wasn't." I kiss the top of his head, still feeling his little body wracked with sobs. Holding him tighter, I continue, desperate to make him feel the depth of my love, even though I know it won't be enough.

"The second I found out I was pregnant, I was the most excited I've ever been. You were like this special gift, given to me when I least expected it. And I've never stopped being so grateful to have you as my son."

His small arms wrap around me, holding me just as tightly as I'm holding him. I won't say anything else about Tim; even though he's the one who broke Cooper's heart, I'm the one who said the words I can never take back. The words my sev-en-year-old now has to process and make sense of.

We stay like that in the tree house, holding each other for a long time. Finally, Cooper lifts his head and looks at me with red eyes. "Can we go inside now?"

I stroke back his hair and kiss his forehead. "Of course."

I climb down first, and Chloe starts dancing around my feet. Her excitement grows when Cooper reaches the ground, and he picks her up, hugging her to him. We make our way inside in silence, and Coop disappears to his bedroom with Chloe.

I force myself to finish preparing dinner, reheating the sauce and cooking up some pasta. When it's all done, I go down the hall to Coop's room. He left the door open, and I peek inside to see him on the floor, doing something with the LEGO scene he and Sawyer were working on the other day.

"Hey kiddo, dinner's ready."

He nods and pushes the fire truck into a spot by a building that I'm guessing is their version of a fire hall. I make a mental note to buy him the fire station set for his birthday.

We make it through dinner, Coop's homework, and then bedtime. I'm starting to think we're over the worst of the emotional heartache of the evening. Until I'm tucking my son in and he looks up at me.

"Mom," he starts, twisting his blanket in his hands. "Am I a bad kid if I wish my dad wasn't my dad?"

"Oh, honey," I reply, at a bit of a loss as to what to say. "No, I don't think you're a bad kid. You're hurting right now, and when we're hurting, we feel big things."

Coop nods, seeming to accept that. "I wish Sawyer was my dad instead."

My body goes cold. If I was at a loss before, now I'm completely in despair. There's no good response to that. Nothing I can say to either comfort or clarify.

Thankfully, Coop doesn't take my silence as a bad thing, and he lets out a little sigh, closing his eyes. I lean down and kiss him goodnight, hoping he doesn't pick up on my internal panic.

I wait until I'm out of his room before going straight to the kitchen and out into the backyard.

"Holy shit." My hands are shaking as I sink down on a chair on the patio and try to calm my racing heart.

I knew I was falling in love with Sawyer. If I'm honest with myself, knew Cooper was, too.

But my kid has just found out his own father doesn't want him and never did. And here I am, his only stable parent, in a relationship with a man who, up until very recently, made it abundantly clear he was not cut out for commitment. A man who could decide at any moment he doesn't want to do this anymore.

Because being in a relationship with a woman? That's one thing. Being in a relationship with a single mom... That's another. And for someone like Sawyer, who's clearly got deep-seated reasons he has *never* been in a relationship before, that level of commitment is bound to be a lot to take on.

The problem is, how are Cooper and I meant to handle it if Sawyer hits that point of not wanting the responsibility and commitment that comes with being with us?

My son has been abandoned by the man who donated half of his DNA. He's never known a true father figure. And now, thanks to me not controlling my anger on the phone with his grandmother, he's all too aware of just how little Tim has ever cared about him.

If his own biological father could walk away from him, what's to stop someone like Sawyer from doing it? Only Cooper's feelings for Sawyer run a lot deeper than his feelings for Tim.

Which means the heartache he's feeling now would be magnified immensely.

A sob escapes me and I clap my hand over my mouth to hold back any more from breaking free. But there's no fighting the tears that start to roll down my cheeks.

I've always stayed true to one thing. Cooper comes first. And how can I uphold that if I don't protect him from further pain? There's no way to know how long this thing between Sawyer and I will last. But the longer it does, the higher the cost to Coop's heart — to say nothing of my own — when it inevitably ends.

Which means there's only one thing to do.

I put on an award-winning performance the next morning, if I do say so myself. I get Cooper dropped off at school, come home, and hold it all together until I get in the shower. Only then do I let myself fall apart and grieve what I'm about to lose.

The hot water washes away my tears but does nothing to fill the gaping hole in my heart. I go through the motions of getting dressed, tossing my wet hair up in a bun, then putting Chloe in her cage.

I drive slowly across town to the fire station, alternating between hoping the trucks won't be there so I can delay the inevitable, and hoping they are so I can get this over with and go home to cry some more.

I pull into the parking lot; all the engines are parked behind the open bay doors.

"You can do this," I whisper to myself as I climb out of my car. As I make my way over to the station, I realize I didn't think this through. Coming to him at work? What the hell was I thinking, how selfish can I be? I start to turn around when he shouts across the parking lot.

"Tori!"

I freeze. I hear his footsteps as he jogs up to me, and then his hands are on my shoulders, turning me to face him. His easy grin lights up his face, but as soon as he sees how wretched I must look, it falls.

"Angel, what's wrong? Is it Cooper? Is he okay?"

I'm already shaking my head, and I manage to whisper, "He's fine," before I stupidly let Sawyer tug me in to his firm chest. His uniform is scratchy under my cheek and it's a struggle not to sink into the comfort he's offering.

But now that he's here, I have to go through with it.

I break away and take a step back. His arms fall from my body, and confusion is etched across his handsome face.

"Tori, what's going on? You're freaking me out." He moves to step closer and I hold my hand up to stop him.

"Sawyer, stop. I can't..." I gulp back a sob. "I can't do this anymore. It's not going to work."

"What?" he says, his hand raking through his hair. "What the hell are you talking about, angel?"

"It's not you, you've done nothing wrong. It's me. I always said I couldn't be in a relationship because I need to put Cooper first. That hasn't changed. And maybe the reason I've had a hard time figuring out how to tell him about us is because I shouldn't." I'm grasping at straws and I know it. But how the hell do I tell the man I've fallen madly in love with that I can't be with him because I'm terrified he won't ever feel the same way and that someday he'll break my heart — and my son's.

"Tori." He sounds broken and I drag my eyes up from the pavement to meet his gaze. That was a mistake, because if I thought he sounded broken, it's nothing compared to how he looks.

"I'm sorry," I whisper.

He crouches down, dropping his head into his hands before looking back up at me, despair and confusion all over his face. "I don't understand. What changed? I thought we were good...better than good." He springs back up. "You're scared, aren't you? That's what this is, you're scared. Well, so am I, angel. Why can't we be scared together? We're meant to be together, I know it. We can figure this out."

He has no idea how right he is. I am scared. Terrified. But I can't admit that without saying what I'm scared of. "I can't." Taking the step to turn away and move toward my car is the hardest thing I've done in a very long time, if not ever. Knowing he's there, watching me end us with no good explanation fills me with more grief and guilt than I've ever felt.

I keep my hands gripping the steering wheel and my eyes pointing forward as I drive out of the parking lot and away from Sawyer. When I get home, I drop down on my couch and wrap up in the blanket that's draped over the back of it. Then I grab my phone and make two calls. The first one is to my parents, asking if they'll take Cooper and Chloe for the weekend, starting today after school. I make up an excuse about needing the time to write, and they eagerly accept.

The next call is to Willow. "Can you come here for the weekend?" I whisper, and being my best friend, that's all I need to say for her to agree.

"Oh, babe. I'll be there tomorrow and you can tell me who I need to hurt," she says, and fresh tears start to fall.

"He doesn't deserve any more pain," I manage to say. "I hurt him enough."

Willow's silent for a beat. "Okay. Hold yourself together until tomorrow morning. I'll be there."

"Thank you."

I may not have Sawyer anymore, but I have my family, and I have Willow. That has to be enough, just like it always has been.

Chapter Twenty-Seven

Sawyer

Don't ask me how I manage to work after Tori drops her bomb, but I do. I'll be damned if I'll be like Lance and let this put me or anyone else in danger.

She's running scared. Once I got over the initial shock of her breaking things off between us, I could see that clearly. She didn't want to end our relationship. Her heart was hurting just as much as mine. But she's scared.

And the thing is, I understand. I'm not a good bet when it comes to relationships, and she's been burned badly in the past. It makes sense that it was only a matter of time before she'd panic and worry that I'm not in this for the long haul. She's protecting her kid, and I can't be mad at her for that.

I can be hurt and disappointed that she doesn't trust me yet, but that just fuels my desire to prove myself to her.

When I get home after my shift, I text my brothers to see who wants to meet me at the gym. It's late but there's not a chance in hell of me sleeping tonight unless I completely exhaust my body.

Beckett and Hunter take me up on the offer, but Jude's out of town with his hockey team, and Max is working the night shift.

By the time the boys get to the gym, I'm already in the middle of a set of sprints on the treadmill. The guys step onto the machines on either side of me.

"Hey man." Beck starts off at a jog. "Everything cool?"

"Nope." I increase my speed.

"Okay, are we gonna talk about it?"

"Nope."

Thankfully, they let me run in silence, their company all I really need right now as I work out in my mind how to move forward. When I finish my set, I slow the pace down to a walk, and the two of them immediately do the same.

"How 'bout now?" Hunter asks.

I exhale loudly. "Yeah. So, Tori broke up with me." Turning off my treadmill, I turn and walk over to the weight bench, setting it up for a bench press. The guys scramble to follow, and Beckett comes into position to spot me as I lay down on the bench.

"What happened?" he asks gently as I lower the weight.

I press it back up, then lower again and press up once more before I answer succinctly. "She's scared I'm gonna walk."

"Are you?"

I shoot a glare at Hunter. "No, you dumbass. I'm pretty fucking sure I love her and her kid. I have zero intention of walking away."

"Well, did you tell her that?" Beckett adds, and my glare intensifies as I turn it on him.

I grunt as I push the weight up again. "When exactly was I meant to do that? When she was trying not to cry as she ended it, or when she drove away from me?"

I finish my reps and set the weight back down before setting my hands on my chest. Hunter and Beckett are silent, waiting for me, I guess.

"She showed up at the station and said she needed to end things. That it wasn't working. But that's bullshit, and she knows it."

"Okay, but her feelings aren't bullshit. And if you say she's scared, then there's a reason for that," Beckett says, taking my place on the bench once I stand up. Hunter moves to spot him while I grab a set of dumbbells and start some curls.

"I get that," I grind out. "But how am I meant to prove to her this is serious, that my feelings are serious, if she's pushing me away?"

"Grand gesture."

The two words Hunter says make me pause mid-lift. "Grand gesture. Wait, like, from romance books." For the first time since Tori drove away from me, a smile crosses my face. "Hunter, you're a fucking genius, my brother."

I set the weights back down and walk over to the two of them. "Thanks for meeting me, but I gotta go. I have a grand gesture to plan."

I'm already walking toward the changeroom when I hear Beckett yell at me. "You called us here for a workout and now you're bailing on us?"

All I do is a backward wave. "I've got a woman to woo. See you fuckers later."

The next day, I pull up at work, eager to get my shift done and dusted so I can go to Tori's house. Even after the gym, I didn't go to sleep for a long time, my mind racing with ideas of how I can make her believe this is it for me. That she and Cooper are what I want, now and forever.

Nothing can stop me today. I'm joking with the guys, shooting the shit, doing what needs to be done. We answer a call for a kitchen fire, and I lead the crew through the easy job of putting it out, proving yet again that I can one hundred percent balance a relationship and my job.

I may not know exactly how I'm going to prove my intentions to Tori, but I do know I'm not leaving her house tonight until she at least agrees to give me a shot.

The alarm goes off for a medical — a car accident on the highway, and the guys and I jump into action. Like a well-oiled machine, we load up and head to the scene. Once there, we're efficient, setting up cones, making sure everything is safe, and start to triage the injured. It's a bad one, multiple vehicles involved, and there's several people that need attention. But the ambulance crew is right behind us, and everything's going smoothly.

Until I hear Sloan shout my name, but it's too late.

When I wake up in a fucking hospital bed, the first thing I register is the supremely annoying beeps coming from some machine on the wall. The second thing I notice is how numb my leg feels. The third thing is the worried faces of several family members staring at me.

"Sawyer? How you doin', brother?" Max lifts my eyelids, even as I swat his hand away.

"What happened?" I mumble.

"You got hit by a dumbass who couldn't keep his eyes on the road," Hunter says from the foot of my bed. "I was just pulling up to help with traffic, saw the whole damn thing happen."

My eyes drift down to my leg, elevated on a stack of pillows and looking very bulky. "My leg?"

"Broken in two places, which is why you needed emergency surgery," Max says grimly.

"But you're okay, and that's what matters."

My head lolls to the side. "Mom?"

She gives me a watery smile. "Hi, baby. You scared me. Your dad had to stay home with Violet, but he'll be so relieved to know you're awake."

"I just texted the family group," Hunter says, looking up from his phone.

The pain is starting to hit me now as I become more conscious and aware of, well, everything. I remember being at the scene and Sloan yelling at me, but then it's all a blur. "Did I hit my head?"

Max is the one who answers. "Yeah, you were unconscious at the scene for about a minute, apparently. The paramedics that brought you in said when you woke up, you were asking for Tori. I think the girls were going to call her once we tell them you're awake."

"Shit." I wince and turn to my mom. "Sorry."

"It's okay, you've earned a curse word or two. But don't you want them to call her?" Mom asks, her brow furrowing. "I thought you two were together now."

"No? Yes? We are, well, I think. I don't know. I need to talk to her, and doing so from a hospital bed isn't exactly the way I planned it."

Mom stands, leaning over to kiss my forehead. "You'll work it out." Just then, the door opens, and some dude wearing scrubs comes in.

"Hello there, Sawyer, glad to see you're awake. That means we can move you to the ward soon." He looks at Max, Hunter, and my mom. "You'll be able to *officially* have more than one visitor there."

Max shakes his hand while Hunter looks a little embarrassed. Even as my pain is growing in intensity, I can easily read between the lines and realize Max used his hospital privileges and Hunter pulled the cop card so they could all be with me.

"Thanks, guys. Go back to work, I'll be fine."

They both lean down to give me a hug before leaving, Hunter reassuring me he'll update my crew on my status.

"I'll go and check in on your father, and the rest of the family will see you once you're settled." Mom gives me a longer hug, and I let her, knowing this must be bringing back some painful memories from Dad's accident.

Once I'm alone, it isn't long before a nurse walks up just in time to see my grimace as I try to shift in bed. "Hold on there, Mr. Donnelly, let me help." I manage to get into a more comfortable position, but the effort leaves me out of breath from the pain.

"I'm going to give you something that will help. It'll make you sleepy, so when you wake up, don't be surprised if you're in a room on the orthopedic ward instead of here, okay?"

I muster up a nod and close my eyes. Pain or no pain, I'm still fucking terrified of needles and I know she's about to push a syringe filled with clear liquid into my IV. Thankfully, it works fast, and my eyes start to droop as the fiery pain in my leg eases slightly.

Chapter Twenty-Eight

Tori

Thank God Willow is with me when I get the call.

"He *what*? Oh my God." My hands start to shake as I listen to Kat tell me over the phone that Sawyer was hit by a car while at work a few hours ago. I didn't think I had any more tears left in me, but somehow, more well up as she manages to calmly share that he had surgery to repair a broken leg and is now awake. "Thanks for telling me," I manage to get out before hanging up, my phone falling to my lap.

"Woman, you better fucking tell me what's going on before I jump into panic mode," Willow demands.

"Sawyer's in the hospital," I whisper, dashing away the tears on my cheeks. "He had surgery. I...I need to go to him. I can't..." I break on a sob, and Willow pulls me sideways into her arms.

"I know, honey. I know. But he's okay, right? He's okay, and we'll get you to him, and everything will be fine."

Somehow, I pull myself together enough to grab my purse and keys, which Willow promptly takes out of my hand. "As if I'm letting you drive right now."

Westport really isn't that far away, but at this moment, driving to Sawyer without knowing what I'll find when I see him feels like it's too far and yet not far enough. I have no idea if I'll be welcome at his side or if he'll push me away.

But I need to see him. I need to know he's alright. Then, if he wants me to go, I'll leave.

Willow pulls up to the main entrance of Westport General Hospital and gestures to the doors. "Go find your man."

I should be rushing to get out of the car. Instead, I'm frozen. "What if I'm too late. What if I pushed him away and he's decided I'm not worth the trouble."

"Then he's not the man either one of us thought he was. You'll see that he's alive, and you'll leave, and we'll go back home and drink margaritas and denounce all men." She leans across me and opens the car door. "But you won't know if that's the truth or just a really shitty story you're making up in your head if you don't go in there and find him."

I gulp down a deep breath and give her a feeble nod. "Strong margaritas?"

"The strongest."

I get out of the car and walk through the sliding glass doors of the hospital. Kat said he was on the orthopedic surgery ward, so I follow the signs through the halls that smell of cleaner and that unmistakable hospital aroma. The elevator ride up to the fourth floor gives me enough time to psych myself up to see Sawyer again. When I reach the nursing station, I realize I forgot to ask Kat which room he's in. It turns out, I didn't need to because I hear an achingly familiar voice, yet not the one I want to hear, call my name.

"Hey Tori, over here."

I turn to Beckett, who's come to a stop outside of a room, a cup of water in his hand.

His face is unreadable, so naturally, I start to overthink everything. Is he angry that I'm here right now? Does he know I ended things with Sawyer?

"I should warn you, he's pretty doped up right now. Apparently, when they moved him to the ward, they realized his IV line wasn't working, so they removed it. But when they went to re-insert, he panicked. They weren't prepared for a grown-ass man to be so terrified of needles." Beckett shakes his head. "They gave him some sort of short-acting sedative a few minutes ago, and I think they're about to try again."

I give him a nod but can't find words to say as I follow him into the room. Max and Heidi are there, both in scrubs, indicating they're on shift right now as well. Heidi walks over and gives me a hug, while Max flashes me a quick smile from beside Sawyer. I drag my eyes over to the hospital bed and the man lying on it, who's currently got his eyes half closed and a dopey expression on his face.

"Angelllll," he slurs. "You came." His head droops to one side, as if his neck is nothing more than a limp noodle.

Beckett snorts to hide a laugh, I'm guessing, as Max shakes his head. I approach the bed slowly, and his head rolls upright again as he blinks his eyes open.

"Hi." I look him over, taking in the scrape on his forehead and the bandage covering what I assume is the old IV site on his arm. His leg is propped up, the blankets off it for now, revealing a bulky cast.

"Hi." He giggles. "I'm soooo happy you're here. You should always be here, okay? Like, always."

I glance over at Max. "Is this normal?"

He shakes his head with a low chuckle. "Not exactly, but we never really know how someone will react to medications. And Sawyer here has clearly never had Ativan."

A hand tugs at mine, and I look back to see Sawyer trying to lift it, I assume to kiss it the way he likes to, except he keeps missing and kissing the air instead.

I suppose it's better than him immediately kicking me out of the room, even if I don't quite trust his actions right now. After all, will he still be as happy to see me when the sedation wears off?

A nurse chooses that moment to walk in. "Alright, the Ativan should be working, shall we try this again?" She looks to Max. "Are you and your brother willing to help restrain him?"

My eyes bug out at that word. "Restrain?"

Heidi smothers a laugh. "Yeah, he, umm, really didn't like it the last time they tried to insert an IV. Wouldn't let anyone do it, not even me or Max."

"Needles are scary, angel." Sawyer pouts, tugging on my hand again. "But I'll be okay if you hold my hand."

Max curses under his breath. "You're telling me all we needed was her? Not two staff members and a dose of benzos?"

Sawyer turns his floppy head to the side and grins at his brother. "Yuuuup."

Slipping into mom mode, I sit down in the chair that Beckett brings over, and with my free hand, tilt Sawyer's head to face mine. "Okay, I'm here. I'm right here, and you're going to let them do their job and put the IV in so you can get the medicine you need, right?"

"Gimme a kiss?" he slurs, and I can't help the twitch of my lips turning up. Leaning forward, I press a light peck to his mouth. When I settle back, he's got another dopey grin on his face, and his eyes are closed. "Your kisses are the best. I want all of them. Forever, 'kay?"

Stroking the uninjured side of his face, my own smile grows wider. I might not know if this is how he'll feel when he's not drugged up, but for now, I'm going to let myself bask in his goofy affection. "Okay." Flashing my eyes to Max and the nurse, I give them a sharp nod. Max holds down Sawyer's other arm, and I turn my focus back to the adorable man I'm madly in love with.

"You're going to have to let Cooper be the first one to sign your cast," I say, continuing to gently stroke his cheek. "He's with my parents this weekend, but I'm sure he'll want to come and see you when you feel up to it."

"Yeah, Coopzilla's my little maaaaaaan. Ouch!"

Sawyer jerks slightly, and I lean in and kiss him more firmly this time, holding my lips to his until I hear the nurse say, "Done."

"Good boy," I whisper against his lips before kissing them one more time, then sitting back in the chair. He blinks his eyes open, looks over at his arm, then back to me with a triumphant expression.

"I did it."

I laugh and hear his siblings laugh as well. "Yeah, you did."

"Will you call me a good boy again?" He giggles, then his head falls to the side and something that sounds a lot like a snore comes out of him.

I flush bright red because I'm pretty sure he didn't mean to say that quite as loud as he did, but then again, with Sawyer, who knows. "How long is he going to be this...um...unfiltered?" I ask, turning my head to Max.

"Probably a few more hours," he replies with a grin. "We've got to get back to work, are you good to stay with him?"

I nod just as the door to Sawyer's room opens and Willow pokes her head in. She takes in Max, Heidi, and Beckett before turning to me. "So everyone in the family is gorgeous. Got it." She walks in and wraps her arm around my shoulder. "Everything okay?"

"Yeah, he's just a little dopey." I introduce her to everyone, then Max and Heidi leave.

Beckett lingers, his eyes going from his now definitely snoring brother to me. "It's none of my business, but then again, he's my twin. Which is the only reason I'm saying anything." He pushes his glasses up his nose. "Sawyer might not know how to show it, or even how to say it, but he cares for you. A lot. Whatever you need to work out, I hope you can, because he's a good man. He'd be a good man for you if you give him a chance."

He walks to the door, then pauses and looks back at his brother. "For what it's worth, we *all* hope you can work it out. You're a good fit with our crazy family. You and Cooper both."

He leaves and as the door shuts behind him, Sawyer choses that second to snore extra loud, making both Willow and I giggle quietly.

"Well, it seems his family is Team Sawri."

"Team *what?*" I ask, looking over to the window ledge Willow's perched on.

She lifts her shoulders in a shrug. "Not my fault your names don't blend easily." Hopping down from the ledge, she moves to the door. "I'm gonna go find some coffee. Give you two some time."

Then Willow also leaves, and it's just me and a sedated Sawyer, snoring away.

I take several long minutes to just watch him, drinking in the rise and fall of his chest, and the steady beat of his pulse. All the reassurances that he's alive and he's going to be fine.

It's sadly ironic how I pushed him away because I was so scared of him leaving us, only to have the biggest threat of losing him come from something completely unexpected. If things hadn't turned out the way they did, if he hadn't been so lucky to only break a leg, this all would have ended with him never knowing how I feel.

Suddenly, I can't bring myself to wait another second. Carefully, I climb onto the hospital bed and lie down on his uninjured side, resting my head on his shoulder.

"Whaa?" he mumbles, rousing slightly.

"Shh. It's okay. I'm here," I whisper, laying my hand on his chest. "I'm here and I love you. And I'm so sorry for what I said yesterday. You were right, I was scared. Scared you would wake up one day and realize you never wanted this. A relationship, a kid, all of it. But I've realized, I'd rather have a short time loving you than no time at all. So if you'll have me back, I would love a second chance."

My voice is cracking by the end of it, and it's silly to even say it now since I know he probably isn't even conscious enough to hear it. Which means I'll have to repeat it all soon, anyway. But it feels so good to say the words that have been heavy on my heart.

"I love you."

I lift my head at his quiet but clear expression. His eyes are still droopy, but he's staring at me with a soft smile.

"I love you, angel. And I plan on loving you for a really long time."

I feel ready to burst with happiness and relief and most of all, love, but I'm very aware I need to be careful. Moving gingerly, I shift up slightly so I can kiss him again, pouring every emotion, every ounce of love into that kiss.

"We're gonna be okay?" I ask, and he nods drowsily.

"Yup. Just needa sleep some more."

"Okay. You sleep." I move to get off the bed.

"Noooo. Stay," he mumbles, his hand coming over his body to stop me. Except that tugs on his IV and he winces. "Ow."

"I'll stay right here. You sleep."

"Love you, angel." He turns his head to mine, so the words are mumbled against my forehead. Then I feel his body relax back into a medicated sleep.

"I love you, Sawyer Donnelly."

Chapter Twenty-Nine

Tori

I don't tell Cooper about Sawyer's accident until the next morning, when the man in question is no longer loopy and sedated, but is still grumpy, growly, and in pain. The doctors cleared him for discharge today, but it became clear he couldn't go home to his apartment.

Which is why I begged my parents to keep Cooper one more night, thankful he had no school today. Coop wasn't happy, begging to talk to Sawyer, but as soon as I told him he needed to stay with his grandparents one more night because Sawyer would be moving in with us temporarily, his face lit up and he was much more agreeable.

I spent the morning racing around, cleaning my house with Willow's help, and getting things as set up as I could for him to recover here. I fully expected his family to protest when I offered to take care of him. After all, I'm just the girlfriend.

Kat's the one who pointed out it made the most sense, seeing as I work from home. Still, I figured his parents would want him there, but when we were discussing it in the hospital hallway outside his room, Claire Donnelly leaned over and whispered that she wished me luck. According to her, Sawyer's a terrible patient, and she was more than happy to let someone else deal with him.

Did that lead to some trepidation on my part? Yes, but I still wanted to help.

Two of his brothers have just finished dropping off a load of stuff from his house, including food from his fridge that would have gone bad and a suitcase of clothes. I'm putting the shirts and pants away in my room when Willow wanders in.

"How are you going to explain to Coop why Sawyer's sleeping in your bed?"

My hands still. That *is* the one thing I hadn't quite figured out. "Good question, got any ideas?" I finish putting his T-shirts in the drawer and slide it shut. "It's not like he'll be upset when we say we're dating. I think he's hoped for this for a long time. If anything, he might be mad I didn't tell him sooner. But dating is different from sharing a bed, and how much does a seven-year-old boy understand about that, anyway?"

Willow holds up her hand. "Babe, you're rambling. Slow down. Why don't you stick to the truth? There isn't a guest bed, so he's sharing with you, just like I do when I come to stay."

I start to scoff at that simple answer, then pause. "You think that's good enough?"

Folding her arms across her chest, she smirks. "As long as you keep the hanky-panky to a minimum around him, then yes.

Coop will be fine. He loves Sawyer, and like you said, he's been 'shipping you two from the get-go."

We leave the bedroom, and she picks up her bag. "Tell Coop I said hi and let me know if you need me to come back next weekend." We embrace, and I hold on to her tightly. She's my best friend who dropped everything to be here for me when I thought my heart was breaking, and she stayed as it was put back together.

Words can never express how much she means to me.

"Thank you, Wills, for everything."

After she leaves, I head back to my bedroom to finish unpacking Sawyer's clothes. I've just emptied the suitcase when the doorbell rings.

It's a little embarrassing how fast I race down the hall to unlock the front door. Beckett is standing behind Sawyer, who's on crutches and sporting a four-day old scruff that is wildly sexy on him. Enough to make me wish he wasn't an active firefighter so he could keep it longer. Then again, he's not exactly on active duty right now...

"Wherever your mind went, angel, hold that thought till we're alone."

I blush bright red and step to the side to let them inside. "Sawyer, stop."

He pauses beside me and leans over to kiss me. "Never gonna stop loving you, angel."

I blink open my eyes as his lips leave mine to see him crutch into my house and over to the couch. I hurry after him in case he needs help, but with his upper body strength, it seems easy for him to set the crutches to the side and sink down with the barest of winces. Then he does look up at me with a puppy-dog expression.

"Can you help me lift my leg? Who knew casts were freaking heavy."

"Don't listen to him, Tori," Beckett brushes past me and drops a bag on the coffee table. "He can move his leg just fine." Beck comes to stand over Sawyer and folds his arms across his chest. "Stop milking it, Sawyer."

I bite my lips to hide my laugh as Sawyer pouts at his brother. "You're mean, Becky-boo. I'm a broken man."

"Not that broken," Beckett mutters. Then he turns to me and gestures to the bag on the table. "All his prescriptions are in there, discharge paperwork, follow-up, all of it. You're a brave woman to take this on; if you need a break, just call any of us. We went through something similar with Jude, but he was just a grumpy asshole, not the annoying fucker this one is going to be."

Now it's really hard not to laugh, because between his mom and Beckett, I'm starting to wonder just how much work it's going to be with Sawyer staying here.

"Thanks, Beckett. We'll be okay." I try to sound reassuring, but Beckett just raises his eyebrows and shakes his head.

"Good luck."

Sawyer gives his twin a middle finger salute from the couch as Beckett leaves, and I turn to him, hands on my hips. "You're not going to be any trouble, are you?"

The smile he gives me is so sweet it could give me a cavity. "Definitely not." His lips curl down slightly. "But could I please, pretty please, have a cup of coffee? Hospital coffee is gross."

My face softens at his plaintive request. "Of course." I move to go to the kitchen, just for him to call after me.

"Got any cookies? Maybe some Oreos?"

This time, I let my laugh ring free. When I reach the kitchen, I make him a quick cup of coffee, debating whether to take him seriously on his cookie request. On impulse, I do, reaching for the package I purchased at the store last week before everything in my world went sideways.

I place two on a plate and take it back to him, along with the coffee. Setting it down on the table, I say primly, "You'll need to practice your tongue dexterity with these until you can have the real thing again."

Those delicious chocolate eyes glint wildly. "Doc didn't say anything about abstaining, angel." He leans forward, at least as much as he can with a broken leg, and I dart back with a shriek of laughter.

"Stop, you'll hurt yourself!"

"Then come here and kiss me properly," he rumbles.

I'm not turning down that offer, so I move back over and bend to meet his upturned lips. His hands thread in my hair, holding me in place while he greedily plunders my mouth.

A knock on the door has him growling against my lips, but I know who it is, so I pull back.

Sure enough, I open the door to admit the whirlwind of a little boy and his puppy, my mother following behind more sedately.

"Careful, Coop!" I call out as he beelines to the sofa. Sawyer's ready, however, his arms open wide as Cooper flings himself into them.

"Well, isn't that the most precious thing I've ever seen." I turn at the sound of my mom's voice as she loops her arm in mine. "I can see why my grandson didn't stop talking about Sawyer all weekend."

I turn into her hug. "Hi, Mom. Thanks for bringing him home."

"Our pleasure, honey. I must admit to being a little eager to meet the man who's charmed my daughter *and* my grandson so thoroughly."

We move inside, and I lead her over to Cooper and Sawyer. "Hey Coop, why don't you take your stuff to your bedroom and unpack."

"But Mom," he starts to whine, then Sawyer nudges him.

"Little dude. C'mon, listen to your mom."

Cooper huffs but gets up from the couch and moves to get his bag from the front door. "I'm gonna get some markers to draw on your cast, okay?"

Sawyer flashes him a thumbs-up before turning to my mother. "Hi, Mrs. Charles. I'd get up, but..." He gestures to his leg with a rueful grin. "Hoping you'll excuse me this time."

"Of course. And call me Sonya. It's lovely to meet you, I am sorry to hear about your accident. I won't stay long, I know you're just settling in. But you'll have to come to Westport sometime for dinner with Tori's father and me."

Sawyer flashes her a charming grin. "That would be great. I'm sure my mom would love to have the two of you join one of our family dinners, but I should warn you, with five of us kids, plus our partners, it gets a little wild."

Have I entered an alternate universe? My boyfriend is inviting my mother to family dinner with *his* family? I shake my head, trying to make sense of the madness as Cooper runs back out of his room with a fistful of markers.

"I'm ready, Sawyer!"

"I'll get out of your hair," my mom says, moving to the door. "Hey, Coop? Can I get a hug goodbye?"

Cooper darts over to her. "Bye Grandma, thanks for a fun weekend, love you." Then he darts back and settles in on the floor at Sawyer's side.

"Nice to meet you, Sonya," Sawyer calls with an easy grin.

"You, too. Take care, Sawyer."

I walk my mother out the front door and down to her car where she turns to take my arm. "Victoria Charles, that man is a gem. I can tell from just a few minutes with him."

I smile. "Thanks, Mom, but I already know."

She squeezes my arm gently. "Good. You and Cooper deserve to be happy."

We hug, and I watch as she gets in her car and drives off before turning back to my house. The front drapes are open, letting me look right in to see Cooper bent over Sawyer's leg, no doubt drawing something on his cast.

And I'm filled with an overwhelming wave of love. This is what I've waited so long for. This feeling of happiness, of completeness.

This is my happily ever after.

Sawyer manages to prove everyone wrong and is a model patient and house guest over the next two days. Don't get me wrong, it's been stressful, but not because of him. I've been a nervous mess, worried he'll hurt himself further somehow. Which is why tonight, which happens to be book club night, I'm not exactly excited about leaving. But no matter what excuse I come up with, Sawyer and Cooper are refusing to let me back out of going.

"Mom, if you don't go, then they have nothing to talk about."

I arch my brow at him. "They can talk about my book without me just fine. I don't know if I should leave you two."

It's Sawyer's turn to help me realize I'm being foolish for no reason. "Angel, you have to go. They're excited to talk to a famous author. Don't let being scared of something make you push it away." The meaningful but loving look he gives me breaks my resolve.

"Fine, you're right. But I'll have my phone with me the entire time, and if you need anything —" There's an unexpected knock at the door that has me frowning. "Who the heck is that?" I move to open it, and to my surprise, Cam and Beckett are on my front porch.

"Um, hi guys," I say, glancing back to see a knowing look on Sawyer's face. "I'm guessing you're here to take me to book club." I sigh.

"Beck is going to hang out with me and Cooper, so if I need any help, he's here. Cam's driving, so you can have a glass of wine and relax, angel. You've earned it."

I walk back over to him and lean down to kiss him. I hear Cooper's "Eww, Mom" but ignore it. He's going to have to get used to me kissing this man. To be fair, when we told him Sunday night that Sawyer and I loved each other, he very matter-of-factly said, "Okay, cool. It's about time." And that was it. Apparently, my kid saw this coming a mile away.

I straighten up and ruffle Coop's hair before picking up the bag that has some prizes and giveaways for the book club members and move back to the front door.

"Alright, let's go. Be good, boys."

"Where's the fun in that?" Sawyer teases.

"Don't worry, I've got them," Beckett says quietly, standing by the door. I flash him a grateful smile, then follow Cam to her car.

A couple of hours later, I've forgotten why I was so hesitant to come here tonight. The women raved about my book, asked incredibly insightful and fun questions, and we had a blast with the games and giveaways I planned. It's been the perfect reminder of why I love writing. It's not just for myself, it's for my readers. It's their happiness, and escape, and inspiration that fuels my own.

Cam and I drive back to my house, and I'm in a happy, slightly wine-buzzed state. We pull into my driveway and I hop out, eager to go in and see Sawyer.

I throw open my front door to see Beckett and Sawyer on the couch, watching a movie. "Where's Cooper?"

Beckett stands up and starts gathering his things. "We got him to bed about an hour ago."

My jaw drops. "He went to bed on time?"

Sawyer smirks. "Yes, angel. I've been paying attention. I knew it was bedtime, so I put him to bed."

"He brushed his teeth?" I ask. Sawyer nods.

"Went pee?" Another nod, and a growing grin.

"And he didn't ask for a hundred snacks and a glass of water?"

Sawyer chuckles. "Woman, your kid doesn't do that. He knows better."

That makes me smirk. "That's true." I make my way over and lean down to peck him on the lips. "Thank you for getting him to bed."

Turning to Beckett and Cam, I say, "Thanks for coming to stay with them, Beckett, and for the ride, Cam."

Cam walks over and gives me a hug. "We knew you wouldn't want to leave them alone, and honestly, we'd all feel the same. Sawyer in charge of a kid at the best of times is risky business, but when he's injured?" She pretends to shudder.

Something in me wants to defend Sawyer. "He's great with Coop. I trust him completely. It was more if he needed something…" I trail off as I realize they're all grinning at me. "What?"

Beckett shakes his head. "Nothing. You two have a good night." They let themselves out, and I go to lock the door behind them before turning back to face Sawyer.

"Why were they smiling? I meant it, I really do trust you with Cooper."

The heated look he gives me is full of pent-up desire and so much love, it's overwhelming. We haven't done anything intimate since before his accident, and I know we're both feeling it. "I know you do, angel. And that means so fucking much to me, you can't even imagine. Get over here."

I walk over to him, and he tugs me down so sharply that I have to react quickly so as not to land on his injured leg.

"I love you, Tori Charles. I love your kid, and I love you. Thank you for trusting me and loving me in return."

The kiss he gives me is more than I can take, and I pull back, breathless.

"Bedroom. Now."

CHAPTER THIRTY

Sawyer

I hobble down Tori's hallway, trying not to drool at her curves swaying in front of me. She truly has no idea just how alluring she is without even trying. And hearing her defend me to my brother and his wife, hearing her tell them how much she trusts me? That might have turned me on more than her hot little body in those jeans she's wearing.

She trusts me. With her kid, no less. And she loves me.

There's no greater gift. And I'm going to spend a lifetime repaying her, one orgasm at a time.

Starting now.

In her bedroom, I drop my crutches to the floor beside the bed before maneuvering myself onto it. How Jude managed being one-legged for his long recovery, I do not know. I'm an impatient fucker and this is already annoying just a few days in. I'm starting to understand why he was so goddamn grumpy.

But I'm resourceful. And no broken leg is gonna stop me from making Tori see stars. "Angel, get that pretty little ass over here and sit on my face." I whip my shirt over my head and thank the gym gods for my upper body strength as I manage to shift down so my head is on a pillow. I make some grabby hand motions that have Tori giggling as she strips out of her clothes, but when I see what she was hiding underneath, I growl.

"Stop."

Her hands freeze, fingers looped in the blue lace that barely covers her pussy.

"Keep it on."

Her cheeks flush but she withdraws her fingers and slowly walks to the side of the bed closest to me. "Someone's feeling bossy tonight," she murmurs when she finally reaches my side. I grab her by the hips and move to lift her onto my lap, but she doesn't fully let me, climbing up herself and settling right on my hardening cock.

"Someone's feeling needy, not bossy. I haven't tasted your pussy in days. I almost died, you know." I pout, batting my eyes like a fool. But my joke lands flat as Tori smacks my chest with a frown.

"Don't joke about that. You scared me."

"I'm sorry, angel." Curling up to a seated position, I tangle my hands in her hair and stare into her eyes. "I promise to do everything in my power not to scare you like that again. My job isn't without risk, but I swear to you, I'm focused and careful. You and Cooper mean everything to me. I don't have any intention of leaving you."

Her face softens as she leans her cheek into my hand. "Good."

I tilt her head and kiss her sweetly, then deeper, our tongues tangling together as the passion from earlier comes roaring back. Letting myself fall back to the pillow, I bring her with me, and she starts to grind her hips down on my lap. Her kiss muffles my groan.

Lifting her head, I can tell her heart is racing just like mine. "Pretty sure I told you where to sit." I wink. Grabbing a handful of her ass, I pull her up my chest. "Hold on, angel." Her panties are already damp with her arousal, the scent of her heavy in the air, her hips right above my mouth now. I run my nose up the crease at the top of her thigh making her shudder as she falls forward and grabs the headboard. "Fuck, you're addictive."

"God, Sawyer," she moans as I lick her slit over the lace of her panties, making them even more soaked. I do it again, and she squirms, her hips instinctively rocking back and forth along my tongue. I grab her ass, holding her there for a minute as her taste floods my mouth. I need all of her, so grabbing the side of her skimpy panties, I tear them down the seam and toss them to the side.

Tori's hand comes down and grips my hair, and I wrap my arms around her waist, holding her down to my mouth.

"Shit, oh my God, Sawyer that's... Oh my God!" She shrieks as quietly as she can as I tunnel my tongue and plunge it inside of her in shallow thrusts. Letting go of her with one arm, I snake my hand through so I can tease her from the inside with my fingers. But as I brush over her ass, dipping in between her cheeks, she shivers.

"Mmm," I rumble against her pussy. "Are we gonna check off a bucket list item, angel?"

Her answering moan is all the answer I need. My mouth goes into overdrive, sucking and pulling at her clit, alternating with long sweeps up and down her slit, lapping up her drops of moisture. Lifting my hand up to her, I growl, "Suck."

She pulls my fingers into her mouth, swirling her tongue around them in a way that makes me even harder than I already was. I pull them free and move them to the puckered entrance between her cheeks. Rimming around the edge, I test her out by gently pushing into the tight muscle, then backing off out. "Relax, angel," I say, and I feel her let go a little.

Returning my attention to her pussy, I work her over with my tongue some more before pressing my finger in her ass a little more, feeling her tense, then release and let me in.

"Holy fuck!" she cries out as I slide just the tip of my finger in and out. Her head is thrown back, her tits heaving with every breath.

"More?" I ask, pulling away from her sex slightly. She looks down at me, her eyes glazed with pleasure as she nods.

I nip at her clit, then lave it with my tongue as I press my finger inside her back hole even further this time, feeling her squirm around me. This time, I don't move it in and out, I just hold in place and focus my attention on her pussy. She's on the edge, her legs trembling and tightening around my head. As much fun as it would be to keep her here for a while, driving her wild, I don't know if I can hold out much longer without feeling her heat around my cock. So, with a few more swipes of my tongue, I put suction on her clit and pull once, twice. Then she's damn near pulling my hair out as she makes a strangled noise and her orgasm overtakes her.

I slide my finger out of her ass just as she sags back onto my chest, crumpling over my face. I'm not complaining since it brings those tits, still covered in blue lace, right over my mouth. I suck one, then the other, before she trembles and slides off me.

"I think I'm dead," she says shakily. "I think you've officially made me explode into orgasmic dust."

My chest rumbles with laughter. "Nah, I wouldn't go that far. Not sure how I'd explain that to Cooper."

She giggles and lifts her head to rest it on my chest. "You do owe me a new pair of panties."

"Angel, I'll buy you a hundred pairs of panties if I get to rip them off you every night."

"Deal."

I swing my legs to the side and sit up carefully. Looking over my shoulder at the goddess lying beside me, my heart fills with so much love. "I'll be right back, and then you're gonna ride my cock like a fucking rodeo cowgirl, got it?"

I hobble with one crutch into the bathroom to wash my hands, then turn back to the bed, where my queen, my angel, my love, is stretched out on her side, watching me.

"You're wearing far too many clothes, Sawyer Donnelly." She lifts up onto her knees as I approach, her hands coming to the top of my shorts. "Here, let me help you." Climbing off the bed,

Tori turns me around before sliding my shorts and boxers down past my hips. Then she takes my crutch and sets it down before pushing me to sit. I let her take the lead, pulling my clothes all the way off as I lean back on my hands. As soon as my cock springs free, her little hand wraps around it.

"Didn't I tell you to rodeo it up?" I ask gruffly, but she just flashes me an impish smile.

"Ah, but I've been practicing with my lollipop, getting some scene inspiration for my book. Don't you want to see my new moves?"

I bark out a laugh as she lifts up my broken leg, helping me spin back around so it's elevated and not aching so badly from being dependent. "Oh angel, you're fucking amazing."

Tori takes her place beside my hip and bats her eyelashes at me as she licks her palm, then wraps it around the base of my cock. "All in the name of book research."

I fucking love book research.

A few nights later, we drop Cooper off at a friend's house for a sleepover on our way to Hastings to meet up with my siblings. Personally, I was all for skipping it. A night with Cooper out of the house means Tori doesn't have to hold back her reactions when we make love. And I love *loud Tori* sex. But she insisted we go and spend some time with my family, not taking no for an answer, even when I pointed out we see them all the damn time.

When we get to Hastings, everyone is already there, but there's two empty chairs at the long table waiting for us.

"Hey!" Kat says, leaning in to give Tori a side hug when we sit down. "Glad you guys could make it."

"Same," Tori says with a sound of contentment as she accepts a glass of beer from Max. "Perfect timing with Coop having a sleepover tonight."

"I'm surprised you left the house," Lily teases from across the table and I point at her.

"See? We shoulda stayed home, angel."

Tori shoves at my shoulder, rolling her eyes. "No, I wanted to see everyone. We've got all night to ourselves; we can spend a couple of hours being social."

I let out a huff as those around us laugh at our expense. But the truth is, I fucking love it. I love not being the odd man out anymore, being able to wrap my arm around her shoulders and pull her in for a kiss. I love seeing her with my family, laughing and talking with so much joy on her face. And I love that when we leave here, we're going back to her house and I get to fuck her all night long.

There's a lull in conversation when Kat winces.

"You okay, Kat?" Max asks, a slight frown furrowing his brow.

She waves him off. "Yeah, just Braxton-Hicks. They're annoying, but it's nothing to worry about. Our midwife says we're all good."

I lean in front of Tori and point at Kat's stomach. "Kid, it's your favourite uncle talking. Give your mom a break, okay? You've got a lifetime to annoy her, no need to start early."

Kat bats away my hand with a laugh. "Thanks, Sawyer. If only they would listen."

Jude crosses his arms and props them on the table, a rare grin underneath his beard. "So. How are you gonna manage to be favourite uncle now that you're with Tori?"

My brothers all jeer as I look at him calmly. "If you really think my relationship is going to impact my position as favourite uncle, you're a fool, Beatle. I'm clearly the front-runner. I'm the most fun, I have access to fire trucks, and Tori has a kid and a puppy for them to play with when they're old enough."

"Yeah? Well, I have access to hockey," Jude fires back. "Maybe they won't care about silly fire trucks, and they'll be into sports instead."

I open my mouth to retaliate but Tori beats me to it. "We have access to pro baseball players, thanks to my best friend."

"Yeah." I smirk, holding my hand out to Tori for a high five. She doesn't leave me hanging, slapping her hand on mine.

Damn, it feels good to have a partner in crime. I get it now — *relationships are awesome.*

Chapter Thirty-One

Tori

Two weeks go by in a blur. A happy, laughter-filled blur.

It hasn't all been perfect. I finally discovered that Claire wasn't exaggerating after all when she said Sawyer was a difficult patient. The number of times I had to use my mom voice to get him to take his painkillers, elevate his leg, or use his damn crutches instead of hopping on one foot, is starting to border on ridiculous.

But even with those moments of frustration, there's no denying the positive energy Sawyer has infused into my house.

Sawyer's tucking Cooper into bed tonight, and once I finish tidying the kitchen, I head down the hall to say goodnight. When I overhear Cooper asking Sawyer if he could just stay here forever, even after his leg is healed, I hold my breath, waiting for Sawyer's reply.

"You know, bud, that would be super cool. But me and your mom, we're still finding our way together, and I want to do it right. My priority is making sure everyone is happy, and that includes you, but your mom's job is to put you first, which makes it my job to put *her* first. And that means letting her take the lead on those kinds of decisions. The last thing I want is for you and your mom to get sick of me."

I peek around the corner to see Cooper squeezing Sawyer around the neck tightly, and my hand comes up to my chest.

"She loves you. Like, really loves you, the way she loves me. And you don't get sick of people you love like that. It's not possible."

Coop's words ring true. And I watch Sawyer's body language for a reaction but can't pick up on one. Then they break apart, and Chloe darts into the room, drawing their attention to the doorway — and my presence.

"Hi, guys," I say, walking into the room as if I didn't just eavesdrop on the sweetest moment. Sawyer grabs his crutches and stands up, and when he turns to me, I see his eyes glistening.

Ohhh. There's the reaction. I give him a private, loving smile as I squeeze his bicep and switch places with him on Coop's bed.

"Are you ready for tomorrow?" I ask my son, whose eyelids are already drooping. He nods slowly.

"G'night, Mom. Love you. G'night, Sawyer. Love you, too."

"Love you, buddy." I lean down to kiss his forehead, straighten his blanket, and move to stand. Sawyer's standing there, awe written all over his face. Balancing on his good leg, he bends over and pushes back the hair on my son's forehead.

"I love you, too, Coop." His whisper is filled with so much joy, and I realize this is the first time he and Cooper have said those words.

Dang it, now I'm tearing up.

Sawyer and I make our way out of Cooper's room, Chloe ambling behind us. Without a word, we settle on the couch in what's become our typical nightly routine, Sawyer with his leg stretched out and me nestled in against his chest.

"I don't know what to say," he starts, his voice wavering. "Other than to say that was, hands down, one of the best moments of my life." He inhales a shaky breath, his arms tightening around me. "Thank you for sharing your son with me."

I break out of his hold and turn to straddle his lap, taking his face in my hands. Raw, unbridled love is shining out of every part of him and I hope he can see it echoed back from me. "There's no one in this life I would rather share him with. He loves you, and I love you. You've completed our family puzzle when I was ready to live with a missing piece."

Sawyer lets out a laugh. "That's exactly how it feels for me. Like I was building a puzzle without knowing what the final picture would be, until I realized it was you. You and Cooper, with me forever."

My head dips down and our lips meet in a kiss. "It only took one night with you to know you'd be etched into my heart and soul," I murmur against his lips. "One night for you to win me forever."

Showing off the strength that makes me feel safe and cherished, Sawyer surges up. "I need you, angel. I need to show you just how that makes me feel."

I scramble off his lap, put Chloe in her crate as he grabs his crutches, and we move quickly and quietly to my bedroom. We learned our lesson the other night not to get too lost in each other while in the living room after Cooper came out for a drink of water and almost caught me with my shirt off.

But behind the locked door of my bedroom, my shirt isn't the only thing that comes off.

Dogwood Cove's Summer Solstice Festival is hands down my favourite part of moving to this town — after Sawyer, of course. It's the perfect sunny day, not too hot, but warm enough for shorts and a sweater. The other day, when Sawyer asked Cooper if he wanted to take his spot in the fire truck for the parade, I thought my kid was going to faint with excitement.

"Really? Like, seriously? They want *me* to ride in the truck?" His eyes are as wide as saucers as he stares at Sawyer, who gives him a solemn nod.

"It's a lot of responsibility. You have to sit safely and listen to the driver. But if you do that, I've heard he might let you turn on the lights and siren."

"Or you can stay on the side and watch the parade with us if you'd prefer," I tease, knowing exactly what kind of a response I'll get.

Sure enough, he scoffs. "Yeah right, Mom." He turns back to Sawyer. "This is so freaking cool. Thank you!"

They go through their high-five routine, which I've now seen enough times, I'm pretty sure I could do it myself.

When we show up at the fire station, there's more surprises. Sawyer's coworkers are waiting for Cooper with a DCFD T-shirt in his size. I stand to the side, watching my son beam with joy and pride as he basks in the attention of everyone. It's what every kid deserves. To feel important, supported, and loved. And the man responsible for all of it is the man finally making me realize I deserve the same things.

He crutches over to me, a silly grin on his face. "Angel, you look like you've just seen heaven, but I'm still fully clothed."

I choke out a laugh as he bends down slightly to kiss me. "You're ridiculous."

"But you love me."

I nod as he kisses me again. "I really do."

We step back and watch as Cooper and the firefighters load up, my kid enthusiastically waving out the window at us. They drive off to the parade staging area, and we make our own way back to my car and drive to the reserved parking spot next to Cam's art studio. Beckett, Cam, and the rest of Sawyer's family are waiting for us with a chair for Sawyer to sit in to watch the parade.

"Is Cooper excited?" Kat asks me, rubbing her giant belly.

I nod as I eye her stomach. "Absolutely thrilled. How are you doing? Maybe you need the chair more than Sawyer."

She shifts to the side, and I see a second chair and chuckle. "Oh. That's good. End of pregnancy can be a beast."

Kat grunts in acknowledgment. "Seriously. I had no clue my ankles were capable of swelling this much. But the end is in sight. Just a few more weeks."

Cam wanders over to join us. "Hey Tori, I'm almost done with the first sketch for your alternate covers. I think they're going to be amazing."

My eyes light up. When Cam first offered to design some special edition covers for my most popular series, my jaw dropped open. Custom-drawn covers? It's basically every author's dream. "Really? I can't wait!"

"Come over next weekend for dinner? I should have them done by then."

We firm up plans just as the parade starts. The fire department is at the very end of the parade, so it takes a while before we hear the *whoop* of the sirens. But as they slowly drive past, every single person in our group cheers for my son. No one louder than Sawyer, of course.

We moved here for a fresh start. To be closer to my family and give Cooper a better life. But never in my wildest dreams did I picture that life including a man who loves us fiercely, as well as his family, who welcomed us with arms wide open.

This life is everything I hoped for, and so much more. And it all started with just one night.

Epilogue

Sawyer

"Did you buy every single item in the team store or something?" Willow says as we climb out of the SUV she sent to pick us up for today's game, courtesy of her uncle.

I spread my hands and smile back. "Listen, there's no shame in my fan game. I love the Tridents, and having box seats to the season closer? That basically required me to go all out."

Willow arches a brow and turns to mock whisper to Tori. "Your boyfriend's a total dork."

My angel just giggles. "Yup, he is. And I love him for it."

I glance down at my outfit. So what if I'm decked out in head-to-toe Tridents gear? So is Coop, and I must say, we look great.

"Listen, Wills, I'm basically a walking advertisement for the team in this getup. If anything, you guys should be paying me right now." I turn in a slow circle. "Hat? Check. Jersey? Check. Matching joggers? Check." I pull up the bottom cuffs of my pants and point to my feet. "I'm even rocking the socks."

"Subtlety really isn't your strong suit, is it Sawyer?" Willow tugs Cooper into a quick hug. "You, on the other hand, look fantastic. Perfect amount of team spirit."

My mouth falls open in mock outrage, seeing as the only difference in our outfits is that Cooper's wearing plain track pants instead of the team colours I've got on. "You're just sayin' that because you like him more than me," I grumble as we head toward the stadium.

Willow shrugs. "That's true, I do."

Cooper looks from Willow, to me, and then back again. "Aunt Willow, Sawyer's just excited. He's never sat in your fancy seats before."

I lean over and fist bump my little dude. "That's right, Aunt Willow, don't ruin my excitement."

That earns me an eye roll from Willow and a gentle shove from Tori. "Behave, you two."

Jokes about my outfit aside, Willow's offer to have us as her guests for the season closing game tonight is seriously fucking cool. I've been a Tridents fan for years, and I've been to several games. But watching from box seats right over home plate? This is going to be fucking amazing.

We enter the stadium and wander around for a while, enjoying the pregame festivities until Willow takes Cooper to throw the first pitch. *Lucky kid.* But I'm not mad about having a few minutes with Tori to myself. Well, me and a stadium full of people. Wrapping my arms around her from behind, we stand in place and watch Coop walk out on the field with the Tridents' pitcher. "He's going to remember this for a long time," I say, kissing her ear.

Her head falls back on my shoulder. "Yeah, this year definitely goes down in history as an amazing one for our family."

I grin, knowing I'm lucky enough to be a part of the reason why it's been such a great year. "I still can't believe he got his first home run last weekend." Cooper joined the Dogwood Cove Minor League Baseball Team for some summer training camps, and then their fall season, which started last month. The kid's a natural on the field, but even still, we were all shocked when his bat cracked the ball so hard, he stood there staring at it for a second before jumping into action and running around the bases.

I've never been more proud of anyone in my life, not even when Jude's hockey team won the championships. *Not that I'll tell him, of course.*

But watching Coop cross home plate, then turn to run over to the dugout and be swarmed by his teammates? Not gonna lie, my eyes got watery. He may not be my son biologically, but I love that kid with every fiber of my being.

Almost as much as I love his mom. She calls this year amazing, I call it life-changing. It started out with me feeling confident in my bachelor ways. I never would have imagined I'd find a woman, a single mom, no less, that would turn my life upside down, my heart inside out, and complete a part of me I never knew was missing.

We cheer as Coop throws a beautiful pitch straight into the catcher's glove, then he and Willow are escorted off the field and over to where we're waiting. Tori pulls him in for a hug first.

"That was a great pitch, buddy."

"Thanks!" Cooper breaks free from his mom and turns to me. "Sawyer, guess what? The catcher said I should play for the Tridents some day!"

Willow ruffles his hair. "Monty doesn't say things like that unless he means it. You really did impress him."

We make our way up to the box Willow reserved for us, and I let out a wolf whistle as I take it all in. "Wills, this is incredible."

She takes a little bow, then leads us over to the bar area. "Yeah, there's gotta be some perks to being related to the owner. This is one of them."

We grab food and drinks and settle in to watch the game. The Tridents win with a strong lead, and the stadium erupts in cheers. The postgame celebrations are fun to watch with the players and their families flooding the field. But then Willow leans forward, peering down at something going on.

"You've got to be freaking kidding me," she shrieks as one of the veteran pitchers, Rafe Montego, pulls a woman and a teenage boy over to an open spot on the field and drops down on one knee.

Willow grabs the handheld radio attached to her hip and starts barking orders into it. "Tell me you've got a crew on this, Roger! Why the hell did no one tell me this was going on? What do you *mean* no one knew? That idiot. I'm going to kill him.

Yes, I know it's very romantic, *but this is the kind of thing the media team needs to know about!*"

Cooper leans over. "Aunt Willow is really mad. What's going on?"

I look at Tori. "You can take this one, Mom."

Tori's eyes are dancing between her best friend, who's storming out of the box while still yelling into her radio, and the field. "Well, it certainly looks like that player is about to ask his girlfriend to marry him. And I think Aunt Willow is mad because she didn't know."

"Why does she need to know? He's not proposing to *her*," Cooper astutely observes. I hide my laugh and gesture at Tori to handle this one as well.

"That's true. But her job means she has to be aware of these kinds of things because of the attention everyone is giving them. Aunt Willow needs to help handle it."

Cooper thinks about it for a second, then shrugs. "'Kay. I'm gonna get more popcorn." He wanders off just as another loud cheer goes up. We turn to see Rafe stand up and the woman throw her arms around him.

"Guess she said yes," I comment, wrapping my arm around Tori's waist.

"That is so unbelievably romantic." Tori leans her head on my shoulder. "I couldn't have written it better myself."

"I dunno," I murmur into her hair as I press my lips to the top of her head. "I think our story is even more romantic."

She tilts her head up and I press my next kiss onto her upturned lips.

"That's true."

I kiss her again. "Our happily ever after is the only one that matters to me. And some day, I'll be asking you the same question he just asked her."

Her mouth turns up as she initiates another kiss. "And when you do, I'll say yes."

Sawyer and Tori are still working on her sex bucket list. Curious to know what they cross off next? Get their spicy bonus scene by signing up for my newsletter.

https://bit.ly/JuliaJarrett_ONTWY_bonus

And if you need your next read...Have you checked out my Dogwood Cove series? Start with **Always and Forever**

https://bit.ly/JuliaJarrett_AF

Curious what's coming next? Keep on reading for an (*unedited and subject to change*) sneak peek at my brand new series of spicy baseball romance coming in 2024, The Vancouver Tridents. It starts with **Break The Rules**, which has a familiar heroine...

Prologue

Willow

My bag is buzzing, and it's not coming from my phone.

Shit... Maybe putting my favourite vibrator in my carry-on wasn't the smartest choice. But, oh well, nothing to do about it now.

All that stands between me and sun, sand, and relaxation is a five hour flight. Oh, and this damn security line at Vancouver International Airport, where everyone around me now knows I've got a sex toy in my bag.

"Oops," I smile at the female guard eyeing the small suitcase. "Sensitive power button, you know what I mean?"

She gives me a nod, but I see the hint of a smile she's fighting to hide. Picking up my suitcase, she beckons me forward. My new friend opens the bag, and is after a quick look inside, reaches in and turns off the toy. She gives me a subtle wink before passing my bag over to me. "Enjoy your trip, ma'am."

I wink back. "I most certainly will."

Suitcase, and vibrator, in hand I leave the security area, intent on finding the nearest Starbucks and caffeinating myself. My best friend Tori likes to give me a hard time for my coffee addiction, but I don't care. Ever since university, pulling all nighters as I balanced working part time, playing recreational fastball, and trying to maintain my GPA, I've been a three cup a day kind of girly. Maybe four if I have a decaf at night.

The lineup at Starbucks rivals that of security, making me glance at my phone more than once as the minutes tick by to when my plane will start loading. If I hadn't hit snooze on my alarm clock I would've been here sooner, instead I'm going to be rushing.

As soon as I've got my liquid gold warming up my hands, I hurry over to step on the escalator that will take me up to my gate. Lifting my coffee cup to take a sip, my gaze drifts over to the escalator carrying passengers back down to the main airport concourse. My gaze locks onto a face that is both startlingly handsome and vaguely familiar. It's the man from the security line, only this time he's facing me. And oh, what a face.

He's got deep brown hair poking out from under a Toronto Wolverines ball cap, with thick scruff covering a strong jaw. The cap hides his eyes, but my imagination fills in the blanks and pictures them as a dark brown or green, something with depth and fire in them.

There's no hiding the bulge of his arms under the Henley he's wearing. And best of all, even on an escalator going the opposite direction from me it's clear he's a head taller than anyone around him. And there is nothing hotter to me than a guy with some height. After all, I'm five-nine, and I love heels.

His stare meets mine as we pass each other, *green - I was right,* his lips quirking up into a sexy as fuck grin as we pass each other. *Hello dimples...*

"Who are *you*?" I whisper to myself as I crane my neck around to keep sight of him as long as possible. The only thing making my actions not completely mortifying is the fact that I catch him twisting to watch me as well.

I have a moment where I actually consider abandoning my holiday, getting on the escalator going down, and chasing the captivatingly handsome stranger through the airport. But that's crazy, even by my standards. Although if there was ever a man worth sacrificing a week in Hawaii for, it would be him. Who needs holiday hotties when I could have... him. There's handsome, and then there's whatever he is. Looking like that, I'm going to say a god among men, guaranteed to be next-level sinful, and a wickedly good time.

Instead of giving in to lust-fueled insanity, I mentally give my head a shake, step off the escalator, and make my way to the gate. Sure, he was hot, but there will be an island full of hot half-naked men on the beach where I'm going. I have no doubt I'll soon forget about the escalator god.

Except, I recognize him. From somewhere. Or do I? I wouldn't have thought I could forget a man as delicious as him.

Reaching my gate with thankfully half an hour to spare, I sink down in a seat and let my eyes flutter closed as I sip from my coffee. Of course, just then, another buzzing starts up, but at least this time it *is* coming from my phone. The notifications I have set up for any baseball headlines.

"Management shake up at the San Diego Devils."

"Free agent frenzy: Who's up for grabs this offseason and who wants them."

"Star pitcher Colt Waterstone wows crowds at the World Series"

I skim the headlines quickly, and when none of them have anything to do with my team, I heave a sigh of relief and turn on my out-of-office for the first time in over a year. I am officially on vacation, and any news surrounding the Vancouver Tridents baseball team, possible off-season trades, or player drama, will have to wait a week.

Between the ongoing work one of our players likes to create with his drama, and the surprising discovery that our veteran – now retired – pitcher, Rafe Montego, had a secret kid no one knew about, the media relations team was run off our feet constantly this past season. And as the assistant director of said team, no one felt it more than me.

My work-life balance was nonexistent at times. But the next seven days will be the reset I need and deserve. I plan on lying in the sun, drinking icy beverages served poolside, and maybe finding a holiday hottie or two to have some fun with.

No better stress relief than an orgasm.

And if the hotties don't deliver, the toys I packed will.

At that moment, a young family enters the waiting area for our flight. The little boy runs past me, wearing a Toronto Wolverines shirt, and I gasp as realization slams into me.

Holy shit, escalator god is Ronan Sinclair.

The first baseman caught my eye a few years ago when I was on the field after a game, coordinating interviews. From afar, I noticed he was tall dark and handsome, not to mention kind, humble, and respectful toward the media and support staff.

Knowing that my escalator god is a baseball player makes things both easier and harder for me.

I might not see him again today, but I will undoubtedly see him during the season, and now I have to make myself forget the way he made my mouth water with nothing more than an upturn of his lips.

I have a rule about dating baseball players. As in, *I won't.*

A short while later, I'm settled in my first-class window seat and pull out my e-reader that's stocked with all the books I haven't had time to read these last few months. While the rest of the plane boards, I lose myself in the science fiction saga I've been dying to start.

The vivid storytelling sucks me in immediately, and I don't even notice someone sitting down in the seat beside me until a husky rumble of a voice stirs something deep inside of me.

"Seems you are going my way, after all."

I look up. And into the mossy green eyes of my against-the-rules escalator god.

Bring on the Baseball Hotties!

Willow and her escalator god get their HEA in April 2024.

Preorder Breaking The Rules Today: **https://bit.ly/JuliaJarrett_BTR**

The end of a series is bittersweet for authors. We've spent so long with these characters in our head, that saying goodbye to them feels like losing an old friend. But what better way to say goodbye, than with a man like Sawyer?

Thank you to all of my readers for being on this journey with me. I hope you love Dogwood Cove as much as I do, and that the Donnelly family feels like home – if home is full of handsome men who make you swoon and women you want to be best friends with.

As always, my thanks also goes to my work wife, ride-or-die writer BFF Chelle. I couldn't do this without you. Alex and Theresa, for putting up with my crazy. The KKSB girls for always being there. Jess, Erica, Kelly, Chris, Andrea, my editing team extraordinaire... Your input and advice is always amazing. Carolina, my brain. You keep me sane.

And my family... I love you forever.

Also By Julia Jarrett

<u>Dogwood Cove</u>

Always and Forever

Rumours and Romance

Work and Play

Truth and Temptation

Then and Now

Passion and Promises – A Dogwood Cove Novella Collection

<u>The Donnellys of Dogwood Cove</u>

Dare To Kiss You

Hate To Want You

Pretend To Love You

Promise To Marry You

Dare To Marry You – A Donnellys of Dogwood Cove Holiday

Novella

One Night To Win You

<u>Standalone</u>

Seductive Swimmer - A standalone novel set in the Cocky Hero

World, inspired by Vi Keeland and Penelope Ward's Cocky Bas-

tard series

About Julia Jarrett

Julia Jarrett is a busy mother of two boys, a happy wife to her real-life book boyfriend and the owner of two rescue dogs, one from Guatemala and another one from Taiwan. She lives on the West Coast of Canada and when she isn't writing contemporary romance novels full of relatable heroines and swoon-worthy heroes, she's probably drinking tea (or wine) and reading.

For a complete listing of Julia Jarrett books please visit www.authorjuliajarrett.com/books

Follow Julia:
Instagram @juliajarrettauthor
Facebook Reader Group: Julia Jarrett's Nutty Muffins
TikTok @julia.jarrett.author

Made in United States
Troutdale, OR
01/12/2024

16918419R00184